Perfectly Matched

Heather Webber

Other books by Heather Webber:

The Lucy Valentine Novels

Truly, Madly

Deeply, Desperately

Absolutely, Positively

The Nina Quinn Mystery Series

A Hoe Lot of Trouble

Trouble in Spades

Digging up Trouble

Trouble in Bloom

Weeding out Trouble

Trouble Under the Tree

The Wishcraft Mystery Series

(written as Heather Blake)

It Takes a Witch

This is a work of fiction. All of the names, characters, locations, organizations, and events portrayed in this novel are either the products of the author's imagination or are used fictitiously and are not construed to be real.

Perfectly Matched: A Lucy Valentine Novel

www.heatherwebber.com

ISBN: 1477471006
ISBN-13: 978-1477471005

Dedication

To all of you who love Lucy as much as I do
and pushed me to continue writing her stories.
Thank you.

Chapter One

There was nothing like a brutal heat wave to flush the kooks out of hiding.

For the fourth day in a row, it was pushing ninety degrees outside at almost nine o'clock in the morning—abnormally hot for the beginning of June—and I could attest that the crazies were indeed out and about in Boston.

In fact, six of them sat around a conference table in my office at Valentine, Inc., my family's matchmaking firm.

Including me.

On my left, roving reporter Preston Bailey leaned forward, adjusted her digital tape recorder, then leaned back and swiped her forehead with a wadded tissue. It was also ninety degrees in my office.

The air conditioner had broken the second day of the heat wave, and the part to fix it was on backorder. I had three tall oscillating fans set up, and even with their blades working overtime, they barely made a dent in the hot, humid air.

"Whose bright idea was it to have the meeting in Lucy's office?" Annie Hendrix asked as if I wasn't in the room.

She tucked a damp lock of her eggplant-colored chin-length hair behind her ear.

She sat directly across from me and I watched in utter fascination as perspiration dripped down her full cheeks, dribbled down her chin, snaked into the deep line of her cleavage and disappeared. Her halter dress was so low-cut her boobs were practically splayed on the table along with notepads, pens, and a stack of photos of a missing little girl.

I felt a tap on my leg—a subtle kick from Preston. She had nicknamed our odd assortment of kooks as the Diviner Whiners. For a good reason.

We were a bunch of psychic complainers.

"I did," Orlinda Batista, our mentor, said tartly. She glanced at her watch and adjusted the position of her wheelchair to be more in line with the airflow from the fan behind her. "And I have only twenty minutes more before I have to leave for the airport so I'd appreciate it if you all focused on the task at hand and not on the heat. Or on Annie's bosom, *Graham*."

Sitting on my right, Graham Hartman hadn't been able to drag his gaze from the bodacious breasts since he sat down. I couldn't blame him. They were rather mesmerizing. Personally, I had spent the last ten minutes trying to figure out how Annie kept them from popping right out of her dress. I was convinced she was a sneeze away from a major wardrobe malfunction—and making Graham's day.

Graham's cheeks reddened at the chastisement, and he quickly refocused his attention on the picture of a missing girl in front of him. But a second later, his gaze was back on those breasts. I noticed, too, that Annie kept throwing him flirtatious looks. Maybe being in a matchmaking office had given her romantic ideas.

Next to Annie, Dr. Paul McDermott let out a frustrated breath, ran a hand over his sweaty bald head, and said, "Maybe we should just call it quits for today?"

Orlinda, who sat at the head of the table, whipped her laser-sharp gaze to him. "We are not finished." Snapping her fingers, she said to me, "Lucy Valentine, what are you picking up?"

Technically, this was the fifth meeting of our little soothsaying class.

I was getting psychic lessons, and I was flunking out.

Staring at the picture of the little girl in front of me, I tried to concentrate. She was a sweet little thing, with blond hair, straight near the crown, then turning to curls at the ends. Brown almond-shaped eyes twinkled at the camera, and blue cake frosting covered most of her chubby cheeks, her lips, and teeth. The pose, caught in mid-laugh as she gazed up at her parents standing behind her, nearly broke my heart. It was taken on the girl's fifth birthday—the last celebrated with her family.

She'd been missing for two years now.

I looked into her parents' faces. At her mom, who looked like a cool suburban soccer mom with her blond-streaked dark hair. At her dad, who stared at the girl as if she was the most precious thing on earth.

I could only imagine the anxiety her parents felt now. The anguish. Running my hand over the picture, I silently cursed my limited psychic abilities. Sure, I had been working with the Massachusetts State Police for the past eight months to help locate missing persons, but the way I found those people wasn't through photographs.

I had the ability to find lost *objects*. Fortunately, sometimes those things led to lost souls.

Glancing at Orlinda, I shifted uncomfortably. I'd met her, a practicing psychologist and highly gifted psychic, a few months ago while working on another case—that of a missing man. In the months since, I wasn't convinced that our meeting had been happenstance. It was as if fate had put us together.

I looked away from her probing gaze. I didn't want to fail her. She had taken me—and Graham, Annie, and Dr. Paul—under her prodigious wing. Each of us had limited psychic abilities, but Orlinda was convinced that we all were capable of more. That there were other gifts within us and that she was just the psychic to nurture—or browbeat—them out of us.

Running my finger over the picture, I focused on the girl. Stared into her eyes.

From Annie, we had learned the girl's name started with a B.

From Graham, we learned that she had been kidnapped in front of her house after being dropped off by the kindergarten school bus.

From Dr. Paul, we learned that there was a man with a dark beard involved in the crime.

All of which Orlinda had validated.

From me...we had learned nothing. Absolutely nothing. I wasn't picking up a thing, except for Preston's nervous energy.

I could feel the jiggle of her leg beneath the table.

Over the past eight months, reporter Preston had gone from sworn enemy to friend. For a long time, she had tried to get the inside scoop on my family, convinced we were keeping secrets. She planned to use the headlines to make it big as an investigative journalist.

It was true—my family was keeping secrets. Lots of them. Some of which Preston had discovered and written about, and some she still didn't know.

She'd been the one who exposed my psychic abilities. But she didn't know the whole story behind how I'd come to acquire my particular gift.

She didn't know that my father, and generations of Valentines before him, had the psychic ability to read auras. The talent had been parlayed into a highly successful matchmaking company, Valentine, Inc. It was the top matchmaking company in the world, and it had made my father a very rich and famous man.

However, very few knew that my father's success came from matching people based on the colors he saw surrounding them. Blues matched with blues. Yellows matched with yellows. It was fairly simple, and up until I was fourteen, I'd been expected to continue in his footsteps of matchmaking. Then the unthinkable happened. A lightning strike had taken away the auras I had been able to see…but left me with the ability to find lost things.

"Lucy?" Orlinda pressed.

Putting the picture back on the table, I shook my head. In the last five weeks, I'd not had any luck whatsoever in broadening my psychic abilities. While Graham, Annie, and

Dr. Paul were making headway, I lagged behind. I was still only able to find lost objects—but only if I touched the hand of the person who either currently owned the object—or *had* owned the object at one time. I found a lot of missing people by using presents as a conduit because it was often the only time an object belonged to two people. Most recently, I'd found a missing teenager because I'd touched her mother's hand and was able to see the Ugg boots the mom had bought her daughter for Christmas. That case had a somewhat happy ending—the teen had been a runaway but was now home, and the whole family was receiving counseling.

Feeling like a complete failure, I didn't dare look at Orlinda. "Sorry. Nothing."

Disappointment stung my nose, and I sniffed it away. Under the table, Preston rested her fingers on my arm—she knew better than to hold my hand. The energy I used to find lost objects came from palms, so I rarely touched people's hands if I didn't have to.

Across the table, I heard a frustrated sigh—from Annie, though I suspected Graham and Dr. Paul felt the same way. The three of them hadn't made it a secret that they believed I should have been kicked out of our group weeks ago. I was holding them back from exploring their true potential.

But Orlinda had nipped all that talk in the bud. She believed in me, believed I possessed undiscovered abilities, and wasn't going to let me quit—as the three of them had wanted me to after only two weeks of embarrassing classes.

The thing was, even though I was failing, *I* didn't want to quit. Because I believed there was more within me, too.

In fact, I *knew* there was. There were times I could see into the future; flashes of visions destined to come true. The caveat was that *those* insights only came to me when I touched P.I. Sean Donahue's hands. He was a partner with me in Lost Loves, my division of Valentine, Inc. Together we used my psychic abilities and his P.I. skills to reunite long lost loves. We were also dating. Dating seriously. Just thinking about it made my stomach tingle and my palms sweat. I was giddy about it, but at the same time, I had a serious fear of commitment, thanks to a pesky family curse. Thankfully, Sean was a patient man—and had issues of his own to work through.

"Take another minute, Lucy," Orlinda said softly, encouragingly.

Dr. Paul muttered, "For crying out loud."

I glanced at him—but he wouldn't meet my eye. Huh. There was nothing worse than a cranky gay man.

"Seriously. I have an appointment for a showing soon," Graham, a real estate agent, said sourly.

Huh. Except for a cranky straight man.

I glanced at Graham. He had finally stopped staring at Annie's cleavage and met my gaze straight on. His pale face was flushed, and his blond fancy hairdo had wilted a bit from the heat. Blueberry-colored eyes flashed with irritation. Like an ornery little kid, I felt like sticking my tongue out at him but managed to refrain.

Orlinda whapped the table loudly. "Enough!" she said sharply. "If I've said it once, I've said it ten times already. We are all in this together. Perhaps supporting your peer would be better than your remonstration."

I heard someone whisper, "Teacher's pet." Dr. Paul, maybe. It had come from the opposite side of the table. I was grateful Orlinda hadn't heard it, or she might have had a cow right there in my office.

"Try again, Lucy," Orlinda said.

I felt all their eyes on me as I stared at the picture, willing myself to see something. Feel something. Anything. But I didn't.

After a long minute, I shook my head. Again, I fought back tears. Stupid, frustrating tears. I refused to let the others see how upset I was.

"Do not be discouraged," Orlinda said. "It is possible that photographs are not your path. However, there are many trails leading to the top of the mountain." She reached behind her, to the knapsack attached to the back of her wheelchair.

As she searched for something in particular, I checked my watch. I had an appointment with a Lost Love client in ten minutes.

Even though I had my long hair pulled back, I could feel the sweat dampening my hairline, and droplets sliding down my back. This place was a like a kiln, and my agitation had amped up the temperature by a good ten degrees.

Preston anxiously tapped her pen on a notepad. She was a fidgeter, and especially so around Orlinda. The woman made Preston skittish. Maybe because when Orlinda first met Preston, she predicted a huge upheaval in my friend's life.

The reading had come true almost immediately. After she had written a huge art-theft exposé that had gone national, Preston had been offered a monthly column in the *Mad Blotter*, a national magazine that was part *Reader's Digest*, part *New Yorker*. The *Mad Blotter* had loved Preston's previous human interest stories, which were mostly about my clients (a deal she had set up through my dad). The magazine's offer was pretty much everything Preston had been dreaming of and she'd readily agreed to become a columnist. She had already written two stories for them, and now she was working on another—one about this class.

So far, she hadn't gleaned much, except that we were complainers.

Preston was getting antsy for a juicy breakthrough in our learning. But that wasn't from where her current nervous energy stemmed. More recently, Orlinda had predicted another upheaval in Preston's life—and so far, nothing big had happened. It was driving Preston crazy. This in turn drove me crazy, because Preston was a constant pestering presence in my life. Not only did I work with her (kind of), she was also dating my brother. There was no escape. Thankfully, we'd long ago put our contentious past behind us and had become friends. Or I might have had to throw her out the window or something.

"Ah," Orlinda said, finally pulling a small bundle from her pack. She made a grand show of setting the package on the table, keeping her hands wrapped tightly around the plastic bag. Orlinda had a flair for drama.

Preston asked the question on all our minds. "What's that?"

"Another path," Orlinda said. She slowly slid the parcel

toward me.

I gingerly reached for it. Plastic crinkled as I untwisted the bag's handles. Nervously, I looked within, where there was another bag—this one a clear plastic type with a zippered top. I pulled it free and my heart clenched tightly at what was revealed.

A forlorn pink teddy bear. It looked well-loved, with its matted fur and threadbare paw. Maybe eight inches high, it was short and squat, with an adorable nose, two black eyes, and a thin smile that probably once looked cheerful but now appeared so terribly sad.

"Does that belong to the missing girl?" Graham asked. He looked like he wanted to snatch the bear away from me.

"It does, yes," Orlinda said.

Dr. Paul leaned forward, his bald head glistening. He was obviously eager to get his hands on the teddy as well.

Boobalicious Annie, however, appeared more interested in flirting with Graham than anything. I was pretty sure they were playing footsies under the table.

"Psychometry," Orlinda boomed. "It is the ability to communicate with a person by holding an object that belongs to them."

Next to me, I felt Preston perk up. She had once goaded me into trying psychometry, but believing that it was impossible, I hadn't put forth much effort. Maybe I *could* get readings from objects. Why not? I could get readings from people *about* lost objects. It wasn't that much of a stretch.

"I want you to remove the bear from the bag, Lucy," Orlinda advised, "and hold it between both your hands."

I slowly slid open the zipper of the plastic baggie and reluctantly reached inside. My stomach was in knots. Part of me didn't want to touch this piece of the little girl's life. Another part was terrified that I would fail yet again. But the biggest part couldn't help feeling hopeful. Maybe with the right guidance, I could uncover hidden abilities.

Letting out a breath, I pulled the bear free of the plastic. I settled it between my hands.

Orlinda's voice dropped two notches. "Let the energy flow from your palms. One to the other. Visualize the little girl. See her playing with this bear."

The only sound in the room was that of the fans, their blades whirring. My heart beat so loudly, I was surprised the others couldn't hear it. I stared into the eyes of the bear.

Please let me see her.

I often carried around guilt for all the people I couldn't help. All the children I couldn't find. But if I had a new ability...I could help so many more.

Please.

"Close your eyes," Orlinda said.

I let them flutter shut. I tried my best to drown out the doubts screaming in my head along with the endless chatter of my internal thoughts.

Think. Focus. Breathe.

The fans whirred. I rested my chin atop the bear's head and took even, deep breaths. My palms tingled, and behind my closed lids, I found myself looking through a strange set of eyes. I glanced around, taking in the new sights, absorbing details.

Suddenly, I felt a poke on my arm.

"Do you see something?" Graham asked.

Just like that, the view was gone.

My eyes popped open. I felt woozy—I always felt dizzy after a vision.

Orlinda groaned. "Psychic rule number one, Graham. Never interrupt a reading."

"You never gave us any rules," Annie said, flipping through her notes as if she'd forgotten a lesson.

Orlinda rolled her eyes.

"Well?" Dr. Paul asked. "Did you see something, Lucy?"

Preston had her pen at the ready.

I focused on Orlinda. "I saw..."

Orlinda beamed. "What did you see?"

"I saw a school bus. And I saw a man. The man with the dark beard."

"What else?" Orlinda asked.

There hadn't been much else—not that I could immediately decipher anyway. I shook my head. "It happened too fast. I'm not sure." Hopefully I could go back to the vision later, when all was quiet again, and study the details.

"You will, Lucy," Orlinda said. "It just takes practice."

Annie gave me the stink eye. "We already knew a man with a beard took her after school. How do we know you had a real vision and didn't just copy what you learned from us?"

"Yeah," Dr. Paul said, crossing his arms over his narrow chest.

I was beginning to dislike the whole lot of them.

Preston scribbled away. I could only imagine how she'd spin this conversation in her article.

"I—" I glanced at Orlinda. "Is that even possible, to have a vision of what they saw as my own?"

Even as I asked, I knew that wasn't what had happened to me. I'd seen the scene. I had the wooziness. I hadn't made that up. In fact, I was pretty sure I'd been looking at it through the eyes of the little girl.

"Possible, yes, as a type of psychic transference," Orlinda said, "But doubtful. It isn't unusual for multiple psychics to have similar readings. You're picking up on facts, on feelings. Those are unchangeable."

"Could it have been telepathy?" Dr. Paul asked. "Maybe one of the three of us unconsciously sent Lucy the images?"

"Again, possible," Orlinda said, "but doubtful."

"Well, I'm doubtful," Graham said loudly, pushing his chair back. He shoved his pad of paper into a messenger bag and draped it over his shoulder.

"Big surprise," Preston said drily.

He threw her a withering look and said to Orlinda, "I need to get going."

"Me, too," Annie said, standing. I could have sworn I heard a suction sound as her breasts lifted from the table.

"I, as well," Dr. Paul piped in. "I have patients to see." He glanced at Preston. "Are you ready?"

She reached for her tape recorder and shut it off. "Hold your horses."

I held in a smile. Preston was shadowing Dr. Paul today, Graham tomorrow, and Annie on Friday for her *Mad Blotter* article. I didn't know who to feel most sorry for—them or her. She was an acquired taste, but they were meanies.

"Well, go," Orlinda said, dismissing them all with a wave of a hand.

Graham said, "Are we still on for Sunday?"

"Noon, at my office," Orlinda said. "Do not be late."

Other than Preston, none of them said goodbye to me as they trooped from the room.

"I need to be on my way as well," Orlinda said, packing her knapsack. "I have to catch the water taxi to Logan."

She was attending a psychology conference in Chicago and would be gone until early Sunday morning.

I continued to hold the bear. The electricity in my palms had vanished. I felt nothing.

Nothing at all.

I handed the teddy back to her.

"No, no," she said. "Keep it. Practice. You're on the cusp, Lucy. More than anything, you need to trust and believe in yourself."

I tucked the bear back into its pouch but didn't say anything. My emotions were all over the map. Up, down, around. Inside out.

I'd been looking through the girl's eyes. Even now, I was starting to pick out more of what I'd seen in my vision. But I was also worried that I wouldn't be able to recapture the process—and that I didn't have enough information to find where she was now.

Orlinda spun her wheelchair around and rolled toward the door. "Noon. Sunday."

I followed her to the door. "I'll be there."

"Do not let the others get to you," she warned over her shoulder.

"I won't," I assured her. "If they get out of hand, I'll just sic Preston on them."

Amused, Orlinda nodded. "Good plan. You don't have to see me out, Lucy."

"Okay, but let me know if you have trouble with the elevator." It was the only elevator in the building and could be a little tricky.

"I will."

She was halfway down the short hallway leading to the reception area when I called out to her.

She stopped and swiveled her chair so she could see me.

"Her name is Bethany," I said, my voice cracking. "It was on her backpack."

The corners of Orlinda's eyes crinkled as she gave me a knowing smile. "Very good, Lucy Valentine. Very good."

Chapter Two

I had just turned to go back into my office, when I heard a happy squeal from the reception area.

My curiosity piqued, I headed down the hallway to see what the commotion was all about.

In the reception area, Valentine, Inc.'s go-to gal, Suz Ruggieri, sat behind her desk, her eyebrows raised so high they nearly disappeared into her dark chestnut hairline. She knew all my family's secrets, including the biggies like the fact that my father used his psychic ability to find his clients true love, that I used my psychic gift to reunite lost loves and help solve missing person cases for the Massachusetts State Police, and that I had an illegitimate brother the public didn't yet know about.

She gave a quizzical shrug about the scene playing out before us.

A man was bent over Orlinda's wheelchair, and she appeared to be squeezing the life out of him.

But on closer look, it was just a hug.

"Can't breathe," the man gasped.

Orlinda laughed, a loud barking sound. "Oh you," she said, playfully pushing him away.

When he stood, I tried not to be taken aback. He was six feet of striking man. Long, lean, and muscled in all the right places. Brown hair, grass green eyes. He wore nicely-fitting dark jeans and a black T-shirt. There was a dangerous edge about him that had me easily picturing him as special ops...or career criminal. His presence screamed "bad boy." Especially with the deep scar that ran along his jawline.

I noticed he had a black gym bag on the love seat and wondered what was in it. Machine guns? Grenades?

"Lucy," Orlinda said, whirling around, "have you met Jeremy Cross?"

The name triggered recognition. I'd never met the man, but he was my newest Lost Loves client. "Not yet," I said, inwardly cringing as I reached out to shake his hand.

"Lucy and Suz, this is Jeremy," Orlinda said.

His rough, calloused hand grasped mine in a firm quick shake. I saw nothing, and let out the breath I was holding.

Suz gave him a finger wave. I noticed a newspaper was spread open on her desk. She'd been reading the biggest story around—the serial arsonist who was on a fiery spree. Really, *everyone* in the city had been reading the story. Three weeks, four fires—all set after midnight. The last one had almost claimed the life of an elderly man. So far, there had been no link found between the cases, and the randomness had put everyone on edge.

"We've met," he said, smiling at Suz. "Informally."

Suz, a happily married woman, giggled like a school girl.

His smile. His voice. Either one could make a girl's knees weak. And *had*, obviously, with Suz, since she remained seated. What was it about women loving bad boys?

I, thankfully, was somewhat immune. I had Sean.

"Jeremy, I'm surprised to run into you here," Orlinda said.

He lifted a dark eyebrow. "Are you really?"

Ah. So he knew about Orlinda's psychic abilities. I gave him another once-over (someone had to do it). Was it possible he was psychic as well? There was no way for me to know unless someone enlightened me.

"Lucy, Jeremy is a former student of mine."

Someone like Orlinda. I had no doubt she had tapped into my thoughts. Better mine than Suz's—I could only imagine with the goo-goo look in her eyes what she was thinking.

Jeremy sat down on the couch, so he was at eye level with Orlinda—a nice gesture, I thought. She once mentioned how she hated craning her neck to look up at people.

"A student like me?" I walked over and sat in the chair opposite Jeremy. Eyeing his bag, I was dying to know what was in it and hoped it was something more interesting than gym clothes.

The reception area wasn't nearly as hot as the back offices. Suz had window fans in place to help stir the stale air. Sidewalk noises drifted up. People talking, horns honking. Traffic along Charles Street.

From up here on the second floor, I had a clear view of

the Public Garden and some of Boston Common. The heat wave had brought out tourists in droves.

Orlinda said, "Exactly like you."

"Really?" I glanced at him and wondered what kind of abilities he had.

Suz said, "You mean, he's psychic, too?"

Orlinda nodded.

Suz threw her hands in the air. "Psychics here, psychics there, psychics everywhere. I can't escape you people." Her voice warmed. "Would you like some iced coffee, Jeremy? I made coffee cake, too. From scratch."

Jeremy said, "Maybe some iced coffee. Thank you."

As soon as Suz's foot hit the hallway, Orlinda said with a touch of pride, "Jeremy graduated from my class with flying colors."

I glanced at Orlinda. "Did you know he'd be here today?"

Orlinda smiled and rolled toward the open doorway leading to the stairs and elevator. "Hadn't a clue."

By her grin, I suspected she was lying.

She said, "I have to go—I'm pushing my luck as it is. Jeremy, it's always a pleasure. Be nice to Lucy. And Lucy, don't forget Sunday." She gave us a wave as she rolled away.

Be nice?

What did that mean, exactly? Now I glanced at him with less appreciation and more caution.

"Shall we go into your office?" He picked up a clipboard with his registration information and his black bag.

His tone had shifted to no-nonsense, take-no-prisoners.

It made the hair rise at the back of my neck. For some reason, I was now very uncomfortable with Jeremy Cross—despite Orlinda's obvious affection for him—and was eager to get rid of him. I'd make this meeting a quick one.

"All right," I said grudgingly.

Suz came back and handed Jeremy a tall glass of iced coffee. He smiled as her, and she nearly melted on the spot.

Oh brother.

"Shall we?" Jeremy said again to me. His gaze was steady, never wavering.

Not really, no, I wanted to say. But he was a client, so I nodded. The sooner I knew his background, and he revealed the lost love he was looking for, the sooner he could be on his un-merry way.

Jeremy walked ahead of me as if he knew already knew which was my office—and maybe with his type of psychic gift he did. Reluctantly I followed behind, eyeing the black bag he carried at his side. He went straight to my office, set his bag on the ground, and sat in the chair I'd occupied during the meeting with Orlinda.

"Sorry about the disarray," I said, gathering up loose pens and collecting the images of Bethany into a neat pile on one side of the table.

Jeremy picked up the baggie holding the pink bear, looked at it for a long second, flinched, and then handed it to me.

I wasn't sure I wanted to know why he flinched, but I couldn't help asking, "Did you pick up a reading on the bear?"

"I don't do missing persons cases anymore," he said.

That hadn't been my question, but I thought his answer was rather telling. He obviously knew the case revolved around a missing person—had he seen Bethany? Did he know what happened to her? And if so, how could he *not* get involved?

I tucked the bear into my tote bag to take home with me and sat across from him. "Why not?"

His jaw set and his eyes narrowed. "Because I don't."

All-righty then. I picked up a pen and grabbed a fresh pad of paper. I was ready to get this meeting over with. The sooner, the better. His dark energy was making me extremely uneasy.

Condensation dripped from his glass. He'd yet to take a single sip.

I reached for his client questionnaire and was more than a little surprised to see all the lines blank. He hadn't filled it in.

Glancing at him, I found him studying me intently.

It ramped up that uncomfortable feeling. "Why are you here?" I held up the clipboard. "It's not to find a lost love, is it?"

"Not really. It's more a favor."

"Did Orlinda send you?" Was she testing me yet again?

His clasped hands rested on the table and continued to look me over. "Not to my knowledge."

Two could play his game. I studied him right back. There were random sparkly silver strands in his short hair, but not too many lines around his eyes. I guessed his age to be late-thirties. A healthy natural tan told me he spent a lot of time outdoors—but probably used sunscreen. No stubble on his jaw; however, his sideburns were a bit long—which hinted that beneath his rigid exterior there might lurk a bit of a rebel.

His clothes were newer, unwrinkled, and clean. Short trimmed fingernails. Calloused hands. No visible tattoos. No wedding ring.

When I met his stare, he quirked an eyebrow acknowledging my inspection, but he remained silent.

"Why are you here?" I asked again.

The heat in the room—and in my irritated gaze—didn't seem to bother him in the least. He looked cool, calm, collected, and completely detached.

"I was told to come here."

"By whom?" Not Orlinda—we'd already covered that.

"You'll see soon enough."

"You like to be in control, don't you?" I said, abandoning my pen. This appointment clearly was going to be unlike any other.

My division of Valentine, Inc. specialized in reuniting lost loves. Usually a client would come in, questionnaire already filled out, and we'd go over the specifics of the case: who the client wanted to reconnect with, and all the when-where-whys. Then I'd collect all contact info, ask the client if he or she had ever given the lost love a gift, and try to get a psychic reading on that gift's energy to pinpoint a location. If that failed, Sean and I would tackle the case using traditional tracking methods.

We had a strong success rate of finding lost loves, and

we'd already been invited to two weddings this summer for couples we'd reunited.

Jeremy Cross was proving to be quite the anomaly, however. I couldn't help but feel that something was off. Way off.

A hint of a smile pulled at the corner of mouth. "What I want, and what I have, are two entirely different matters."

"Do you always dance around direct answers?"

This time, he did smile. "Why do you ask?"

I rolled my eyes and wiped at my brow with a tissue. My sundress was starting to stick to my back again. "You don't seem the type to let someone boss you around, yet you say someone told you to come here—and you came. Unwillingly, apparently, but still… you're here."

I noticed he squeezed his hands together—the only indication I'd seen so far that he was the least bit uncomfortable.

A truck rumbled in the service alley below my windows, rattling the steel fire escape. The scent of diesel fuel wafted into the office, but I didn't dare close the windows. The risk of my office becoming a furnace was too great.

"There are times," he said, "when it is best just to do as someone wants than deal with the consequences."

It was logic I wanted to argue but couldn't. I often capitulated to my parents and my grandmother for that very same reason. It was easier to give in.

I had drawn the line with my grandmother Dovie, however, when it came to her constant nagging that Sean and I have babies as soon as possible. She didn't care that we weren't married—or even engaged. She was desperate for a great-grandchild, and though I was desperate for her to leave me alone, I *was not* giving in.

Which meant I was dealing with the consequences.

This week, I discovered a beautiful bassinet on my front porch.

My grandmother was anything but subtle.

"Did your grandmother send you here?" I asked.

His brows dipped. "My grandmother? No."

"Mom?"

His face darkened like a stormy sky. "I don't have any family."

There was a story behind his words—I could tell by his tight tone. "None?"

"Are you always this nosy?"

"With clients, yes." After a brief second, I added, "Actually, always."

"It's annoying."

I smiled, enjoying our give and take. "You can feel free to leave. *I* certainly didn't tell you to come here."

Again, he squeezed his hands.

I was starting to like him a little more since realizing he wasn't as cool, calm, and collected as he seemed. "Maybe you should go?"

A noise came from the bag on the floor. I looked under the table, then back up at him. "What was that?"

"Nothing."

"It sounded like..." I wasn't sure. Familiar, though. I shook my head. I couldn't place it.

His jaw was clenched again, and I would bet that he

grinds his teeth while sleeping.

He shoved his chair back, and for a hopeful second I thought he was leaving, but instead he picked up the bag and put it on the table. I realized it wasn't a normal duffel at all—it was a pet carrier.

Through a mesh side panel, two glittering green eyes stared at me.

Jeremy stood, unzipped the top panel, and reached inside. He pulled out a small black fluff ball and set it on the table.

The long-haired cat continued to stare at me.

I glanced between it and Jeremy, wondering where the hell this meeting was going. "Anomaly" was starting to look like a huge understatement.

Jeremy set the carrier back on the floor and sat down. He gestured to the cat. "This is Ebbie."

"I don't understand," I finally said.

His fists clenched, unclenched. "*She's* the one who told me to come here today."

Chapter Three

The cat flicked her tail.

I didn't quite know where to begin. "What kind of cat is she?"

He shrugged. "She was a stray that Orlinda found and brought to my farm a little before Christmas."

"You have a farm?" I asked.

"I have a few acres in Marshfield."

That wasn't too far from where I lived in Cohasset, on Massachusetts's South Shore. "What kind of farm?" I mostly asked because I was still a bit stunned about the cat sitting on my conference table, and I needed time to process that information.

"It's a small hobby farm."

"What kind of hobby farm?"

He glared. "Nosy."

"Evasive," I countered.

The cat continued to flick her tail.

"Ebbie's been quite adamant I come to see you," he

said.

Just to keep my hands busy, I picked up my pen again. She was young, maybe a year or two old, and hadn't taken her gaze off me. "She talks?"

"Not aloud," he said simply. "But I hear her just fine."

She twitched a whisker.

Ah. "You're a cat whisperer?"

"I'm an animal communicator," he corrected.

Orlinda had told my little soothsaying group about animal communicators, and Annie even claimed to have a few conversations with a local squirrel (he was probably looking for a nut and found a big one), but I'd never met a full-fledged communicator personally. Until now.

"Among other things." Again with the fists. Clench, unclench. Clench, unclench.

He was a bundle of repressed energy, I realized. Holding everything in. I wondered why. And what would happen if he dared let it all out. "And Ebbie told you she wanted to see me?"

"Yes."

"Why?"

"Apparently," he said as if mocking her, "only you can find my soul mate."

I needed some ibuprofen. And maybe a stiff drink. Or four. "You said Orlinda dropped her off?"

"She found her roaming around her neighborhood and took her in. However, Orlinda couldn't keep her. She's allergic."

I stared at him. He stared at me.

"I know what you're thinking," he said.

"That Orlinda gave you this cat specifically so the cat could bully you into coming to see me to find you a mate? Then yes, you know what I'm thinking."

He drew in a deep breath. "Ebbie takes offense at the bully comment."

She twitched a whisker.

"Sorry," I said to her, wondering what kind of rabbit hole I'd fallen into.

"Look," he said. "I don't know if we're pawns in some sort of game by Orlinda or not. All I know is that Ebbie has made it quite clear that you're supposed to help me."

"Help you find your soul mate?"

"Right," he said.

A trickle of sweat slid down my spine. I could only imagine what my hair looked like. Humidity wreaked havoc on my curls. Even though I'd pulled it up today, I knew strands had probably escaped, twisting this way and that. In fact, one strand dangled in front of my left eye. I tucked it behind my ear and drew corkscrews on the notepad.

"Okay, then, let's figure this out." I wasn't one to back away from a challenge. "Let me ask the obvious. Do you think you've met your soul mate yet? Is there someone from your past that you've loved and lost and want back? Someone you're pining for?"

Stiffening, his shoulders drew back, his chin came up, and I thought I saw a split second of all-consuming pain in his eyes.

"I don't pine."

"Of course not," I said sarcastically.

Clench, unclench. "But, no. There's no one."

I drew a triangle to go with my corkscrew. I looked at Ebbie. "Does she have any thoughts about who your soul mate might be?"

"She says that you can find her."

An octagon joined the shapes on my pad of paper. A stop sign. This meeting was going nowhere. "I think there's been some confusion somewhere along the line. I can't match-make. You're going to have to meet with my father. He's the expert in that field."

"No," Jeremy said. "Ebbie said it has to be you. Only you."

None of this made sense. As soon as he left, I was going to call Orlinda and get to the bottom of this. "What, exactly, has Ebbie done to convince you to come here?"

"The whining. I can't take it anymore."

Her tail swished. She looked so sweet and innocent, but I could hear the exasperation in Jeremy's voice. Suddenly, I was very glad I couldn't hear what the little cat had to say.

I walked over to my desk and riffled through the bottom drawer. I found one of my father's questionnaires. It was an extensive quiz of likes and dislikes, of personality traits and habits. He insisted every client fill one out—even though he didn't so much as look at it. He didn't care about compatibility—at least on paper. He cared only about people's auras. If their colors matched, they matched. Period.

A pigeon bobbed along my windowsill as I closed the drawer. I took my time walking past one of the fans (*ahhhh*) and sat back down at the conference table.

"What kind of woman do you prefer?" I asked, pen poised. "Tall, small? Blond, brunette, redhead? Curvy or skinny?"

Honestly, I was only going through the motions. I had already hatched a plan to get my father involved somehow. All I needed was for Oscar Valentine, King of Love, to get a glimpse at Jeremy and tell me his aura color. Then, a quick look-see through Dad's files would lead me to Jeremy's perfect match.

And if for some reason Dad couldn't come through for me, then I'd rope my newfound brother, Oliver "Cutter" McCutchan, into taking a peek at this mystery man. He could also see auras, but he wasn't a matchmaker (long story), but was a successful artist who incorporated auras into his paintings.

One way or another, I was going to find out Jeremy's aura color so I could be rid of him—and his cat—once and for all.

Clench, unclench. "Tall, blond, in shape but not too skinny, and obviously, she has to like animals."

A small spiral of anxiety twisted through my stomach. "Like me?" I asked warily. Was this why Orlinda was involved? Was she trying to match him with me? Because I hated to break it to her, but it wasn't going to happen.

I had my perfect match already.

"You're okay," he said.

"Flatterer."

"You're not really my type," he added, not even trying to soften the blow. "You're a little too..."

"Careful now, Dr. Doolittle."

"Chatty."

It was one of the nicer insults I've had slung at me. I dabbed the tip of the pen on the questionnaire. "You don't think Orlinda is trying to match us, do you?" I wanted to warn him if that was the case, I wasn't playing this game.

"Ebbie says no."

"She's sure?"

"She's absolutely adamant."

Well...good.

With a quick look at his watch, a black high-tech brand, he said, "I have to get going soon. Can we hurry this along?"

I managed not to roll my eyes, and quickly read off questions, taking notes as I went along. So far, on paper, he seemed normal. Sitting across from him, I knew he was anything but.

A night owl, he preferred jazz music and liked reading nonfiction. Yet he was psychic, a modern-day Dr. Doolittle, and he refused to work on missing person cases.

I had to admit, I was intrigued. Who *was* Jeremy Cross?

"Where did you grow up?" I asked.

"I really have to go."

There were still a lot of empty lines on the questionnaire. "We still have a lot to cover."

He stood up, plucked Ebbie from the table, and cradled her in his arms. As natural as could be. Adoringly, she gazed at him.

And in that instant, I knew that despite how "bad boy"

Jeremy Cross seemed, he was a good guy. I had to help him. Some way. Somehow. I was afflicted with the Love Conquers All syndrome, and Jeremy had just become my latest project.

Trying not to make it sound too important, I set the bait for an "accidental" run-in with my father. "You'll have to come back for another meeting."

"Fine." He tucked Ebbie into the carrier.

"Doesn't it get too hot in there for her?"

"Ice packs."

Ah. I had no knowledge of cat carriers. My cat, Grendel, was a twenty-plus pound Maine Coon who, thankfully, had a vet who made house calls. Because there's no way Grendel would fit into one of those bags. Maybe if it was a steamer trunk...

His vet was Marisol Valerius, one of my best friends since childhood. I had to confess that for a fleeting second I thought she might make a good match for Jeremy, what with their connection to animals. But no. She was the opposite of tall and blond. And she had curves that could make a man dizzy. Plus, Jeremy wasn't her kind of man, either. She liked the Matt Damon type. Blond. Boy-next-door with a heart-stopping grin.

Not tall and dark with a dangerous edge.

I eyed his scar. "What happened to your jaw?"

"What happened to your leg?"

Beneath the hem of my dress, a raised scar stood out against the tan skin of my left calf. I'd once been stabbed by a psychopath. I studied Jeremy. Was he saying his scar had come from a psychopath, too?

His eyes gave nothing away. "I'll call you," he said, setting the carrier on the chair. "To set up another appointment."

"That's fine." I wanted to ask more questions, probe what he meant about the scars, but on second thought, I wasn't so sure I wanted to hear the answers.

Voices floated down the hallway. Male voices. Maybe I could save Jeremy another visit... "Can you hold on one sec?"

"One," he said.

As soon as I turned my back on him, I rolled my eyes. He was used to getting his way. How that was going to translate into dating I couldn't be sure. I could only hope a soul mate was going to love him the way he was.

I headed down the hallway, hoping my father had come in. I wanted to waylay him and put my plan into motion. Operation Read Jeremy's Aura. But as soon as I stepped into the reception area, I saw Sean and his brother, Sam, sitting on the loveseat looking decidedly uncomfortable.

"What's wrong?" I asked, knowing immediately something was.

Sam stood up. Intense blue eyes narrowed on me. "We need to talk to you."

Sean said, "It's important."

In his face, I searched for a hint of what was going on and saw something that made my heart clutch. It was something *big*.

"I'm just about done with Jeremy Cross," I said, "our new clie—"

I was cut off my Jeremy's sudden appearance in the room. "Sorry, but I really have to go. I'll call about that appointment," he said, rushing for the door. "It was nice to meet you, Suz."

He threw her a smile, and I swear she melted right there in her seat. A Suz puddle. Giving a nod to the rest of us, he disappeared out the door.

Something about his sudden departure was bothering me as his hurried footsteps echoed on the wooden stairs. I turned to Sean. "Well, I guess I'm done with Jere—" Shock rippled as I realized what it had been that nagged me. It was what he *hadn't* been carrying. "Oh no he *didn't*!"

"Didn't what?" Sean asked.

"No, no, no!" I cried, dashing back into my office, wobbling on my wedge heels. I slowed down a bit before one of my ankles gave way.

"Who? What?" Suz called after me.

I stopped in the doorway to my office and stared.

Oh, but he *had*. Sitting on my conference table was the black bag.

Two green eyes stared out at me from behind a mesh panel.

Jeremy Cross had left Ebbie behind.

Chapter Four

I couldn't believe he'd left her with me.

Five minutes had passed since Jeremy walked out, and now Sam sat in my seat at the conference table in my office, Sean stared out the window, and I was still mulling over the note Jeremy had left.

Ebbie said she needs to stay with you for a while. I'll be in touch soon.

That was it. No other explanation. He'd dumped and run.

I'd asked Suz to call the number we had on file for him, but it turned out we didn't have a number—he'd never filled out that portion of the client questionnaire.

Damn him.

I'd tried getting in touch with Orlinda, but my call was sent straight to her voicemail.

It looked like, for the time being, I was going to have to take Ebbie home.

Grendel was not going to be happy.

Currently, Ebbie sat on the table, staring at Sam. And for a second there, I wondered what it would be like to hear what she was thinking... It was an interesting ability.

Sam drummed long fingers on the table top. "That cat is freaking me out."

"I think she likes you," I said.

Ebbie's tail swished against the table.

"I'm a dog person," he said to her.

She flicked an ear.

Frowning, he swiveled his chair so he could look directly at me. "I know you have a lot going on, but we have a problem, Lucy, and you need to be made aware."

Sean's voice was low and steady as he said, "There's still a chance you may be wrong, Sam."

Sam said, "We've been over this."

I adjusted my chair so I could see the both of them. Tension pulsed through the room. The whirr of the fan blades was the only thing cutting through the silence.

They both looked like they'd just come from a funeral. "What's going on?"

I'd learned only a few months ago that Sean and Sam weren't blood brothers, but had been adopted by the same family as teenagers. Sean didn't talk much of his early years—especially the time after his mother died and he'd been placed in the foster care system.

After they'd been adopted, they flourished under the care of the Donahues. Both graduated high school and college. Sam joined the military while Sean followed his adopted father's footsteps and became a firefighter.

Sam eventually left military service behind and settled down to have a family. And it had only been a couple of years since Sean had to leave firefighting behind because of a dangerous heart condition, one that required a defibrillator to be implanted into his chest.

Fate had eventually led them both to private investigating. Sam opened SD Investigations (SDI), and rented the third floor office space from my father. Over the past eight months, our two companies had become intertwined.

As happy as Sean was these days, childhood scars that didn't show on the surface affected him almost as much as the visible scars on his chest.

My heart beat just a little faster as I recalled how Sean had been shocked back to life by his defibrillator a few of months ago. I'd been terrified. For him. For me. Because as much as I feared commitment, I feared losing him even more.

His pearly gray eyes stared out the window, seeming to focus on nothing at all. A muscle in his jaw jumped. Their silence was making me extremely nervous. "What's going on?" I asked again.

Sean carried a lot of emotional baggage, but until today I hadn't seen much of it firsthand.

Today, I saw him scared.

And it terrified me.

Six plus three is nine.

I gave myself a mental shake. It was a longstanding childhood habit that when I was stressed, I solved simple math equations in my head. I'd been working really hard to break the habit—I hated math—but sometimes when I was really on edge it slipped back in.

Sam sat rigid on the edge of his chair. There were only a few times I'd seen him so stressed. Usually, he was an easy-going, go-with-the-flow guy. "You've heard of the Beantown Burner?"

The Beantown Burner was the ridiculous nickname the media had given the recent serial arsonist. "Of course."

Sean and I had just been discussing the case over breakfast. As a former firefighter, his interest in the arsonist bordered on obsession. Especially since he was very familiar with the neighborhoods where the fires had been set—he'd grown up in and around those very places.

"Sean and I noticed a pattern today while talking about the case," Sam said.

"What kind of pattern?" I asked.

After a long second, Sam said, "I think the firebug is someone I know, and I think I'm being targeted."

I looked at Sean. He was still staring out the window. His jaw was still clenched.

"You're serious?" I said. It seemed like quite a leap to make.

"Maybe someone out for revenge," Sam added, dragging a hand over his face. He glanced furtively at Ebbie.

She was still staring at him.

He frowned.

"I think you'd better explain," I said softly.

He propped his elbow on the table, rested his face in his hand, and used his long fingers to block Ebbie from his peripheral vision. "I didn't put it together until this morning when the *Globe* published the addresses of the places that had been targeted. The first fire was set in an apartment I rented off-campus during college. The second fire was at one of the high schools I attended. The third was Sean's and my grandparents' old corner store where I used to work. The fourth, this latest one that almost killed the old man while he was sleeping, was the first house Lizzie and I bought together."

Sean pushed his hand through his hair, raising spiky tufts in its wake.

My mouth had gone cotton-ball dry. Now that he'd explained, his leap didn't seem all that big. "Have you called the police?"

He nodded. "A detective is coming by today to talk with me."

"I've also been in contact with an old fire buddy, Curt Meister," Sean said. He looked at his watch. "He'll be here in a few minutes."

I recognized the name. Sean played poker with friends from his old firehouse once a month, and Curt was one of the ones Sean talked about most. They'd been close before Sean's heart problems, going through the fire academy together, working at the same station, vying for the same jobs. I was immensely relieved that Sean had a contact within the firehouse. Maybe Curt could share some information that hadn't yet been released by the public.

Grim lines bracketed Sam's mouth. "I've been making lists all morning of potential enemies."

Of which he'd have many. Being a private investigator

had its downfalls.

"I've sent Lizzie and the girls away to visit family in California," Sam said.

The ramifications of his being a target were setting in. Sending Lizzie and his twin daughters away was a good idea. If someone was specifically going after him, his home would be at risk. His family.

So would his business.

A surge of fear zipped down my spine. "You think SD Investigations is in danger." It wasn't a question—I could already see the answer in his eyes. That was why he was here, filling me in.

"It makes sense," he said.

The building, owned by my father, consisted of three floors. The first floor housed the Porcupine, a busy restaurant owned by Maggie Constantine, who was practically like family; especially now that she was engaged to Raphael, my father's personal valet of over twenty-five years.

Since meeting Maggie, Raphael had drastically cut back on his hours working for my father and spent more and more time at the restaurant. My father hadn't minded the shift too much since it was about the same time he'd reconciled with my mother. She was a great diversion.

My family dynamics were complicated to say the least, but Raphael was like a second father to me, and the thought of anything happening to him made my blood run cold.

On the second floor was the Valentine, Inc. office space. I had a sudden image of flames trapping me, Suz, and my father in the building and wished I didn't have such an overactive imagination. My heart was beating wildly, and that was before I even thought about Sam and Sean on the third floor. Their company, SD Investigations, had rented that space for years.

Nine times nine is eighty-one.

Damn it!

I suddenly felt strong hands settle on my shoulders and looked up to see Sean standing behind me.

"It's all conjecture at this point," Sean said calmly, belying the look in his eyes. "The arsonist may have nothing to do with Sam. It could be a coincidence."

I knew what he was doing—trying to ease my fears. It wasn't working. This building was old. Centuries old. And though it was up to fire code, I'm not sure it could withstand an arsonist's attempts to burn it to the ground.

"Too much of a coincidence," Sam said.

I agreed. Sure, lots of people went to that same high school. But the apartment off-campus? And his starter home? And his grandparents' shop? Unlikely that someone would pick those spots randomly.

Sean's hands remained on my shoulders as I said, "I'll talk to my father about closing up the building for a few days. The air conditioner isn't working, so it makes sense anyway." Maggie wasn't going to like this situation—this was her busiest time of year with all the tourists, but I hoped she'd understand.

Sam nodded and stood. He glanced at his watch and then said, "You might want to start backing up files, too, and moving valuables somewhere safer. I have to go. The detective should be here soon."

He glanced at the cat, furrowed his brows, and strode out of the room. Sean sat down in Sam's vacated seat, and pulled my chair over to his. Our knees touched.

"Stop," he said softly.

"Stop what?" I asked, mentally making a list of things to be moved to storage. My father's valuable artwork, photos, files, computers...

He slipped his hands under my dress and settled them on my bare thighs.

That certainly got my attention.

He said, "I can practically see your mind going a mile a minute."

His thumbs made lazy sweeps against my skin. My brain had practically shut down. "Not anymore."

The corner of his mouth tipped in a knowing smile. "Your skin is hot."

"And getting hotter." Thank goodness I was in the direct line of the fan or I might have self-combusted.

"I'm glad I still have the ability to distract you."

"Was that ever in question?"

We'd been seeing each other for almost eight months now. Exclusively. All-in. He was currently staying in my dad's Boston waterfront penthouse (since Dad was [amazingly] still living with my mother), and I was happy in my cottage on my grandmother's property in Cohasset.

However, the difficult commute between us was getting old so we'd recently resurrected the living-together conversation. It was a big step. Huge. And we didn't want to do anything that might jeopardize the relationship.

He (sadly) removed his hands from my legs and cupped my face. Leaning in, he rested his forehead on mine. "Don't worry about fires, okay?"

"How can I not?"

He kissed a spot near my ear. "Okay. Don't worry *too* much about it."

"But what about Sam..."

He a kissed a line across my cheek and then lingered directly over my lips. "Sam will be fine."

Hot. So hot. But I managed to pull away. There was something in his tone that tipped me off to his inner turmoil. I eyed him warily. "You're not fooling me, Sean Donahue."

Gone was the desire in his eyes, now replaced with barely concealed fury. He leaned back in his chair. "I don't know what you mean, Ms. Valentine," he said lightly. Too lightly.

I was suddenly reminded of Jeremy Cross and his restraint.

Sean, I realized, was acting the same way.

Keeping all his emotions locked inside. It's the way he's always been—even with me. There have been only a few times he's really opened up. He was getting better at sharing, but I was afraid that this threat to Sam was weighing quite heavily on him. Sean Donahue was quite loyal to those he loved. I knew that firsthand.

"You've got something planned," I said. "Tell me."

Gray eyes flashed dangerously.

The fans whirred. Ebbie's tail swished. The truck in the alleyway reversed, piercing the air with an annoying *beep, beep, beep.*

I put my hand on his knee. "Sean?"

His jaw clenched. "This firebug has messed with the wrong family."

"The police will catch him soon. He's bound to have left some clues behind."

"I'm not waiting for the police."

"No?" I asked, getting a sinking feeling.

Sean held my gaze. "No."

"What are you planning?"

A vein throbbed in his forehead. "I'm going to catch him, Lucy. But God help him if he hurts someone in my family before I do."

Chapter Five

On that cheery note, I had to restrain myself from going into full panic mode. To do that, I needed Twinkies, air conditioning, and the ear of a best friend.

I knew what I had to do.

I was on my way out of the office, my tote bag in one hand, Ebbie's carrier in the other, when I nearly bumped into a man coming up the stairs.

He'd pressed himself against the wall so I could pass when I heard Sean call from the third floor landing. "Lucy, wait!"

The man un-plastered himself and smiled at me. "So, you're the infamous Lucy Valentine. I've heard a lot about you."

I had never seen the man before in my life. "Really?"

Sean came down the stairs and thrust a hand out to the stranger. "Thanks for coming, Curt."

Ah. This was Curt Meister. Medium height, thick dark hair, blue eyes. I put him around Sean's age—thirty, give or take a year or two.

The stairwell felt a little bit like an oven, so Sean made the introductions quickly.

I said, "It's nice to finally meet you."

"Same here." He clapped Sean on his back and added, "You've snagged yourself a great guy."

"You don't need to tell me that."

The pensive look was still in Sean's eyes, but I could see how at ease Curt made him feel. "You two are making me blush."

"Just blame this heat," I said.

"Seriously," Curt piped in. "We miss Sean at the firehouse every day, though I'm kind of glad he's not around. I'm coming up for lieutenant and don't need the competition. Did you know Sean beat me out of every promotion that came along?"

I thought I picked up on a thread of animosity in the undercurrent of his words, but maybe I'd been imagining it. "He was good at his job," I said.

"The best," Curt said with a smile.

"Enough about me," Sean protested.

"I've got to run." To Sean, I said, "You'll call when you're done?"

He nodded.

As I rushed down the steps, I heard Curt say, "Great gal you've got there."

Why I felt it wasn't a sincere compliment I didn't know.

***

Fifteen minutes later, I sat next to Emerson Baumbach, who stared at me in horror as I nibbled my way around the oblong golden goodness of a Twinkie—my third in a row.

"Do you know what's in those things?" Em asked.

"Yummy deliciousness?"

"You're a sick woman."

I eyed the bran muffin she was eating. "I'd like to discuss your definition of 'sick.'"

We were in one of the many buildings on the Boston College campus. Em was in-between classes. Last fall she left her job as a pediatric intern to go back to school to become a teacher. Summer school was part of that grand plan.

She tossed a crumb at me. "I don't even want to imagine what your colon looks like."

That made two of us. "You can take the girl out of the lab coat, but not the doctor out of the girl."

She threw another crumb at me, and I smiled when I saw the sun glint off her modest diamond engagement ring.

Detective Lieutenant Aiden Holliday had proposed to her a few months ago while on vacation in Hawaii. Even though she had been fresh off an engagement-from-hell, and Aiden could be considered a rebound relationship, I wasn't surprised she said yes.

She and Aiden had matching auras. My father declared them soul mates, and well, that was about as big a stamp of approval as a couple was likely to get.

I'd met Aiden last fall, during a search for a missing little boy. After that case closed he approached me to work with him as a psychic consultant for the state police.

I eventually agreed, and since then, together we have solved dozens of cases.

Aiden was now one of my favorite people, and I was beyond happy that he was going to marry my best friend.

Em's flaming red hair had been pulled back into a loose braid, and her fair skin glowed. She wore hardly any makeup—just a swipe or two of mascara and some lip gloss—but she didn't need much anyway.

"Have you picked a date for the wedding?" I asked. She and Aiden had been going back and forth about the wedding for a good month now, including whether they should have a big affair or small, local or a destination wedding.

My thoughts of a destination wedding reminded me of a vision I'd had back in the wintertime of Sean and me. In the vision, I'd been wearing a fancy long white sheath, and he'd been in a dark suit. We'd been somewhere tropical, and love had definitely been in the air. I thought for sure the vision meant we would elope while on the impromptu trip we made to join Em and Aiden in Hawaii for a quickie vacation, but I should have known better. Sometimes my visions were misleading. As they had been in this case.

Love *had* been in the air—but the fancy clothes were to celebrate Em and Aiden's *engagement*, not any kind of elopement. Since I hadn't packed anything remotely formal, I'd gone shopping. The white sheath dress had been hanging in the window of a little boutique in the hotel lobby. I'd fallen in love with it at first sight.

Just like I had with Sean.

And just like that, the Twinkies felt like lead in my stomach, and I was back to worrying about him and his state of mind.

"Not yet," Em said. "We just want to let things be for now. See where this crazy thing called love takes us." She glanced at her phone and frowned at the blank screen. "Actually, he's been really quiet these past few days. Not returning my texts or calls for hours. It's not like him."

"Big case?"

"Not that I know of." She wrinkled her nose. "I'm probably just reading too much into it."

"He could be working on something undercover, that he can't tell you about."

"Maybe." She set what was left of her muffin on the beat-up coffee table and peered into the mesh side panel of the animal carrier. "She's a cute little thing."

Ebbie was indeed cute. I still couldn't believe that Jeremy had left her with me and disappeared.

"What are you going to do with her? Give her to Marisol?"

Marisol Valerius, Em, and I had been best friends since we were five years old. We'd actually met when we were three, but couldn't stand each other until a braid-cutting incident in kindergarten cemented our friendship.

Giving Ebbie to Marisol would be fitting since Marisol had a habit of giving me pets-usually an "unadoptable" from one of the veterinary clinics where she worked. She was why I had my three-legged cat, Grendel, and my one-eyed hamster, Odysseus. "I don't think I should. After all,

Ebbie told Jeremy she wanted to stay with me. I can only assume there's a reason why."

Em kicked off her sandals, tucked her legs underneath her, and then leveled an inquisitive gaze on me. "Do you ever find any of this strange?"

"Any of what?"

She waved toward the cat. "ESP, mediums...talking cats."

I smiled. For most of my life, I'd kept my abilities secret from my friends. It was the Valentine way. For centuries, we guarded our gift from unbelievers by maintaining silence on the matter. Only a few trusted souls knew the truth of what we could do. Even now, very few outsiders were aware of the auras; however, the whole world knew (thanks to Preston) that I could find lost objects.

My friends had been more supportive than I could have ever asked, but I could see skepticism in Em's eyes as she stared at the cat carrier.

"She can't *really* talk," I said lightly.

Em whacked my arm playfully. "You know what I mean."

I did. And truth be told, it *was* strange.

"Can you hear her?" Em asked, placing a finger on the mesh.

Ebbie stared at it as if wondering how she was supposed to react. She settled for turning her head disdainfully.

Em knew I'd been taking psychic lessons, so her question wasn't out of the ordinary—except maybe to someone eavesdropping. I glanced around. Remarkably, we were alone.

"No." Not yet at least, but I kept that part to myself.

"Do you really think this guy Jeremy can communicate with animals?"

I bit the inside of my cheek. "Part of being in my line of work is to trust that people are who they say they are."

"Isn't that a little dangerous, too, though?" she asked. "How do you know if someone is really psychic—or if they're full of baloney?"

"Baloney?" I smiled.

"I'm hungry." She scrunched her nose. "That bran muffin...blah."

I offered her one of my Twinkies. I'd bought a whole carton on the way over. She eyed it with contempt. "Not on your life."

Waving the box under her nose, I said, "You sure?"

"I'd rather eat another bran muffin."

Laughing, I set the Twinkies on the table. "Suit yourself."

"So, really, how do you know if someone is psychic?" she asked.

Inwardly, I sighed. I'd hoped she wouldn't pick up the conversation. I wasn't comfortable talking about things I couldn't explain—but could only feel. "There is no definite way. Jeremy has Orlinda's stamp of approval, though, and that's good enough for me."

Her reddish eyebrows rose. "Well, then, that makes it all right."

Em didn't care for Orlinda. I figured the dislike

stemmed more from not being able to figure out the woman than anything. Em's scientific mind wanted tangible answers as to how Orlinda knew the things she knew; how she could do the things she did. There were no answers—and that frustrated Em beyond belief.

Before she could dig deeper, I blurted out, "So, Sean's brother Sam thinks the Beantown Burner is after him."

She blinked pretty blue eyes, opened her mouth, and then closed it again. I could practically hear her brain spinning as she calmly evaluated and processed what I'd just said. "Is there any merit to his thinking such a thing?"

Em was exactly who I needed right now. She provided a cool, calm, collected viewpoint. I explained about the location of the fires.

Tapping her chin, she stared at me, blinked again, and said, "Well, shit."

Groaning, I flopped against the back of the couch. What happened to cool and calm?

"Does he have any idea who it might be?" she asked.

"Not yet. When I left, he was meeting with a detective on the case. And Sean was getting together with a former fire colleague to get any information that may have been withheld from the public."

Her brows dipped. "Let me put on my psychologist's hat for a moment."

The fact that she wasn't a psychologist needn't be pointed out. She had, however, taken a few psych classes, and that was also good enough for me. "Go on."

"The fact that the arsonist targeted locations from Sam's childhood, i.e. his grandparents' store and his high school, reveals a deep-seated hatred that dates back decades."

I narrowed my eyes on her. "Did you just make that up?"

She twisted the cap off a stainless steel water bottle and gave me a little grin. "A little, but you get the gist."

I did, and it made sense. Why target places from Sam's childhood if the arsonist hadn't known Sam back then? There was a familiarity to these fires. Burning down his grandparents' former shop was intensely personal.

She took a sip of water and then said, "I'm sure the detectives in charge of the case, as well as the arson investigators, are already thinking along the same lines. It will be a tough investigation, especially if Sam doesn't keep in close contact with people from back then."

"I don't know if he does or doesn't. Having been a foster kid might make it a bit difficult." I gestured to her water bottle. "Can I have some of that?"

She passed it over. "I'd forgotten Sean and he were in the system. That adds a new spin on things."

"How so?" I removed the cap, set it on the table, then poured water to its rim.

"Have there been any fires related to places Sam lived before the Donahues adopted him?" She eyed me as I set the cap inside the cat carrier. "What are you doing?"

"Ebbie might be thirsty." I smiled innocently at her. "You wouldn't want her getting dehydrated, would you?"

She sighed. "My God, it's a good thing I love you."

"I know," I said as Ebbie sniffed the cap. "As for Sam, I'm not sure. I don't really know enough of his history. Are you thinking it could be someone from the time he was on the streets?"

"Could be," Em said, peeking in at Ebbie, who was delicately lapping the water. "It makes sense. If one of those kids didn't get adopted like Sam, didn't do something with his or her life... That could certainly breed hatred, especially if the arsonist has been watching Sam all these years. Beautiful family, successful business. It may have come to a breaking point. The arsonist might want to take all that away, starting with places from Sam's childhood."

Sunlight flooded through the tall floor-to-ceiling windows, but I could see clouds on the horizon. "How many psych classes did you take?"

Glancing at her thin gold watch, she gathered up the remnants of her bran muffin. She had class in ten minutes. "It was my minor, remember?"

"Right." I didn't want to believe her theory was the truth. Not only because I couldn't fathom a lifetime of loathing, but because I hated the thought of any child suffering, of not having the opportunity at a good future.

Yet, I knew it happened. All the time. I had a Lost Loves case not too long ago that drove home exactly that point.

Along with her muffin debris, Em grabbed my Twinkie wrappers and walked over to the trash can. "If I'm right, and I think I am, because I always am, then Sam is in very real danger."

"Always right?" I asked, eyebrow raised.

"No time to go into that," she said dismissively, sitting on the arm of the sofa. "Sam. Danger. Don't get sidetracked."

It was impossible to get sidetracked. My stomach was churning. My mind was ticking off math problems like it was going through a stack of flashcards.

"My point is," Em continued, "that it's not only Sam in danger."

"He already sent his wife and girls to stay with relatives in California. And I'm going to talk to my dad about closing down the building for a few days, in case the arsonist targets SD Investigations."

"What about Sam himself?" Em asked. "Where's he staying for the time being?"

He hadn't said anything about that. "I don't know."

"And Sean?" Em asked, gathering up her backpack.

"What about Sean?" I asked, feeling my stomach freefall.

"Lucy," Em said softly, "*anyone* associated with Sam is in danger, including Sean."

Chapter Six

"Who thought this was a good idea?" Preston whispered. Her agitation, however, was coming through my cell phone loud and clear.

"You did," I reminded her as I adjusted my cell to my ear and held it in place with my shoulder.

It had been two hours since I met with Em, and I was back at the office. The only way I was getting through the rest of this afternoon was by going into complete denial about any potential danger Sean might be in. I'd been keeping busy by trying to get another reading from Bethany's pink bear, but hadn't had any luck whatsoever.

I'd also tried calling the phone number for Jeremy again, with the same results, and Orlinda's phone kept going to voicemail. For now, Ebbie was mine.

I had thought Sean would be done visiting with Curt by now, but apparently they'd taken a field trip and Sean hadn't yet returned.

Preston had called while I'd been packing up my office,

awaiting my father's return from a lunch date with my mother.

Their relationship never ceased to amaze—and slightly traumatize—me.

Technically they'd been married for almost thirty years. However, for a good twenty-five of those years they had lived happily-separate lives. They hadn't divorced because of the stigma it would have caused the family business (aka the bread and butter)—because there was nothing worse than the world's most famous matchmaker being unable to make his own relationship work.

However, a few months ago, they'd started dating again, then moved in together at my mother's place... The fact that the two of them were still together almost four months later surprised the hell out of me. I was actually starting to believe that they might make a go of it this time around.

Yet, I knew better than to count those chickens...

"This place is creepy," Preston said. "*He's* creepy."

She was still tagging along with Dr. Paul at the hospital where he worked. "What's so creepy about him?" I asked as I shoved files into a moving box. I didn't ask what was so creepy about the hospital. It was a hospital. Enough said.

"Did you know he's a gerontologist?" she said.

"Nope." I had only known he was a doctor—not what kind. Honestly, with the unfriendly vibes I'd received from my whole soothsaying group, I really hadn't gone out of my way to get to know any of them.

"Well, did you ever read that book about the cat that could predict death?" Her voice sounded echoey, as if she was cupping her phone with her hand so people couldn't overhear what she was saying.

"No..." I glanced at Ebbie. She was curled up on my office chair, sound asleep. I'd stopped at a pet boutique on Charles Street and picked up a kitty litter box, some food, and other supplies I might need to keep Ebbie happy for a while.

Em had let me keep the water bottle, so I was still using its top as a water dish.

So far, if Ebbie had any sort of cosmic message for me, she was keeping it to herself. Though, I had to admit, I spent a few extra minutes checking out the nice clerk at the pet shop as a possible match for Jeremy. I had to assume that Ebbie's presence in my life was going to lead me to his soul mate—one way or another.

Unfortunately, the woman was married. Matrimony tended to put a damper on dating.

Unless you were my father.

Well, at least how he *used* to be before this current reunion with my mother.

I should also admit, I'd spent a good half hour holding up colored fabric swatches—one of my father's tools for matching clients—to Ebbie, in hopes she'd paw one, giving me a clue as to who would be Jeremy's best match.

She'd only blinked lazily at me and yawned.

"Well," Preston said, "there was this cat that lived in a nursing home, and it could sense when people were going to die. It would cuddle with them, then *poof*! A couple of hours later they're goners."

I shoved another file in the box. There were already six boxes stacked near the door, ready to be taken to storage.

The movers would be here later this afternoon. "Where are you going with this, Preston?"

"Dr. Paul is that cat!"

Amazingly, I understood her reference, but I couldn't help having a little fun with her. "He cuddles with his patients? That is creepy."

"Lucy Valentine, so help me. You don't know what I've been through this morning. Dr. Paul has already predicted two deaths, and those patients are now in the morgue. The morgue! He says he gets a vibe from them and knows when their death is near. There's nothing overtly medical about it. The patients can appear perfectly status quo, but he gets this glazed look in his eyes, and an hour or two later, there are nurses running everywhere…crash carts…chaos! He's creeping me out. Creeping! Me! Out!" She dropped her voice even more. "I think he might be a serial killer. One of those angels of death doctors. Can't you see it?"

"No." I really couldn't. Squeaky-clean Dr. Paul? No way. "Did he tell them they were going to die?"

It was a big psychic no-no to predict death. There weren't many beneficial outcomes to such a reading, and would most likely only cause pain—something most psychics strove to avoid. The only exception to this rule was when the outcome could be changed in some way, a preventative measure—as in a potential murder. Even then, dealing with death was tricky.

Thankfully, I didn't have death visions (and hoped I never would), so my conscience was (somewhat) free and clear. I would probably always carry guilt that I couldn't help more people with my limited abilities...

But I was working on that.

The pink bear jutted from my tote bag, and I couldn't help the bubble of hope that was growing inside me. Maybe I could find Bethany.

"Oh," Preston said, "he was all kind and compassionate about it. Asked the patients what their favorite food was and then ordered it. Called their families and said a visit might be a good idea..."

"And you think those things are the hallmarks of a serial killer?"

"Obviously, he's a smart serial killer. Trying to throw us off his track."

I reached for another file. "I think you've been sniffing too much rubbing alcohol."

"How do *you* explain it?" she asked.

"He's psychic, remember? With his ability, he can predict death."

She scoffed. "I knew you'd take his side. I've got to go. He just came out of another room with that glazed look in his eyes again. I'm going to go talk to the patient before it's too late."

"You're the picture of sensitivity."

"Bite me," she said and hung up.

I laughed. Ebbie woke from her nap and yawned. "Almost done here," I said to her. "Then we'll take you back to my place."

I glanced up when I heard footsteps in the hallway. I hoped Sean was finally back with an update about the arsonist. Instead, my father approached the doorway to my office, looking as suave and debonair as always. In his fifties, he was tall, slim, and old-time movie star handsome. Well, except for the hickey on his neck.

See what I meant by my parents being traumatizing?

"Lucy, Suz said you wanted to see me?" Dark silver-streaked eyebrows drew downward in a deep V as he looked around. "What's with all these boxes?" His face contorted comically and he sneezed.

"Bless you." When Dad sneezed was one of the few times he didn't look refined.

He sneezed again, and pulled a handkerchief out of his pocket. "Is that a..." His eyes widened in horror. "A kitty litter box?"

I was hoping he wouldn't notice that.

He leaned to his left and stared at my chair. "Is that..."

Or notice Ebbie, either.

He was allergic to cats.

"It's temporary," I said as Ebbie stretched and eyed my father like he was a giant cat-scratch post.

"Lucy Juliet Valentine...," he boomed.

I winced. "I can explain."

He sneezed again, and I noticed his eyes had started watering. "In my office. Now."

Reluctantly, I pushed the box I was working on aside and followed him out. I closed the door tightly behind me so Ebbie couldn't escape. Even though that would serve Jeremy Cross right for leaving her with me, I didn't want a lost cat on my conscience.

The short hallway felt like a brick oven as I tromped

behind my father. I could practically see steam coming from his ears like something out of a cartoon. I'd like to say that I'd never seen my dad so furious, but I'd pushed my luck with him a time or two or twelve before.

In all honesty, it was rather easy to do since we were so very different. He was caviar whereas I was egg salad.

I contributed my complete lack of arrogance to being brought up by Raphael (a salt-of-the-earth kind of guy) and my very hippie trippy mother. And even though I'd been raised with every advantage and had access to a hefty trust fund, I knew how very lucky I was. Especially in comparison to the way Sean had grown up.

Even though we spent a lot of time together now, my father hadn't been a huge part of my life in my younger years (his social calendar often took precedence). But all along, even when he wasn't a huge presence in my life and we were often at odds, there was one thing that overcame all that.

Unconditional love. I had always known how much he loved me—even when he wasn't very good at showing it.

Which I was whole-heartedly counting on to save me from a cat-induced tirade as we headed into his office.

When he stopped short in front of me, I nearly walked straight into his back.

Deathly quiet, he said, "Someone had better tell me what the hell is going on around here."

I peeked around him and saw that Suz had already packed all his files. A dozen boxes sat stacked by his door. Priceless artwork had been bubble-wrapped, and even family photos were missing from their frames.

He spun around. "Lucy?"

"It's like this," I said, feeling slightly guilty as I looked into his red, watery eyes. Maybe keeping Ebbie here with me today hadn't been the best idea. I should have had Sean take her upstairs this morning, but I'd been worried that he'd be too preoccupied to keep a close eye on her. As I noticed Dad's eyes starting to swell, I thought about what a bitch hindsight could be. I blurted, "We need to vacate the premises for a few days."

His temples pulsed, his nose twitched, and he sneezed again. "The part for the air-conditioning will be here soon enough."

"It's not that," I said, even though I wasn't going to miss working in an oven. I glanced around. I needed backup. "Where's Suz?"

He sneezed again. "Lunch."

She probably skedaddled right after my father came back to the office. Smart woman.

He stepped around the boxes and into his office, stood in front of his massive desk, and looked around in utter shock. Not all that long ago, he'd had a heart attack. By the look of his red face, throbbing veins, and wild eyes, I could see another one looming.

I quickly explained about Sam.

Dad sat on the edge of his desk, and tried to stare me down. Ordinarily, it was a look that would have me backing quickly toward the doorway, but today with his watery, puffy eyes and that hickey on his neck, it didn't so much as make me wobble.

"Even if—and I stress the word if—Sam is a target," he

said, "that is no reason for us to close down this building. Others count on us. Not only our clients, but also Maggie and all her employees, and the cleaning crew. And the families of all those people. If we don't work, they don't work. If they don't work, they don't get paid. Not everyone has a nice cushy trust fund to fall back on."

Oh, he was playing dirty.

I folded my arms across my chest. My internal temperature was soaring—hotter than the mercury outside, which was nearing one hundred degrees.

I knew he was right about the employees—we had a responsibility to them, but there was another issue at stake here. "Are you willing to risk the lives of all those people on the off-chance that you're right? Because I'm not."

"The arsonist strikes only at night. The building is closed at night. There is no risk factor."

I hated when he used condescension to try and prove his point. It was almost as bad as when people raised their voices, thinking *louder* automatically meant *accurate*.

"No?" I asked. "Because even though *we* don't work at night, several of Maggie's employees do. And so does the cleaning crew."

His shoulders stiffened. He hated being wrong.

I could play dirty, too, and hit him where it really hurt. His wallet. "Think of the liability factor. The lawsuits that could happen if someone was hurt—or heaven forbid killed—and we could have prevented it?"

One of the muscles in his cheek jumped. He dabbed at his leaky eyes with his handkerchief. "It is highly unlikely that will be the case. And tell me, what happens if the arsonist isn't caught in a few days? Do we stay closed indefinitely?"

I hadn't thought of that. "Maybe, but let's take it one day at a time."

"No. This is insanity. I will not have some pyromaniac chase me from my own company. We're staying." He sneezed. "And what possessed you to bring that cat in here?"

He wasn't going to change the subject so easily. This conversation was far from over. "The cat is a long story, one we don't have time for because we need to finish packing."

"Lucy," he warned.

I couldn't believe he wasn't seeing reason. Out of options, I did the only thing I could do in this situation. I played my trump card. "Don't make me get Dovie involved."

His mother, my grandmother, was a force to be reckoned with. The last thing Dad would want was to go toe-to-toe with her.

His puffy eyes twitched. "You wouldn't," he said darkly.

"Try me." I knew Dovie would side with me in an argument...and more importantly, so did my father.

He let out a deep breath, crossed his arms, and said, "I've been thinking about a vacation anyway."

Victory! I tried not to smile. "Oh? To where?"

"Your mother and I are considering British Columbia."

"Lovely this time of year."

"Indeed."

We stared at each other for a long moment, and then he said, "I'll have Suz cancel my appointments for the rest of the week."

"Already done."

His lips pressed into a thin hard line. "Then I suppose there's nothing left for me to do but go and pack." He snapped his fingers. "Oh, wait. There is one more thing."

I didn't like the mischievous sparkle in his eyes.

"What's that?" I asked, already dreading the answer. No one won a battle with my father without casualties.

"Why, evict Sean from my penthouse, of course."

My jaw dropped. Was he serious? "What? Why?"

"You said Sam is vacating his home. It stands to reason that he'll stay with Sean. And, Lucy Juliet Valentine, you've completely lost your mind if you think I'm going to let some arsonist burn down my five million dollar house. Sean has to go. Today. I'll call Raphael—he'll help Sean pack."

I pursed my lips.

He cocked his head, narrowed puffy eyes, and smiled oh-so-slyly.

And suddenly, I didn't feel so bad about Ebbie anymore.

Chapter Seven

After leaving my gloating father to pack up anything Suz had missed, I left Ebbie in my office and went upstairs to see if Sean had returned yet.

If possible, the third floor, which housed the SD Investigations offices, was hotter than hell itself.

Not that I knew for certain.

But I had a very good imagination.

Andrew, SDI's office assistant, sat behind his desk, holding a battery-operated water bottle fan with one hand, and a copy of a steamy romance novel with the other.

I wasn't sure if the fan was necessary because of the heat from the broken air-conditioner or from the book.

Andrew wore a short-sleeved polo shirt and a pair of khaki dress shorts. His legs stuck out from beneath an antique table that served as his desk. He'd started working here months ago, shortly after a former receptionist had placed a hex on future replacements. Thankfully, he'd only been subjected to one hospital visit as a result before I'd fixed the matter.

All had been fine since then. Except for the fact that Andrew, who was in his early twenties, still wasn't very good at his job. Sam overlooked that because what Andrew didn't know was made up for by his enthusiasm.

A thick lock of hair dangled on his forehead as he looked up at me with wide eyes. "Hey, Lucy."

"Interesting reading you have there," I said. Sun streamed in the front windows, highlighting the burnt orange walls, making them look like the glow cast from a campfire.

Or maybe I just had fire on my mind.

"Aren't you usually a Dennis Lehane, Robert Parker kind of guy?" I added, noticing the boxes of files stacked near the door. They'd been busy packing up here, too.

"Research," he said.

"Into what?" As soon as the words left my mouth, I wished I could reel them back in. I wasn't sure I wanted to know.

His already flush cheeks brightened to a fierce red. "I have a new girlfriend. I don't want to screw it up." He coughed. "I'm not the most…experienced guy. Don't let that get around, okay?"

I smiled. "Your secret's safe with me. But are you really looking for tips from a romance novel?"

"Where better?" he asked.

He had a bit of a point. "Just remember—that book is fiction. Every relationship is different. And a lot of hard work."

"Yeah, yeah," he said dismissively. His eyes were gleaming like he'd already gleaned many juicy pointers.

"Is your new girlfriend anyone I know?"

"I'm not sure. I met her at the Porcupine. She works there."

"Who? No!" I held up my hand. "Let me guess." My mind spun through the options, finally landing on one girl in particular I could see him with. "Annabelle."

He shook his head. "Nope. She's nice and all, but your dad said I should really ask out Grace. Since your dad scares me, I thought it was best just to do what he said even though I hadn't really thought Grace was my type. Amazingly, we hit it off right away. I guess there is a reason your dad is called The King of Love."

A big reason. If Dad had a hand in this match, it was sure to last. Andrew didn't have to worry so much about the relationship working out. My father wouldn't have gotten involved if Andrew and Grace's auras hadn't matched. Theirs was a relationship destined to stand the test of time.

And suddenly I groaned inwardly, realizing I'd shot myself in my foot where Jeremy Cross was concerned. If my father was leaving town, he wouldn't be able to help me identify Jeremy's aura color. I was going to have to get my brother Cutter involved.

"Grace is a sweetheart," I said. Shy, bookish, and a bit socially awkward, she was a hard worker who had an infectious smile.

He nodded and put the book face-down on his desk. "Are you here to see Sean?"

“Is he back?”

“Not yet. Sam’s in his office. Forewarned, though. He’s in a foul mood.”

I could only imagine.

“I guess I would be, too,” Andrew said, picking up his book again, “if there was an arsonist stalking me.”

He and I both. While I was up here, I might as well see if Sam had learned anything from the police. “Thanks. I’ll go back.”

Sam’s office door was wide open. A tall floor fan oscillated, stirring the hot air, but not really cooling it. His back was to me as he stared out the window. I tapped on the doorjamb and he spun around. It looked like he’d aged a good ten years since I’d seen him a couple of hours ago.

He shoved a hand through his short brown hair and said, “Sorry. Didn’t hear you come in.”

There were boxes in here, too, and I noticed that except for one folder and his laptop, his desk was clear. The gun resting on his hip took me aback for a moment. In all the time I’d known Sam, I’d never seen him with a weapon.

Leaning against the doorframe, beads of sweat slid down my back. I didn’t beat around the bush. “What did the police say? Do they think the arsonist is targeting you?”

“Yeah.”

Shit, as Em had so eloquently said.

“They want me to lie low, keep aware of my surroundings, that sort of thing.” The hand he rested atop the back of his leather desk chair squeezed so hard I thought he might puncture a hole in the material. “They also asked me to compile a list of everywhere I've lived and worked in and around the city."

"That's quite a list," I said.

He let out a pained breath. "I can't remember them all. How can I warn the people in those houses now when I can't remember?"

Like Sean, he'd been a foster child, bouncing in and out of the system. Both he and Sean had been living on the streets when they met.

"I'm sure the police can access your records. They'll take care of it."

Angst flashed in his blue eyes "That's what they said."

"You don't believe them?"

"I just want to make sure."

I understood—he didn't want anyone to suffer on his account.

I said, "Did the police talk to you about suspects? Have there been any eyewitness reports?"

"Too many suspects to name. Every spouse I caught cheating. Every con-artist I've helped put behind bars. Sometimes," he said with the barest hint of a smile, "I wish I'd stayed in the military. At least then I knew who my enemies were. Most of the time."

He'd served six years in the Army Rangers before leaving the military. He'd come back to Massachusetts, met his wife Lizzie, and started his PI firm not too long after that. Their twin girls were five, and were his pride and joy. I couldn't even imagine the amount of stress he was under right now—not only trying to figure out who was behind the fires, but the worry of keeping his family safe.

I thought about what Em had said—about these fires being cause by someone in his very distant past. "Did you ever consider…" I trailed off, not sure how to approach this conversation. Both Sean and he hated talking about their lives before the Donahue family adopted them. It was almost as if those children had never existed; that their lives hadn't begun until those adoption papers had been signed.

But we all knew that wasn't true.

They still carried the ghosts of that time around with them. And now it was impossible to ignore that one of those ghosts might have a serious grudge.

"What?" he asked.

"I was with Em earlier, and she mentioned something…" His office walls were painted a deep taupe, and I couldn't help but focus on the spot on the wall where a copy of his PI license had hung. He'd come so far from being a street kid.

"Lucy," he said impatiently. "Just say it already."

"It's just that some of the targets of these fires, like the high school and your grandparents' house, kind of hint that whoever has it in for you…"

He rolled his eyes at that.

"…might be someone who knew you from that time." I bit my lip, then added, "Or before."

The death grip on the chair continued.

"That it could be someone who's jealous of what you've become. Your success." I watched him carefully for a reaction, but Sam had one of the best poker faces around.

Finally, he said, "I don't know. It seems far-fetched. That was a long time ago."

"It makes sense," I said firmly.

"Maybe." He shrugged, brushing me off.

I didn't argue. I could see by the set of his jaw that I wouldn't get anywhere. "Where are you staying tonight?"

"With Sean."

I hated when my father was right. "There, uh, is a slight problem with that."

"What?"

"Sean kind of doesn't have a home anymore." I explained about my dad.

Sam actually smiled. "Oscar is a piece of work."

That he was.

"But," he added, somewhat somberly, "I can't say I blame his reasoning. And if it keeps Sean safe, too, then all the better. It's one less person for me to worry about. Did you talk to your dad yet about closing down for a few days?"

"He agreed." I didn't need to tell him how reluctantly it had been.

"Good."

"You haven't heard from Sean yet, have you?" I asked.

"No. You, either?"

I shook my head.

"He probably got caught up in reminiscing with Curt."

Probably. I knew how much Sean missed firefighting.

"I'm going to go and finish packing. There are movers coming at four to transfer boxes to our storage unit. You're welcome to put your things in there as well."

"Thanks."

I stared at him for a long moment, my heart aching. "It's going to be okay," I said.

He closed his eyes briefly, shook his head, then looked at me. "Lucy, I wish I could believe that were true, but…"

"What?"

"I can't help feeling the worst is yet to come."

Chapter Eight

Suz had gone home, practically floating because she had the rest of the week off. Though she tried to temper her excitement with hugs and well-wishes that the "bastard arsonist" was caught soon, she couldn't keep the smile from her face or the happy glow from her eyes.

With at least six days off, no doubt she would spend most of it on a lounge chair somewhere, with a book in one hand and a cocktail in the other.

She wasn't one to look a gift horse in the mouth, even if instead of strings attached there were flames.

By the time we'd packed the whole office, there were over three dozen boxes and various large items like Dad's paintings and the antique clock that needed to be moved to storage. I'd loaded the elevator three times, bringing big loads down to the vestibule on the first floor.

I could have let the movers do the job, but I was waiting for Sean, and needed busy work to keep my mind from wandering to "what ifs." I had a very good imagination, so it was easy to picture the building going up in flames.

However, after this fourth (and last) load, the boxes would all be downstairs, and all that remained in the office would be the big items.

I knew my limits. The movers could handle the heavy stuff.

After settling Ebbie's carrier on one of the boxes in the elevator, I wiped the sweat from my brow, and wrestled with closing the decorative exterior brass door.

The elevator was older than my father and just as fussy. It needed finesse.

For some reason, Orlinda never had a problem with this door in all the times she visited me at my office. But whenever I tried to use it, the elevator put up a fight.

And usually won.

Ebbie meowed from her carrier as I tugged.

I wasn't sure if she was berating my efforts or giving me encouragement.

Finally with a big *whoosh*, the door slid to the left. The interior steel scissor door slid easily, and I let out a breath as the herky-jerky mechanics of the elevator assured me it was working.

If I hadn't been on this elevator a hundred times, I would be scared for my life. But by now I knew its personality and didn't mind the bumpy ride.

Thankfully, the downstairs exterior door opened easily, and I made quick (but sweaty) work of the boxes, stacking them high in the vestibule.

By the time I was done, I needed a cold drink, a shower,

and possibly a nap. The two latter options weren't on my agenda anytime soon, but the drink was immediately doable.

I grabbed Ebbie's carrier, went outside into the hot humid day, and took a hard right. I pulled open the door to the Porcupine, and went inside, infinitely grateful that Maggie, the Porcupine's owner, had scrounged up portable air conditioners and had them going at full blast.

It wasn't as icy cold as I would have liked, but it was about twenty degrees cooler than upstairs and felt like the inside of a fridge after what I'd been through.

I set Ebbie's carrier on the stool next to me at the lunch counter and set my tote bag on the floor. I was checking for messages from Sean (none) when Raphael bustled through the swinging kitchen doors. He took one look at me and turned back around.

Usually my appearance didn't send grown men scurrying, but I could only imagine how I looked. I could feel that my hair had frizzed, and I knew my makeup had long since melted away.

I glanced around. The restaurant had a good crowd gathered. I didn't see Maggie anywhere and figured she was in the back, helping with the cooking. She was doing that more and more now that Raphael was working here part-time. Her love was in the kitchen, and it was a relief to her that she could trust the front of the Porcupine to Raphael.

He was a trustworthy guy. One of the best I knew. Maybe, possibly, *the* best.

Maggie was lucky to have him. Theirs was a match I thought *I'd* made, but it turned out that my father had a hand in their romance as well. Still, I liked to take credit. Often.

A second later, Raphael was back. He set a tall glass of iced tea in front of me along with a tiny plate of lemons.

The man knew me well.

I squeezed a lemon. "Thank you. I'm dying of thirst."

"You should have let the movers lug the boxes, Uva," he said.

He'd been calling me "Uva," Spanish for "grape," since I was five years old and threw a tantrum that turned me as purple as a Concord grape.

In turn, I called him "Pasa," Spanish for "raisin." Because any good grape knew that raisins were older and older meant wiser. Much, much wiser.

"I know," I said. "But I needed a distraction."

He glanced at the cat carrier. "I'll refrain from teasing about what the cat dragged in."

I guzzled some more tea and held the cold glass to my hot cheek. Eyeing him with as much consternation as I could muster in my current state, I said, "You need to work on your definition of refraining, Pasa."

His brown eyes glowed as he smiled. "You do look a little worse for wear."

He was being kind. I totally looked like something the cat had dragged in.

He sniffed the air. "And you smell a bit, too."

I knew he was right about that, also, but I wasn't about to admit it. "To think you used to be one of my favorite people."

Laughing, he said, "I'm still one of your favorite people. Who's your friend?" He motioned to the carrier.

"Ebbie." As I explained about Jeremy Cross, Raphael's eyes grew bigger and bigger, and his smile wider and wider.

"It's not funny," I said, having trouble keeping a straight face. The longer I had Ebbie, the more I was finding humor in this situation.

He tried to school his features into some semblance of solemnity. "Of course not." His lip curved. "You'll tell me how Grendel handles this addition?"

Grendel still hadn't completely forgiven me for bringing a golden retriever into his life a few months ago, even though that had been temporary. "He'll be okay. I mean, look at her." I motioned to Ebbie. "She's a bundle of cuteness."

"I'm sure he'll appreciate that fact." Raphael continued to smile.

It wasn't a reassuring smile, either.

In truth, I was trying not to think about Grendel's reaction. He was going to pitch a kitty hissy-fit. To keep from thinking about that, I changed the subject. "Is Maggie in the kitchen?"

"Not today." He rubbed his thumb over an imaginary spot on the countertop and wouldn't look me in the eye.

"Where is she?" I pried. I'm a good prier. Partly from all the investigating I did for a living, and partly because I was extremely nosy.

Pink tinted his olive-toned cheeks. "Shopping."

I used a straw to stir my drink. Ice cubes clunked against

the side of the glass. "Oh? What kind of shopping?"

Rubbing the imaginary spot harder, he said, "Things."

I stopped stirring and stared at him. "What things?"

His eyes met mine, and I saw the pure happiness in their depths. "A wedding dress."

I squealed. And not caring that the whole restaurant was staring, I leaned over the counter and flung my arms around him. "You finally asked her to marry you!"

Almost shyly, he nodded.

Tears welled in my eyes.

"Uva," he said. "No tears."

"But they're happy tears." He'd been a widower for so long now. I couldn't be happier for him.

"Have you set a date yet?"

"Before playoff season."

Swiping at my eyes, I laughed. Raphael was a diehard member of Red Sox Nation, while Maggie was a Yankees fan. It just went to show that opposites can attract. "Smart move."

"Yes, though we might have to live apart during that time."

"Or not watch the games."

His face scrunched in horror. "To say such a thing!"

I rolled my eyes and sucked down my iced tea.

"More?" he asked, motioning to the glass.

"Please."

While he was gone, I checked my cell phone. Still nothing from Sean. His silence was unsettling.

I tucked my phone away and checked on Ebbie. She was

sitting contentedly, staring out her mesh window. "We'll get you out of there soon," I promised.

As soon as I talked to Sean, I would catch the ferry back to Hingham, where my car was parked in the shipyard. It was a short drive home from there.

Looking at my phone, I felt a pang. Not only because Sean hadn't checked in, but because I was missing him. We'd grown so close that it was strange to have no contact over several hours.

I thought about Raphael's big news, and felt a pang about that, too. One that had nothing to do with Raphael and everything to do with me.

Thanks to Cupid's Curse, marriages in my family didn't work out. Plain and simple.

Legend stated that it was Cupid who'd gifted my ancestors with the ability to read auras. With it, however, came a curse. Valentines were not able to see our own auras, or the auras of other Valentines.

That boiled down meant that we couldn't match *ourselves.*

Not a single Valentine relationship had ever worked out. Couples either split up and lived separate lives (like my parents) or they simply dissolved the union (like my grandparents).

So far there had been no exception to the rule. And even though my parents were once again dating, I didn't hold out much hope that this current fling was going to last much longer.

I was a relationship pessimist.

Where that left Sean and me was yet to be determined.

He knew about Cupid's Curse, and I knew all about his disastrous relationship before me. We both had issues with love and marriage. Yet...we were together. We loved each other.

But a wedding? A real marriage? It would be impossible.

Yet, suddenly I wanted to be a bride more than I could ever express. My chest tightened, and I started rubbing at imaginary spots on the counter to distract myself.

Raphael came back with another glass of iced tea and a small plate of fried mozzarella poppers. They weren't on the menu—Maggie preferred healthy foods only—but Raphael knew my favorite food group was junk food and indulged me. Just in time, too, because I was feeling the need for comfort food, and I'd left my Twinkies in my office.

My stomach rumbled as I stuck a popper in my mouth. Bite-sized heaven.

"Your father stopped by earlier," Raphael said. "He mentioned my services were needed to move Sean out of the penthouse."

"Dad's a little uptight about the arsonist possibly burning down his house. Go figure."

Raphael smiled. "How does Sean feel about getting the old heave ho?"

I nibbled another popper. "He doesn't know yet."

"Ah. You haven't heard from him since his meeting this morning?"

I didn't even question how Raphael had known about Sean's meeting. I was convinced he had some sort of superpower. I supposed that's what made him an invaluable right-hand man to my father all these years. "Not yet."

"Your father has given me a deadline... Four o'clock today."

I understood where he was leading me. Raphael was to move Sean out whether he was there or not. Glancing at my watch, I saw it was already after two. "If we don't hear from Sean by then, just bring the things to my place." Maybe this was the push we needed to see if we could—or should—live together.

He nodded.

I finished my drink, stood up, and lifted the cat carrier. "I'm going to go check SDI again. Maybe Sean sneaked in and just hasn't had a chance to call me yet."

Pushing a salt shaker into its proper place, Raphael said, "I spoke with Sam a little bit ago."

There was something in his tone that stopped me cold. "Oh?"

Quietly, he said, "He'll be staying with Maggie and me for a few days."

My stomach clenched a bit at that news. "Really? Maggie doesn't mind?"

"You don't sound pleased, Uva."

It wasn't that.

I loved Raphael more than I could express. He was a second father to me. My rock. If something happened to him...

"Ah," he said, chucking my chin. "No worries. No one other than you, Sean, and Sam will know where he'll be. And he'll be careful. He knows how to lose a tail."

I laughed. "'Lose a tail?'"

"Andrew has been loaning me some of his books. I really enjoy the Spenser ones."

I grabbed my phone from the counter. "You should ask to borrow the one he's reading now."

"It's good?" he asked, curious.

"Definitely. Even Maggie might like it."

He narrowed his eyes. "Why do I think you're up to something?"

"Me? Up to something? Never."

"Hmm."

I leaned across the counter and kissed his cheek. "I'll see you later."

"After you shower, I hope."

"You're off my favorite people list again."

His laughter rang as I pushed open the door and nearly walked straight into someone I never expected to see that afternoon.

Chapter Nine

"Graham?" I asked, wondering what he was doing here.

He'd been frantically ringing the buzzer for Valentine, Inc.

He threw his head back dramatically and said, "Lucy! Thank God. I was beginning to worry that I wouldn't be able to get in touch with you. I've been trying to call, but all I get is a voicemail saying the office is closed, and I don't have your cell phone number."

If he was hinting that I should give it to him, he was wasting his breath. No way was he getting my number. The less I had to do with any of the Diviner Whiners, the better. Especially Graham, who I'd pegged as a playboy the moment I met him. "What's wrong?"

"I lost my wallet. I'm hoping it fell out in your office—it was the last place I know I had it for certain."

His blond hair was slicked back instead of puffed up. It was a much better look than the wilted mess he'd had in my office this morning. I bit my lip. "I packed up my whole office this afternoon, and I didn't see it. But I suppose it can't hurt to take a look. If we don't find it, I can do a reading..."

He was psychic, too, but he couldn't find lost objects like I could. His talents were more as a medium—communicating with the dead. But now that Orlinda had been working with the Diviner Whiners, all except me could also tap into other extra sensory perceptions. Graham could now see visions of past and present events. He was working on seeing the future.

"That would be... Thank you," he said. "I'm just feeling sick about it. Not about losing the money, because there wasn't much in it, but of the hassle of canceling credit cards and getting a new license." He looked at me with such gratitude, I almost felt bad for not giving him my cell phone number.

Almost. I hadn't completely lost my mind.

He rocked on his heels. "Lucy, can I ask you something?"

"Sure."

"Why are you carrying a cat around?"

"Long story," I said, not wanting to explain it to him. "Let's take a look upstairs for that wallet." I reached for my key card to swipe through the lock and realized I didn't have my tote bag.

Panic bloomed until I spun around and saw Raphael coming through the Porcupine's door with my bag.

He was giving me a look I knew all too well. Part chastisement, part "*why am I not surprised.*" "You left it on the floor."

I kissed his cheek. "You're back on my favorite person list." I motioned to Graham and made quick introductions.

I was just about to drop my phone into my tote when a young man on a skateboard rolled straight toward us. Graham pushed me aside before I was knocked over, but as the young man passed, he snatched my tote bag and zipped away.

"No!" I cried. "My bag!" I started after him. I needed my tote back. The pink bear was in there.

I teetered on my wedge heels and was quickly passed by both Raphael and Graham as they gave chase.

As I tried to keep Ebbie as level as possible, I dodged tourists and wondered how on earth the skateboarder could navigate these crowds so easily. I tripped on a crack in the sidewalk and started to fall. Thankfully, a stranger passing by grabbed me before I hit the ground, but a sharp pain radiated up my leg.

After thanking him profusely, I limped to the end of the block. I was out of breath, and Ebbie was voicing her displeasure at being jostled.

I shaded my eyes against the sun and peered down the road. There was no sign of Raphael, Graham, or the skateboarder.

I must have looked truly pathetic because several people stopped to ask me if I was okay.

Although I reassured them I was fine, I most definitely was not.

That bear was my link to Bethany.

My link to finding her.

I needed it back.

Meeowww!

"I'm sorry," I said to Ebbie as I limped to the Porcupine. I couldn't keep carrying her around like this. It wasn't fair to her.

A sudden anger at Jeremy Cross flared within me. I recognized that I was transferring my feelings to him, but I didn't care. Someone needed to bear my wrath, and he was the most convenient target.

Not that there was anything I could do but fume. I had no way of contacting him whatsoever.

As I leaned against the brick exterior of the building and waited, I realized I was still holding my cell phone. I didn't know whether to call the police at this point or not. I decided to wait for Raphael to get back.

Ten minutes later, Graham reappeared, drenched in sweat. "Did you catch him?" I asked.

Shaking his head, he doubled over to catch his breath. Finally, he said, "That friend of yours is one fast guy. He was still following him."

A sinking pit was widening in my stomach. A mix of panic and dread.

"Let me get you a drink," I said. He looked about to keel over from the heat.

He nodded, but as we turned to go into the Porcupine, he grabbed my arm. "Look."

It was Raphael, jogging down the sidewalk. He looked about as bad as Graham, but when I saw what was in his hand, I nearly cried in relief.

It was the baggie containing the pink bear.

When he got closer, I limped over to him and threw my arms around him.

"Huh," Graham said. "How come I didn't get that kind of reception?"

Raphael pulled away. "Uva, I'm all sweaty."

"And smell, too, but I don't care." I reached for the bear and hugged it to me. "I can't tell you how grateful I am."

His eyebrows dipped. "For an old bear?"

"It's not just an old bear," I murmured.

"In that case, I'm glad it bounced out of your bag during the chase. We should call the police," he said. "The thief still has your bag. Your wallet is in there, yes?"

I nodded.

"Come. We have to take action. Cancel credit cards, change locks. There's much to do. You," he said to Graham. "Come inside. We'll get you a cold drink."

"I'd appreciate that," he said, following us into the Porcupine.

While Raphael disappeared into the kitchen, I sat on the same stool I had before, with Ebbie on one side and Graham on the other. I said, "I bet you didn't expect to run a marathon in a hundred degree weather this afternoon, did you?"

"Not hardly." He admired his bicep. "Even though I'm in spectacular shape, I was huffing and puffing after two blocks."

There was no lack of ego with Graham. "Thanks for going after the guy."

"I'm just sorry we didn't catch him." He flashed bright white teeth at me. "Because I know what it's like to lose a wallet..."

Subtle, he wasn't. "Give me your hand. Let's just do it this way because it's really hot upstairs, and I don't want to be responsible if you have heat stroke or something."

Eagerly, he thrust out his hand.

"Think about your wallet, okay? Color, what's in it, that sort of thing."

He nodded.

Taking a deep breath, I placed my hand atop his. The second our palms touched, my mind spun with images. I tried to pick out details and take mental notes of what I was seeing. Finally, I took my hand away and drew in even breaths to chase away the dizziness that always accompanied a reading. "Your wallet is in a taxi, under the driver's seat."

He slapped his head. "The taxi! That makes sense."

"Didn't you realize your wallet was missing when you paid the fare?"

With a sly smile, he said, "Annie paid."

Boobalicious Annie Hendrix, from the Diviner Whiners. "And you let her?"

"Hey, I'm a modern guy. I let girls pay for things."

I bet he did.

After grabbing a napkin and a pen from behind the counter, I wrote down the taxi information and passed it to him.

"Thanks," he said. "I owe you."

I glanced toward the kitchen door, wondering what was keeping Raphael. "Not after chasing that guy you don't. Let's call it even."

"Deal," he said. Then he nodded to my hands. "Can you do a reading on yourself? To find your own wallet?"

With the tip of my finger, I traced the myriad lines on my palms and shook my head. "I've never had any success."

"Want me to try?"

This was unfamiliar territory. I wasn't used to people offering to do readings for me. And I really wasn't used to Graham being nice. "We can try."

He held out his hand, palm up. Slowly, I lowered my hand on top of his. Since he wasn't thinking of anything he'd lost, I had no visions. Instead, I watched him closely. His eyes squeezed shut, and his thick eyebrows drew downward in concentration.

Suddenly, his eyes popped open and filled with wonder. "I think I saw it!"

Shock rippled through me. "Really?"

"It was at a house. Sitting on a kitchen counter. Nice house, too. Two story colonial, pewter with black shutters. The kitchen is top of the line. Stainless steel, Caesarstone countertops." A flash of anxiety crossed his face and he shook his head.

"What?" I asked.

It was as if a dark cloud sat atop his head, blocking out his usual brightness. "It's weird."

"What is?" His sudden unease was starting to make me

feel anxious, too.

"Your driver's license... No. This doesn't make any sense."

"Graham. Just tell me."

His gaze met mine, and I couldn't decipher what was in his eyes.

"It looked like your driver's license is tacked to one of the cabinets." He paused for a second, and then looked away from me.

The hair rose on the nape of my neck, and despite the heat, goose bumps popped up on my arms. "You're not telling me everything."

"It just...it doesn't make sense, Lucy. And I don't want to worry you."

"Telling me you don't want to worry me makes me worried. So you already failed. Tell me. I'm a big girl."

His jaw shifted side to side, the only external sign of the internal war he was apparently having with himself. Finally, oh-so-quietly, he said, "Your license had a red bullseye drawn on it."

Okay, maybe I wasn't such a big girl after all, because suddenly I was scared silly.

"But that's crazy, right?" he added.

"Looney tunes," I said, trying to play it off. "Are you sure?"

He gave himself a good shake. "I don't know. This is all new to me. I could be wrong. I'm sure I'm wrong. It was just a kid who snatched your purse. Probably a druggie looking for some quick cash. Nothing sinister about it. You were an easy target, that's all."

I wanted to believe him, but couldn't shake the heebie-jeebies. "Do you know where the house is? Did you see an address?" It had to be somewhere close since Graham couldn't see into the future. What he saw had to be happening right now.

"I didn't think to look. Do you want to try another reading?"

I nodded and held out my hand. I'd had to teach myself to look for clues that would lead me to the location of a lost object. It was a learned art, and I wasn't the least bit surprised that Graham hadn't seen the address. With more practice, details would become second nature.

I held out my hand again, and his warm palm settled over mine. His eyes squeezed shut, but this time when he opened them, there was no *aha*.

He said, "I didn't see anything. Were you thinking about the wallet?"

I nodded.

"Then I don't understand."

"It's me," I answered. "As much as I'm trying to concentrate, my mind is spinning. It's interfering with the reading."

"Try again?" he asked, holding out his hand.

We did, with the same result. Nothing.

"It's no use right now," I said.

With a quick swipe, he smoothed back his hair. "This psychic stuff isn't as easy as it looks."

No truer words had ever been spoken.

Raphael strode up to us, carrying a tray. He set the tray on the counter and passed us two glasses of ice water. "I finally got hold of the police. Someone will be here shortly." He handed me a bag of ice. "For your foot."

I'd been doing a good job of ignoring the pain, but suddenly it throbbed. I hooked my foot on the rung of Ebbie's stool and winced at the sight. Between the swelling and the purple and blue bruising, I knew this wasn't a simple ankle twist. I balanced the ice bag on my foot, and bit back a curse at the pain.

Raphael *tsked* and shook his head. "This is the third mugging out front in the past week. At this rate we're going to have to hire security."

I was about to tell him of Graham's reading, about how my purse-snatching might not have been so random, but I decided to keep the information to myself for now. There was no reason to worry Raphael when Graham wasn't one-hundred-percent positive of his vision.

But *I* was worried. Yes, readings could be misconstrued, but a bullseye over a picture was pretty specific.

A red bullseye at that.

Red like blood.

And just like *that* I felt queasy.

"Do you think the police will need to talk to me?" Graham asked. "I'm meeting a client in an hour and need to make a stop," he said, holding up the napkin with the taxi info. "And I need to shower. I'm never going to sell a house smelling like this."

"No," I said. "No, you're not."

He gave me a wry look.

"What?" I asked. "I was just agreeing with you."

Raphael said, "We can handle the police. I can give a description of the punk."

At least he hadn't said "perp," what with all the reading he'd been doing lately.

Graham pushed away from the counter. Glancing at me, he said, "You'll be okay? Maybe I should call later and check on you."

I adjusted the ice bag. "You're not getting my cell number, Graham."

He looked at Raphael. "Can't hurt to try, right?"

"It can, in fact, hurt. Especially if Sean finds out." Raphael wiped his forehead with a napkin.

Graham had met Sean a few times at our meetings. "Let's forget I even asked, okay? Here's my number in case the police need to talk to me." He dropped a business card on the table, waved, and walked back into the sunshine.

I smiled as he left, then turned my attention to the pink bear, sitting on the counter next to the salt and pepper shakers. Relief flowed through me. Raphael put his hand atop mine and gave it a squeeze. Then he glanced over my shoulder. "The police are here."

By the time the police took a report of what happened, and I'd called and canceled all my credit cards, it was after four o' clock.

And there was still no sign of Sean.

Chapter Ten

"He doesn't have much, does he?" Raphael set a stack of boxes on the floor and inspected Sean's room at my father's penthouse.

I'd been calling Sean practically nonstop for the past hour. No answer. The calls went directly to voicemail, and after the third message I stopped leaving them. It hadn't seemed right for Raphael to pack Sean's things alone, so I'd tagged along.

"Most of his belongings are in storage," I said, looking around. After his previous relationship didn't work out, Sean and his dog Thoreau, a tiny Yorkie, had moved in with Sam and his family. When they overstayed their welcome, they moved here. It was win-win. My father had someone to watch his beloved penthouse while he cohabitated with my mother, and Sean had a place to live rent-free while we tried to figure out our future.

Thoreau had not greeted us at the door with his usual

yips and bouncing, so I figured that wherever Sean was, he had the dog with him and that Thoreau had not been dognapped (again!).

Taking a deep breath, I let Ebbie out of her carrier and tried not to stress out about Sean.

Raphael lifted an eyebrow. "Your father's allergies..."

I still wasn't feeling too kindly toward my father, so I said, "Just make sure his Epi-pen is around."

Raphael shook his head. "If he finds out..."

Limping, I walked over and closed the door to keep Ebbie confined to the room. After I solemnly promised him I'd have my injury looked at by a doctor, Raphael wrapped my foot with a thick bandage, and I'd abandoned my wedges in favor of a pair of flip-flops bought from a street vendor. "You weren't here."

"I've trained you well, Uva."

Smiling, I gathered up some bubble wrap and went to work. It wasn't all that long ago that Raphael had moved out of this very room and in with Maggie at her home.

I'd had a rough time letting Raphael go, but the transition had been smoother than I thought possible. It helped that he worked downstairs in the Porcupine. I saw him almost every day.

Looking around, I noted that Raphael hadn't been exaggerating when he said Sean didn't have much here; bedding, some clothes, some pictures of us, Sam's family, and his parents—his adoptive parents, that is. I picked up that frame.

"What were their names?" Raphael asked, peeking over my shoulder.

"Daniel and Winifred Donahue."

"Odd how Sean rather looks like Daniel, don't you think?"

"Sean thinks that's why Daniel took such a liking to him; he reminded Daniel of himself."

In the photo, Daniel, dressed in his firefighter blues, stood next to fancily-dressed Winnie. Daniel had an arm hooked around a grinning Sam, and Winnie had her arm around a hesitantly smiling Sean.

Sean once told me about this photo, about how he had been too afraid to believe his good fortune that a family like this would take him in. He'd been afraid to be happy. Afraid to trust. Afraid to believe that nothing else bad would ever happen to him.

I believed he still felt that way much of the time.

Raphael chuckled. "Had Daniel been a scrapper as well?"

"I don't know." I stared at the photo. Getting any information out of Sean about his upbringing was incredibly difficult. I barely knew anything about his real family. And what I knew about the Donahues could barely fill a page.

"Well, they must have been remarkable people." He turned away and wrestled open a cardboard box. He was exceptionally patient as Ebbie tried to help him.

Remarkable.

I'd say so. Taking in Sean and Sam from the streets. Probably saving their lives. Giving them a home. Love. All the nurturing they could stand—and then some.

Until, sadly, Sean's apprehensions about bad things happening had proven true.

He had only ten years with Daniel, a fire chief, before Daniel died during a horrible warehouse fire. Not long after, Winnie had been diagnosed with colon cancer and succumbed quickly. And of course, then there was the day Sean himself had died in the middle of a busy Boston intersection.

He'd been a firefighter called to the scene of an accident when his heart suddenly stopped—a genetic flaw he hadn't known about. His fellow firefighters had brought him back to life. With that, however, came a huge upheaval. He'd needed a defibrillator implanted; he had to leave his job; his girlfriend couldn't handle the stress... To him it felt as though he'd lost everything.

But because of his heart problems, he had taken a job at Sam's P.I. firm—where he found me.

Fate had an interesting sense of humor.

Carefully, I wrapped the frame and placed it inside the cardboard box, alongside Ebbie, who'd climbed in.

After I gave her ears a quick scratch, I went to wrap the other frames.

I nearly dropped one of them when my cell phone rang. Quickly, I set it down and grabbed my phone, hoping the whole time that it was Sean finally checking in.

My ruminating on his heart problems had increased my anxiety about his lack of contact. Did he have an episode? Not long ago, I'd witnessed him being shocked by his defibrillator, and the memory made my hands clammy and my stomach ache. I kept telling myself that if he had been shocked I would have heard by now. Someone would have contacted Sam or me...

Checking the Caller ID, I practically deflated when I saw that it was Suz.

"Don't sound so happy to hear from me," she said dryly when I answered unenthusiastically.

"I thought you might be Sean."

"Now I understand your disappointment. Ha-cha-cha!"

I couldn't help but smile. Suz made it no secret that she thought Sean was one hot tamale. "How come you're not on a beach reading a steamy novel?"

"It started to rain."

I took the phone and limped my way into my father's living room. His floor-to-ceiling glass windows looked out onto Boston Harbor. It was, in fact, raining. "Bummer."

"Tell me about it. Anyway, when I came back inside, I decided to check the office voicemail in case an important call came in or whatnot. You know how I like to stay atop of things."

Rain drops slid down the window panes. Thunder crackled in the distance. "You have to talk to my father about getting a raise, Suz."

"Could you at least put in a good word?"

"I'll see what I can do. I should probably go back to helping Raphael now..."

"Thanks. But a raise is not the reason I called."

Sometimes Suz took the scenic route around a conversation. "No?"

"I was checking the messages and there were about ten

of them from that guy in your group. Graham? Something about a lost wallet. I took down his number..."

"It's okay. I ran into him earlier. The wallet's been found."

"Well, that's good."

"Thanks for letting me know, though," I said.

"Wait. There's more."

I thunked my head against the thick window, and then frowned at the mark I'd left on the glass. I tried to rub it away, but it only made it worse. It just wasn't my day. "What else?"

"Annie Hendrix keeps calling and leaving messages for you."

Oh, for crying out loud. Not Annie, too. There was only so much of the Diviner Whiners I could take in a day. "Did she lose her wallet, too?"

"No, but she's quite insistent that you call her back as soon as possible. She's left about seven messages now."

I didn't really want to call her back, but seven messages hinted that it might be something important. "Give me her number." I jotted it down, and said, "Anything from Dr. Paul?"

"Nope."

Thank goodness for small favors. "Anything from Orlinda or Jeremy Cross?"

"Not a thing."

Of course not. The two people I actually wanted to hear from. I thanked Suz for calling and promised again to talk to my dad about a raise and hung up.

I stared at my cell phone for a long second, willing Sean to call. When he didn't, I walked into the kitchen and picked up my father's landline. I dialed Annie Hendrix's number—I didn't want her to have my cell phone number, either.

After five rings, the call clicked over to voicemail. I left a message that I would try to reach her again later.

What did she want? Had she lost something, too?

Like her mind, for flirting with Graham?

I hoped she didn't think I could match her with him. Just the thought of it made me shudder. Graham was proving to have some decency (miniscule), but dating a playboy like him was only asking for trouble. I didn't know what she was thinking.

Because I was a glutton for punishment, I dialed Sean one more time. Still no answer. But as I hung up, my phone rang.

For a second I was disappointed it wasn't Sean, but then I smiled because it was my brother.

"Oscar called and said I should keep an eye on you while he's gone," he said.

Oliver "Cutter" McCutchan still wasn't comfortable calling our father "Dad." Not surprising, since he only found out that he was the son of Oscar Valentine about six months ago. Otherwise, Cutter had blended into our dysfunctional family perfectly. It helped that the public and the media (except for Preston) hadn't figured out that Cutter was a Valentine. And helped even more that he was on the road a lot—he didn't have to see us very often.

We were a lot to handle.

"Oh, that will be easy with you in San Francisco." He was due home this weekend.

He laughed. "I think he forgot."

I was about to say, "Welcome to my world," but held it in. At least I'd had my father's presence in my life when I was little—even though he was more physically absent than not. Cutter had grown up believing that his father was someone else—a stuffy, starchy executive, who couldn't hold a candle to Raphael when it came to parenting duties.

I'd been the lucky one. And I knew it.

Instead, I said, "He's getting old. His mind is slipping."

"It is not."

"I know, but he'd go crazy if he knew I said it. You should tell him."

Cutter laughed. "Why do I have the feeling he's not on your good side right now?"

"Because you have good instincts."

"Speaking of, have you seen Preston today?"

He'd tried to sound casual, but I picked up an undertone of worry in his voice. "This morning. Why?"

"I haven't heard from her today. It's just strange, that's all."

"She's following around Dr. Paul today, so she's pretty busy. Lots of pre-death patient interviews going on."

"Do I want to know what that means?"

"Probably not."

"Have you noticed that she's been acting strangely lately?"

I smiled. "More than usual, you mean?"

"Lucy!"

"Not that I've noticed. Oh wait, it might be because of Orlinda."

"Your psychic teacher?"

"She predicted Preston was going to have another big change."

He laughed. "Well, that explains some things. Orlinda freaks her out."

I knew.

"Her last prediction…Preston thought for sure I was going to propose to her. She kept leaving engagement ring pictures around the house, dropping hints that she liked round cuts better than square..."

"That's crazy! You've only been seeing each other for a few months."

There was silence on the other end of the phone.

"Cutter?"

More silence.

"Oh. My. God! You're thinking about proposing to Preston?"

He coughed. "No... I mean, I don't think so. But maybe Orlinda knows something I don't."

I needed to sit down. I glanced at my father's fancy sofa and bypassed it. After I witnessed my parents fooling around on it, I could never sit on it again. I flopped into an overstuffed chair.

"Maybe," Cutter went on, "that's why I haven't heard from her. After the last prediction, she was so embarrassed. Maybe now she's playing hard-to-get?"

"This is Preston we're talking about. She's never played hard-to-get in her life. She's about the most in-your-face person I know."

"Well, something's going on. Can you feel her out for me?"

"Maybe I can..."

"Okay, LucyD, what do you want?"

I loved that he used my mother's nickname for me. She (and Dovie, too) had been calling me LucyD for as long as I could remember. It was a shortened version of Lucy Diamonds, which was taken from "Lucy in the Sky with Diamonds." My mother was a rabid Beatles fan and was a little...eccentric. She was Beatnik, flower child, earth mother, and Greek Goddess rolled into one.

"Maybe we can make a trade. Because I need *your* help with something."

"What?"

"Reading the aura of a client, since Dad is out of town."

"Lucy..."

"Oh, stop with that tone. I'm not asking you to give up your career and join the company."

"Good. Because I get enough of that with Dad."

Dad. I also loved that the word slipped into his vocabulary once in a while. "This is a special case."

He sighed. "Okay. Set it up for this weekend, but you better come through for me with Preston."

I was still wrapping my head around the whole engagement angle—and the fact that he'd obviously put some thought into it. "This weekend is perfect. It gives me time to track down my client."

"Wait a sec. You don't know where he is?"

"Not yet," I said. "But I will find him. Make no mistake about that."

Chapter Eleven

An hour later, I was back at the office, watching a locksmith work his magic. He was just about done swapping out the lock on the office door. He'd already reprogrammed the downstairs keycard reader.

I sat on the love seat in the reception area with my foot propped up and my phone in hand. I was going from worried about Sean to being angry with him. He had to know how frantic his absence would make me. It had been over six hours since he left the office—and no one had heard a peep since.

The movers had been here and gone, and Raphael had taken charge of Ebbie and was in the process of bringing her—and all Sean's things—to my place. He promised not to leave Ebbie alone with Grendel, and for that I was thankful. Grendel outweighed the small cat by a good twenty pounds, at least.

I'd promised Raphael I'd take a cab ride home instead of trying to navigate the ferry, even though it was going to cost me an arm and a leg—money that Raphael had loaned me since mine had been carried off by a hoodlum.

Fluffing the pillow behind my head, I wiggled, trying to get comfortable. Over the noise of the window fan, the din of rush hour traffic floated in. Oddly, I found the honking, the sirens, and the *bustle* oddly soothing.

My phone rang and I answered on the first ring. It was my mother.

"LucyD! What is this about your father squiring me away? What isn't he telling me?"

Ah, he hadn't told her about the arsonist. It was probably for the best. My mother was one to dwell on things. I could hear lots of noise in the background. "It's a thousand degrees in the office and Dad doesn't like to sweat. Are you already at the airport?"

"Well, now it all makes perfect sense. And yes, we're at the airport. We're due to fly out in an hour. I could use a vacation, but I knew there was something going on. You'll have the week off as well?"

I felt a stab of guilt that I kept the real reason from her. "Heading home soon."

"How will you survive without me for the week?" she asked dramatically.

"I don't know," I said. "But I'm sure Dovie will be around lots."

She laughed. "Oh, she'll be around. You should see what she's ordered for you and Sean."

"Not a crib, I hope."

"Oh, you'll see."

We said our goodbyes, and she promised to send a postcard. I hung up and looked down. I'd taken the wrap off my foot to let it breathe, and wished I hadn't.

It was one ugly foot.

Even the locksmith noticed. "You ought to get that looked at."

He was as bad as Raphael. "I'm going to."

Just as soon as I found Sean and kicked his ass from here to Nantucket.

With my good foot, of course.

"Soon," he said. "If it's broken, you don't want to have to get it re-broken to fix it."

I glanced at him. He was sixty if a day, with bushy eyebrows and sage green eyes. "Broken? I don't think so. Just sprained maybe."

He tipped his head. "I ain't wrong about these things. I have a sixth sense, you know?"

"Nope," I said. I was sick of anything to do with sixth senses.

He dropped a screwdriver into his mini toolbox. "Well, I do. And dollars to doughnuts, that foot is broken."

I'd already called Em, who promised she'd take a look at it when I got home tonight. It was nice having a best friend who was a former doctor. One who lived right next door—she had been living with Dovie since Christmastime. The arrangement, which was supposed to have been temporary, had turned into something more permanent and was a good thing for both of them. It kept the loneliness at bay.

I rather liked it, too, having her so close. My cottage sat

on the edge of Dovie's property, on a cliff with breathtaking water views. And though I insisted on paying rent, I knew she took the money and funneled it into some sort of high-yield account that would eventually come back to me. Still, it made me feel better to think I was paying my own way.

Now that Em was engaged to Aiden, I wondered how long she'd be around. Not that Aiden lived all that far away, but still. A long engagement would be nice.

I blinked my eyes open and dialed Aiden's number. Em had been worried about him being standoffish lately, and filling him in on the Beantown Burner case might be the perfect reason to call him out of the blue and segue into his relationship with Em.

Which wasn't any of my business, except for the fact that Em was my best friend, and she was worried, so that made me worry.

I was a fixer. I couldn't help myself.

My call went straight to Aiden's voicemail, and I left a quick message asking him to call me back about a case.

I pulled the pink bear from the coffee table onto my lap and stared into its small black eyes. Holding it between my hands, I tried to replicate what had happened earlier in my office, but saw nothing. Felt nothing.

I sighed.

"Just about done here," the locksmith said. "You gonna be okay here? You need a ride someplace?"

"Thanks," I said, "but I'm okay."

His face pulled into a frown as he wiped his hand on a rag pulled from his pocket. "You call me if you change your mind. I've got three daughters of my own, and I'd want someone looking after them."

I smiled. Sometimes I forgot how kind people could be. "Thank you. I have your card if I need you."

With a brusque nod, he packed up his stuff. "I'll send your father the bill."

"I'll make sure he pays it."

The man laughed. He set a ring of keys on the table—he'd already given me several new key cards to hand out. "You take care, Ms. Valentine, and get to that doctor." With a wink, he added, "I'll see myself out."

I debated walking him out just to show I could, but quickly decided against it. In fact, I was seriously considering staying on this couch for the next three days. If not for the extreme heat, an arsonist on the loose, an abandoned cat at my place, and a missing Sean, I might have.

Instead, I stared again at the pink bear.

Orlinda had forbid us from searching for the little girl through other methods besides our abilities. No Googling allowed.

However, I was itching to do a search for a missing little girl named Bethany. Where was she from? Had there been any leads in her case at all? Had any clues been found?

I wouldn't do an online search, however. I'd trust Orlinda's process, as painful as it was.

The office phone rang, and I gave it the evil eye for a long second before I hauled myself off the couch and hopped, one-footed, over to Suz's desk.

I grabbed the phone. "Valentine, Inc., this is Lucy, may I help you?"

"Lucy Valentine!" a woman shouted. "I've been trying to get in touch with you all day."

By the harsh tone, I knew immediately that it was Annie Hendrix. An image of enormous breasts popped into my mind, and I shook my head to get rid of it. "Hi, Annie."

"Don't you 'Hi, Annie' me. You don't know what I've been going through. What I've endured."

Annie was a professional psychic, working full-time at a place on Tremont Street. Her gift was automatic writing—jotting down information guided by spirits who'd passed over. Despite her histrionics, she'd become quite successful in her field.

I sat in Suz's seat. My patience had worn paper thin, so I bit my lip to keep from giving Annie a flip response. My head was starting to ache.

"I cannot afford to lose business, Lucy Valentine. So whatever you've done to me, undo it."

A nice bath. That's what I needed. A glass of wine.

And maybe some morphine.

Rubbing my temple, I said, "You lost me. Undo what?"

"Whatever hex you put on me."

I opened Suz's drawers, hoping to find a wayward bottle of aspirin. "Annie, I have no idea what you're talking about."

"All day, Lucy Valentine! All day. Whenever a client came in, and I pulled out a fresh sheet of paper to do their reading, do you know what I wrote?"

"Enlighten me."

"Your name. *Lucy Valentine*, over and over."

"Why?"

"You've hexed me!"

"I hate to break it to you, Annie, but I'm a psychic, not any kind of witch. I don't have hexing powers."

"Well," she said with a big dose of acrimony, "you kind of seem like a witch to me."

I pulled the phone away from my ear and stared at it, unable to believe what I'd just heard.

The nerve!

My last shred of patience went up in flames.

I hung up.

When the phone immediately rang again, I ignored it.

Even though I was dying to know why she was getting readings on my name, I was done with the abuse. The taunts. The teasing. The snickers. This weekend would be my last meeting with the Diviner Whiners. Orlinda would just have to understand.

As the phone continued to ring, I smiled.

Suddenly feeling good, I rewrapped my foot and turned off all the fans and lights. I grabbed my cell phone, the pink bear, and my new set of keys and locked up the office.

On my way out, I ignored the drone of the ringing office phone and paused on the landing. Looking up the wooden stairs to SD Investigations, I saw the door was open.

Sweat beaded on my forehead as I carefully climbed the steps. Cherry wood stairs creaked under my feet with each tentative step I took.

I tried not to put weight on my left foot, but it was nearly impossible. I thought about what the locksmith said, about my foot being broken, and hoped he was wrong.

The last thing I wanted was a cast during this heat. Never mind navigating the world on crutches.

Then I thought of Orlinda in her wheelchair and felt terrible.

At least my foot would heal.

I tried to ignore the pain as I hobbled into the office. Andrew's desk was clear, and there was no sign of him anywhere. The scent of cinnamon lingered in the air as I headed down the hallway to Sean's office.

Sam stuck his head out of his office door. "I thought I heard someone. I'm just locking up."

"Are you going straight to Raphael's?"

"I'm going to stop at home first and pack some things. I'll take the long way to Raphael's, just to make sure no one is following me."

The pit was back in my stomach. "Be careful, okay?"

"I will."

I nodded toward Sean's office. "I just came up to check on him one more time."

"He's not back yet. What happened to you?" He motioned to my foot.

"Long story." I leaned against the wall. "You haven't heard from Sean at all?"

He shook his head.

I eyed him carefully, picking up on the fact that even though he was stressed, he wasn't stressed about Sean.

"Why don't you seem as concerned as I am?"

"Because I know where he is."

"What?" My tone was sharp. I'd been worried sick all day and Sam had known where Sean was this whole time?

"Sorry, Lucy. I hoped he'd be back by now, and I wouldn't have to be the one to fill you in."

Taking a deep breath to tamp down my annoyance, I said, "What do you mean, 'fill me in?' Where is he?"

I wanted to know so I could get his ass-kicking under way. Then I'd go home, get my foot looked at by Em, deal with Ebbie, and have that bath.

"The cemetery."

Chapter Twelve

Being at a cemetery had a way of knocking the ass-kicking right out of a girl.

I limped along a damp twining path, using an umbrella as a cane. There was a strange feeling in the air, partly due to the fact that sunbeams had broken through the low-lying dark clouds, casting an eerie glow across the city on the horizon.

Here, tombstones rose up around me as trees canopied the path. Because of the clouds, it felt like dusk, even though it was only a bit past six.

The cemetery itself should have been creepy, especially in this light, but the birds were chirping, the breeze rustled the leaves, and I finally felt at peace for the first time all day.

As I passed grave after grave, I couldn't help but think about all these people who'd passed on and wondered what it would be like to communicate with them. One thought led to another and before I knew it, I was thinking about the Diviner Whiners. Annie, Dr. Paul, and Graham could communicate with the dead. Annie through writing, Dr. Paul could see spirits leaving bodies, and Graham could hear them and feel their presence.

I was entirely fascinated by their abilities, but wasn't sure I wanted the responsibility of speaking for those who passed. It was hard enough living with my own ability. *Abilities.* I had more than one now.

I could find lost objects.

I could see scenes from my and Sean's future.

And I could see pieces of a person's life through their eyes by holding something that belonged to them.

I just didn't know how to control that last one. Didn't know how to turn it on and off.

Sam had given me directions on how to find Sean, and had let me borrow one of SDI's cars to get here. He'd also loaned me a tote bag, in which I'd placed my phone and the pink bear. I had a death grip on the bag's straps. No punk skateboarder was going to get this bag away from me. That bear was my link to Bethany.

And my link to figuring out more about myself.

I slowly walked along, thinking about Sean. About why he was here. Sam had said that this was Sean's thinking spot. Where he went when he was stressed out or simply needed time alone. The spot where he worked through his troubles.

The spot where his biological mother was buried.

I debated whether to come. After all, if this was the place he came to be alone, my intrusion might not be welcome.

Then again, it was about time Sean Donahue learned that he didn't have to shoulder his troubles alone—and that I wasn't going anywhere.

A raindrop plopped onto my head as sunbeams lit the path. Another dropped and another.

A sun shower.

One of my favorite things.

I opened the umbrella and stood still, listening to the rain splat against the polyester covering. I breathed deep, loving the smell of the droplets hitting the hot pavement. I drew in another deep breath as I rounded a bend and saw Sean up ahead, sitting on a bench. Thoreau was curled up alongside him, sound asleep.

Sean hadn't noticed me yet, and I took a second to watch him. The way he had his arms folded across his chest, his hands clenched as if ready to throw a punch at any moment. The way his legs jutted onto the path. The sharp angle of his jaw. The curve of his cheek. The waviness in his hair. The way he didn't even seem to notice the rain. The way his gaze was fixated on a tombstone across the path.

The way sadness emanated from him, making my knees weak, my heart ache.

His head turned, and his gaze met mine.

Just like that, my foot didn't hurt. I wasn't worried about the arsonist, or Ebbie, or anything.

My sole focus was him.

And at that moment, I was his.

My pulse thrummed in time with the falling raindrops as

I walked slowly toward him, and his expression darkened when he noticed my limp. Thoreau suddenly woke from his nap as if sensing a change in the air. His head came up and turned left and right as he glanced at Sean, then at me. In a flash, he hopped down from the bench and raced to me, as fast as his legs could carry him.

I bent down to scoop him up and allowed him to slather my chin in doggy kisses. His short fur was damp, and I wrinkled my nose at the sour smell.

When I reached the bench, I sat down next to Sean, my side pressing against his. I held my umbrella over both our heads, and Thoreau busily sniffed my tote bag.

"What happened to your foot, Ms. Valentine?" he asked quietly.

"A skateboarding incident," I said, looking into his troubled eyes.

He shook his head. "Why do I feel there's more to that story?"

"Because there is." I smiled and reached out to wipe a rain drop from his cheek. "Have you been here all day?"

"Most of it."

I glanced across the path, at the simple tombstone facing us.

Holly Cavanagh.

Cavanagh. I committed the name to memory. After all, it had once been Sean's name, too, before the Donahues adopted him.

"Did Sam tell you I was here?" he asked.

"Mmm-hmm."

"He shouldn't have."

"You're right about that. *You* should have told me."

Rain drops dripped off the umbrella and splattered onto our legs. Thoreau curled up in my lap.

"I," he began, then stopped. He picked up my left hand, and turned it palm up. Little zaps of electricity shot down my fingers and up my arm as he trailed his fingertips over my skin.

This is what happened between us—this electricity. If I pressed his palm against mine, I would have a vision. I recalled the first one I'd ever had, where I'd seen us in bed together.

"What's with the smile?" he asked, as he traced the valleys between my fingers.

"I was just remembering the first vision I ever had of us. In bed."

He traced the lines of my palms. My blood raced. "I remember, too."

He didn't *see* the visions I did, but he *felt* the same sparks, the same emotion.

That vision had been one of my misleading ones—we'd been in bed only to fool Dovie, but the thought of him bare-chested atop of me still made my internal temperature skyrocket.

I nudged him with my shoulder. "You should have told me where you were, Mr. Donahue. I was worried."

"I know."

His palm hovered over mine, and I tried to ignore the arcs of electricity flowing between our hands. "Then why didn't you?"

"I don't know that."

I took a breath, folded my hand closed and pulled it away. He wasn't going to distract me. I motioned to the tombstone. "Your mom?"

Slowly, he drew his hand back, too. His jaw clenched, and he nodded.

"She was young when she died," I prompted.

I felt his whole body tense next to me, and knew without a doubt how hard it was for him to talk about this. But it was time.

"Thirty-two."

Only two years older than he was now.

I did the mental math. He was ten when he was orphaned. "How did she die?"

I could hear his jaw working side to side, could feel his discomfort. "She had a heart attack while driving."

Rain splashed against the umbrella, my legs, my feet. I pulled Thoreau a little closer to me. "Heart attack?"

"That's what I was told."

"But not what you believe."

He shrugged. "My condition is genetic."

"Did she know she had a heart problem?" Sean hadn't known about his until *he'd* almost died.

"I don't know."

He sat stock-still, and tension emanated from him in waves. I pressed on. We had to get through this. "What was she like?"

"Lucy."

Thoreau glanced up at Sean's sharp tone. I pet his head, soothing him, and met Sean's gaze straight on. "Sean."

We stared at each other for a bit, neither blinking, neither giving in. Finally, I repeated, "What was she like?"

His Adam's apple bobbed.

"Was she blond-haired? Dark? A redhead? Did she have gray eyes like you? Was she sweet? Tough as nails? Or crazy like my mom?"

"A blonde, but not naturally. I remember the smell when she used those at-home kits."

"Horrible smell," I agreed. "Especially back in those days. Once, Marisol and I tried to dye Em's red hair black. It was her Goth phase, before there was such a thing as Goth. It took five hundred dollars and a hair stylist six hours to fix the damage."

His lip twitched. "Em did not have a Goth phase."

"I have pictures."

"I want to see them."

"We'll make a whole night of it. Popcorn and everything."

He leaned forward and pulled his wallet from his back pocket. Fingers fumbled as he dug through slots to find what he was looking for. Finally, he tugged out a worn photo and handed it to me.

Tears sprang as I looked at the image of a beautiful young woman holding a dark-haired toddler. They both had gray eyes. "You look a lot like her."

He nodded.

I studied her features, and noted the wave in her hair,

the long nose, the high cheekbones. She didn't have the superhero jaw—that must have come from his father, but the rest...he was a spitting image.

"That picture is the only thing I have left of her," he said.

"How is that possible?" I asked. It didn't seem right. What happened to all their family history?

"It was all lost between my moves in the foster system. A piece here, a piece there. One of my foster mothers thought I obsessed too much on my past and threw a lot of my things in the trash. That was the first time I ran away. I was eleven."

I handed the photo back to him. "How many times did you run away?"

He shrugged. "Too many to count. I met Sam when I was thirteen, and we lived on the streets together until one night when we were squatting in a vacant building and lit a fire to keep warm... The place went up in an instant. We tried frantically to put out the fire, but couldn't. Next thing we knew, the roof was caving in. We couldn't breathe. And then a pair of strong hands reached out and saved us."

"Daniel?"

Moisture shimmered in his eyes. "Daniel. I don't know how he managed it, but he talked his way around the social workers and brought us home."

"And kept you."

"We were lucky," he said softly. He glanced at me then, his eyes full of pain. "I can't lose Sam, too, Lucy."

Ah, the heart of the matter.

"You won't," I said.

"Why is someone doing this?" he asked, anguished.

"I don't know, but we'll find out." I cupped his chin. "We will find out."

He nodded and rested his forehead on mine. "I'm sorry I worried you."

"No more disappearing acts, okay?"

"Okay."

"Promise."

I felt his smile down to my soul. "I promise," he said.

"Cross your heart."

"Now you're pushing it."

I laughed and he kissed me. Heat spiraled through me, settling low in my stomach.

When we finally broke apart, he said, "Let's go. I'll make you dinner at my place and you can tell me all about this skateboarding incident of yours."

I was about to explain to him the problem with his suggestion—that he didn't have an apartment of his own any more—when my cell phone rang.

I glanced at the readout. Preston.

I wasn't going to answer until Sean pointed out that she wouldn't let me be until I did. Annie Hendrix had nothing on Preston when it came to persistence.

I was more than a little shocked when a man's voice came over the line. "Lucy?" he said.

"Who's this?"

"It's Paul. Paul McDermott."

Cranky Dr. Paul. Great. "Why are you using Preston's

phone?"

"She asked me to call you."

"Why?"

He sighed. "It's best if you just come down here."

"Where?"

"The emergency room. There's been...an incident."

Chapter Thirteen

The hospital was located in Quincy, just south of the city. I found a parking spot in the visitor garage, and Sean pulled his car in to a spot nearby.

At first when Dr. Paul said Preston had been involved with an "incident," my imagination had run wild with theories ranging from her breaking a patient out of the psych ward to her raiding the pharmacy. One never knew when Preston was involved.

But then he'd knocked the wind straight out of me by saying that Preston had collapsed and was currently in the ER having testing done.

My heart hammered as I threw the car into park and leapt out of my seat. Only when my foot hit the cement floor did I remembered my injury. My leg nearly buckled with the pain.

I swore a blue streak under my breath, inhaled deeply, and stumbled toward Sean's Mustang. The oppressive heat settled over me like a wet blanket. The rain showers only increased the humidity in the air and hadn't knocked down the temperature at all.

Sean cursed when he saw me limping so badly. "You'll get that looked at while we're here."

It hadn't been a suggestion. I brushed him off. "Em will look at it later."

"Only if she's *here* looking at it."

I narrowed my eyes on him.

He tipped his head, his eyes daring me to argue.

It was hard to squabble when pain was shooting up my leg. "Then you'd better give her a call."

He was nice enough not to gloat as he reached into the car and scooped out Thoreau. How we were going to sneak the dog into the hospital, I had no idea, but there was no way we were leaving him out here. Even with the windows down in the car, the temperatures would be unbearable within minutes.

"I called Andrew on the way over," Sean said. "He's coming by to pick up the company car and take Thoreau."

"Take him where?" I asked, trying to ignore the pain in my foot. However, it wouldn't be ignored. In fact, it was screaming like a barely-dressed groupie at a rock concert.

Sean reached out and wrapped his arm around my waist. "Put your arm around my shoulder."

"Bossy." I barely managed to smile.

He kissed my temple. "Watch it, or I'll let you go."

"You'd never," I countered.

Emotion clouded his eyes. "Not willingly, Lucy Valentine. Not willingly."

"Good to know," I said softly.

Warm lips pressed against my temple. "Andrew is taking Thoreau to Dovie's."

Dovie's halfway house for the wayward.

Between Ebbie and Thoreau, she could open some sort of shelter. And although she loved animals, she was going to spin her good deeds into asking favors from us. Undoubtedly, she was going to ask, yet again, that I procreate. Immediately. She was relentless in her quest for a great-grandchild.

Sean and I made our way into the emergency room, and surprisingly no one blinked twice at my gimpiness or at the dog. The waiting area was crowded, nearly every seat taken. Young, old, wealthy, homeless. The emergency room was a great society equalizer.

Sean propped me against a wall, handed off Thoreau to me, and strolled up to a registration desk to a stoic-looking older woman.

Her take-no-prisoners look melted away the more Sean spoke to her. He wasn't beyond using his charm to get what he wanted, and before I knew it he was leading me into a maze of trauma rooms.

"You have a way with older women," I said, hobbling along. This wasn't the first time he'd had a no-nonsense matronly type eating out of the palm of his hand. The last one was a librarian who hadn't wanted to give *me* the time of day.

"You have your gifts, I have mine."

"It's the dimples," I said. "Irresistible."

He smiled, and the dimple in his right cheek popped.

"You think so?"

"Put that thing away before the women in the geriatric ward swarm and carry you off."

Laughing, he led me down another hallway, and I was amazed at how relaxed he appeared to be.

Sean hated hospitals with a burning passion. He'd spent so much time in one after his heart surgery that even the smell of rubbing alcohol sometimes brought out anxiety.

We dodged a man being wheeled toward the elevator, and I threw a glance at Sean. I knew well that appearances could be deceiving. Especially where Sean was concerned. He used to be able to hide his emotions from me easily. Not anymore. I now could see through all his shields, and it had nothing to do with being psychic and everything to do with being in love with him.

"Thanks for coming here with me," I said.

"How could I not? It's Preston," he said simply.

Preston.

At some point over the last few months she went from being a thorn in my side to holding a piece of my heart. I wasn't altogether sure how it had happened, especially since she was a pain in the ass, but there was just something so...lovable about her.

And apparently Sean thought so, too.

I loved him even more because of it.

"There," Sean said, motioning with his jaw since his arms were full of hobbling woman and happy dog.

Dr. Paul stood outside a room reading a chart. He glanced up and his forehead wrinkled as he took in the sight of us.

His gaze dropped back to the chart. "I need a vacation," he said, shaking his head.

"Preston has that effect on people," I joked.

He didn't even crack a smile. "She's in there. Talk to her, will you?"

"About?" Sean asked.

Dr. Paul stared at Thoreau, opened his mouth to say something, then closed it again. Finally, he said, "She's refusing treatment. Won't even let a nurse put an IV in her arm."

"What happened?" I asked.

"Not sure." He wiped his forehead with the palm of his hand. "One minute she's interviewing one of my patients, the next she's on the floor. Scared the hell out of the patient."

"But not you?" I asked.

"People fall at my feet all the time," he said, straight-faced.

I stared at him.

He cracked a smile. "I'm joking."

"Ah," I said.

Dr. Paul frowned. "Anyway, talk to her. People don't usually collapse for no reason."

He had a point.

"What's with your foot?" he asked, bending down for a closer look.

"My shoe went one way, my foot another."

Dr. Paul stood up and said, "The shoe won."

Sean gave me a confused look. "I thought it was a skateboarding incident?"

"I was chasing the skateboarder," I explained.

"I need more details, Lucy," Sean said.

I thought about my missing wallet, and how Graham had seen my license with a bullseye on it. As much as I wanted to, I couldn't keep information like that from Sean. If our roles were reversed I would want to know. However, now wasn't the time or place to talk about it. "I'll tell you later."

Dr. Paul glanced at me, at Sean, at Thoreau, muttered, "Vacation," and turned to walk away. His lab coat flapped as he turned a corner and disappeared.

Sean said, "Personable fellow."

I smiled. "Tell me about it."

I tapped on the closed door.

"Go away!" Preston shouted.

Talk about personable. "I think that means we can go in," I said.

Sean agreed. I turned the handle and pushed the door open. Preston sat, fully dressed, on top of the bed, her arms crossed, her eyes blazing. Her gaze widened as we came in.

"Thank God you're here. Now I can go." She hopped off the bed.

"Whoa!" I said. "Slow down."

"I promised creepy Dr. Paul that I would stay only until you showed up. You're here. Let's go."

"Wait, wait. I need to sit down for a minute." Sean helped me to a chair. I wished that I'd been faking my relief at sitting down, but it had been one hundred percent real. My foot was killing me.

Preston tapped her heel. "Okay? Can we go now?"

I leaned back in the chair. "Aren't you even going to ask me what happened?"

"You can tell me in the car. Let's go."

"Actually," Sean said, "We're probably not leaving for a while. I need to call Em to come and take a look at Lucy's foot."

Preston paled. "You're kidding."

I unwrapped the bandage and winced at the sight. "Does that look like I'm kidding?"

For a brief second, sympathy flashed in her eyes. Then she held out her hand, palm up to Sean. "Give me your keys. I'll come back for you."

"Preston," I said, "sit down. Tell me what happened."

"What happened?" she echoed, gaping. "What happened? I'll tell you what happened. Creepy Dr. Paul is trying to kill me. That's what happened."

Sean sat on the edge of the bed. He still cradled Thoreau, and if the smirk on his face was any indication, he was enjoying Preston's theatrics a great deal.

"He said you passed out. Is that true?" I asked. I studied her closely and noticed she looked a little pale. No, not a little. A lot.

"Lucy, I swear he's the angel of death or something. The Grim Reaper. Did you know he collects tiny skulls?"

"Real ones?" Sean asked.

"Porcelain, but still. That's weird," Preston said, her

voice high. "You can't tell me it's not."

It was a bit...odd. But Dr. Paul was a bit odd, so it didn't seem so strange to me. Wisely, I kept my mouth shut about it though. Sometimes it was best just to let Preston get it all out of her system.

"He's weird," she rattled on. Pulling a small notebook from her pocket, she consulted her notes and added, "He has to wash his hands a certain way, he does this skip-walk thing that makes me nuts, he always takes the stairs. He won't let his food touch; his favorite TV show is *Dexter*. And, even though he's almost forty-five, he still lives with his mother." Her bright eyes flashed between me and Sean. "The man is clearly a serial killer."

"And you've clearly lost your mind," I said.

Jabbing a finger on her notebook, she gaped at me. "Didn't you hear a word I said?"

I needed to redirect her thoughts. "It makes good fodder for your article, don't you think?"

"Yeah, especially after the police dig up his basement and find dozens of bodies."

"Preston..." I said.

"I have good instincts," she insisted.

It was true, but I still wasn't buying that Dr. Paul was the angel of death.

Sean said, "Which of the Whiners are you following tomorrow?"

Ah, I loved that man. He knew exactly how to divert Preston. Work.

"Graham," she said. "And all week I'd been dreading it,

because he's kind of sleazy, but after today, Graham is looking pretty good. He doesn't give me the serial killer vibe at all."

"Good to know," I said, adjusting my tote bag on my lap.

Preston glowered at me. "I don't appreciate your sarcasm."

Biting back another "Good to know," I said, "Dr. Paul says you passed out? What happened?"

She paced. "He must have slipped me something. I don't know when, because I haven't had anything to eat or drink..."

"That could be the problem," Sean said.

She spun on him. "Whose side are you on?"

His dimple popped. "How about I get you a snack?"

"How about no?" she countered.

Unfortunately for him, his dimples had no effect on her.

I took my cell phone out of my tote and started dialing.

"Who are you calling?" she asked.

"Cutter."

She grabbed for my cell, but I pulled it out of her reach.

"Are you out of your mind?" she asked.

"Are you?" I said. "You passed out, Preston. And Dr. Paul is *not* trying to kill you. So that means something is wrong. Maybe it's dehydration. Maybe it's something else. We don't know because you're being irrational."

She gasped. "Irrational? You did not just call me *irrational.*"

"And since you won't listen to us, maybe you'll listen to

Cutter."

"Do not call him about this," she warned.

"Then sit your skinny little self on that bed and let Sean get you something to eat and drink." I'd push for some blood work in a little bit.

Brows furrowed, she folded her arms. Stubbornly, she stood firm.

I continued to dial.

"Fine!" She stomped to the bed and sat next to Sean. Thoreau licked her arm.

I casually put my phone away.

As Sean headed out to find sustenance for Preston, she said, "That was low, Lucy Valentine. Low."

"He'd want to know that you're not feeling well."

"Whatever," she huffed.

I eyed her carefully. "Is something going on with you two?"

She shook her head.

"Preston? Is there?"

When she glanced at me, I was surprised to see a shimmer of tears in her eyes. "I—"

Just then a nurse rolled a wheelchair into the room. "Lucy Valentine?"

"Yes?"

"Hop in."

"I don't understand," I said.

The nurse wheeled the chair closer to me. "Dr. McDermott ordered x-rays for your foot." She handed me a clipboard. "I also need some information from you."

"There's been a mistake. This can wait," I said. "I'm fine."

She stared at my foot. "I don't think so."

"Really, it can."

"Doctor's orders," the nurse said firmly.

"Maybe I could have a word with Dr. Paul?"

"He said he'd meet you in radiology."

"I don't thi—"

"Now Lucy," Preston interrupted, "don't be *irrational.*"

I threw daggers at her.

She grinned at me.

"Fine," I said through clenched teeth. "But just to prove a point to you." I slid into the wheelchair and was suddenly feeling a little anxious. Preston usually had good instincts about people. Maybe it would be a good idea to have someone with me. "Preston, why don't you come along?"

"Uh-uhn. No way. You're on your own."

I clutched my tote for dear life. "Well, you'd better be here when I get back."

She continued to smile. "If Dr. Paul wants to order your favorite food and call your family, make a run for it. Oh, wait. You probably can't run with that injury... I'll give you a good eulogy, I promise."

I groaned as her laughter followed me down the hallway.

Chapter Fourteen

The dimly-lit radiology room was freezing.

My teeth were starting to chatter as I sat atop a table and waited for someone. Anyone. When I couldn't provide proof of insurance, the technician had disappeared. And Dr. Paul had yet to show up.

So I was alone.

Surrounded by humming machinery.

I wanted to jump up and turn on all the lights, but I didn't see any light switches. The room was darkened, and the arms of the machines threw shadows on the walls.

It was eerie, and I was trying not to get creeped out.

Glancing around, I tried to occupy my mind with something else. Anything else.

I tried concentrating on Preston, and what was going on with her and Cutter, but as I sat here in all this eerie wonder, all I could picture was my driver's license with a big red bullseye on it.

I shuddered and thought about making a run—well, a

limp—for it when my phone rang.

Glancing around, I looked for any signage that said I couldn't use it, and didn't see any. Pulling my phone from my tote, I had to smile when I saw the Caller ID.

Suz.

"Let me guess," I said after I answered. "Annie Hendrix is flooding our office voicemail."

"What on earth happened, Lucy? She's in hysterics. She's left dozens of messages ranging from teary apologies to cussing you out. All usually end with her begging you to call her back."

"You might want to shut off the voicemail system," I said.

"Are you kidding? Her calls are pure entertainment. I'm thinking about putting them on YouTube. Can I?"

"No."

"You're no fun."

"I know."

"So, what happened with her?"

"Just teaching her a little lesson," I said.

"And how long are you planning to let her suffer?"

"I haven't decided yet."

I could hear the smile in her voice. "Every once in a while, I get a little glimpse of your father in you."

"I'm not sure that's a compliment."

"I'm not sure, either."

"So much for your raise," I teased.

She laughed, promised to keep me up-to-date on the Annie situation, and hung up. As I tucked my phone away, my gaze lingered on the pink bear.

I pulled it from my tote bag and removed it from its plastic casing. Holding it in my hands, I tried again to get a reading.

The bear's fur, though matted from love and time, was still soft under my fingertips. Closing my eyes, I pictured Bethany holding the bear, serving it tea, reading to it, talking to it. The bear was her clearly her friend, and I wondered if she missed her buddy.

If she was still alive to miss it.

I hugged the bear to my chest and rested my chin atop its head.

My palms tingled, a light flashed, and once again I was looking at a scene through someone else's eyes.

Bethany's eyes.

I saw clearly the man who'd taken her, and the truck he drove. I forced myself to focus on trying to read the license plate. I could tell only that it was a Maine plate—the numbers were obscured with a thick layer of mud. The truck itself was a black Ford. No dents, no dings, no rust spots. A truck that millions of people probably owned.

The man was tall. Dark hair stuck out from beneath a black knit cap. Plain blue eyes. Unruly backwoods beard. Dirty coveralls. Short, clean fingernails. His coat was one I recognized as being from a high-priced designer.

This was no backwoodsman. The clothes, the beard, were part of his disguise.

I jumped as the door to the radiology room opened and nearly dropped the bear.

The visions vanished. Woozy, I rubbed my eyes.

Dr. Paul tipped his head as he came toward me. He glanced at the bear, then up at me again. I was surprised to see the amount of kindness in his eyes. He did not strike me as a kind man.

"Did you see anything?"

"The man who took her," I said, carefully tucking the bear into its bag. "And the truck."

"Maine plates?" he said.

My head snapped to look at him. "You knew that?"

"I saw it this morning," he said, sitting on the edge of the x-ray table.

"You didn't say anything."

He lifted his shoulder in a half shrug. "I don't always believe it's best to reveal your hand all at once. After class, I did call Orlinda to let her know and left a message on her voicemail."

And he'd told me... Realization dawned. "You didn't want Annie and Graham to know."

"They're the jealous sort, and there's only room enough for one teacher's pet in our class, don't you think?"

My jaw dropped. "You don't want them picking on you like they do me."

"Can you blame me?"

"Yes, yes I can."

He laughed, then sobered. "Do you think you could pick the man who kidnapped the little girl out of a lineup?"

I nodded.

"You should call Orlinda, then, and let her know. It

might be time to take our investigating to the next level."

I agreed. "Do you think she's alive?"

"The girl?"

"B—" I cut myself off from saying "Bethany." For some reason, I didn't want to tell him her name. I supposed I wasn't keen on revealing all my cards, either. I nodded.

"I don't know. Usually, I can only feel spirits leaving a body and when departed loved ones visit those close to death."

"Usually?"

"Lately, I've been able to feel spirits around all the time. But I haven't yet learned how to communicate with them."

I was curious. "How do you feel them?"

"A cold wind, a chill right to the bone."

"Is one with me?" I asked.

He shook his head. "No, but..."

"What?"

"Your boyfriend..."

"Sean?"

"There's a strong presence with him. It pulses. You can't feel it?"

I thought about the tombstone I'd just seen and wondered if the spirit was Sean's mother. "Not at all."

"Strange how our abilities are so different. I suppose that's why there can be so many charlatans. It's not as though being psychic comes with a set of rules."

I nodded. "Rules would be nice. Page forty-two," I intoned. "How to speak to the dead. Step one."

He laughed. "That would be useful."

"Preston thinks you're the Grim Reaper."

"I know. I've been having fun with her all day."

I was beginning to like Dr. Paul. First Graham, now Dr. Paul. Next thing I knew I was going to be BFFs with Boobalicious Annie.

"Did you get her to have blood work done?" he asked.

"Not yet. I'm working on it. I have to tell you, though, that she's probably not going to do it. She's stubborn."

"I don't like seeing symptoms and not having a diagnosis. Keep an eye on her." He glanced toward my foot, then looked around. "Where's the tech?"

"Paperwork problems. I don't have my insurance card with me. Or a credit card."

He mumbled under his breath about red tape and said, "I'll take care of it."

In an adjacent glass room, he picked up a phone and made a call. A second later, he was back at my side. "The tech will be here in a second."

"Thanks," I said. I picked at a loose thread on my tote bag. "Can I ask you something?"

"Sure."

"Do you really collect tiny skulls?"

"One for every patient who dies."

I felt my eyes grow wide.

He laughed. "I'm joking! I used to have a collection of cat figurines, but my partner thought I needed to beef up my image a bit. He started the skull collection. It caught on. Now my patients give them to me as gifts."

"Your partner?"

"Martin. He works in the Medical Examiner's office."

"You can't get away from death, can you?"

"Like they say, Lucy. You can run, but you can't hide."

My foot was broken.

Not my ankle, thankfully, which would have caused me to be in a cast for at least six weeks. As it was, I had to use crutches and an orthopedic boot.

Dr. Paul made sure I had the best orthopedic doctor in the hospital look at my foot, prescribed me some pain-killers, and kept me laughing with death jokes.

Maybe it was the medication, but by the time he left for the night, I thought of him as a friend.

It had been hours since my diagnosis, and I was ready to go home. While I was in x-ray, Preston hitched a ride home with Andrew, without even saying goodbye. In retaliation, I'd sicced Dovie on her. In no time flat Dovie had driven to Preston's place, made her pack a bag, and brought Preston home with her.

Home—to the halfway house for the wayward.

Dovie had a full house.

Sean had called Em to fill her in, but insisted she didn't have to come to the hospital since I was just about ready to head home.

As Sean listened to a nurse go on and on about my discharge orders, I fought back a yawn. It had been an incredibly long day.

It was another twenty minutes before I was finally settled in Sean's car, my crutches stowed in the back seat.

He put his hand on my knee. "I just need to stop at the penthouse for a few things before I take you home. I'll stay the night at your place, if that's okay with you."

I glanced at him through sleepy eyes. "Actually, you don't have to stop at the penthouse."

"Why?"

"Because earlier this afternoon, you moved in with me. Surprise!"

His face remained blank, but his fingers drummed the steering wheel. "I'm guessing there's a good explanation?"

Yawning, I nodded.

"Well, I can't wait to hear it, Ms. Valentine. But first, close your eyes and sleep. Don't worry. I'll take good care of you."

Oh, of that I had no doubt.

Chapter Fifteen

I slept all the way home, only waking when the tires of the car crunched over the crushed seashell lane that led to my cottage.

Dusk settled under thin, wispy clouds, and the roar of waves crashing echoed in the night.

A warm welcoming glow filled the windows of my cottage, and I caught sight of Grendel sitting on a sill, peering out. Waiting for me.

I was glad Raphael had been by earlier—Grendel had anxiety issues and being home alone all day would likely mean a disaster for me to clean up.

Sean said, "Stay right there. I'll come around."

I yawned and stretched and glanced toward Dovie's house, set slightly uphill from mine. Her house, nicknamed Aerie, was a glorious sprawling New England manor. Weathered wood and stone, it fit perfectly on the coastline, its many windows glowing like beacons.

Sean opened my door and gently grabbed hold of my

forearms to help me out. I adjusted my tote bag on my shoulder and balanced on one foot while he extricated my crutches from the back seat. I was allowed to put only minimal weight on my foot for the next six weeks.

It was going to be a long six weeks.

"Easy now," Sean said, navigating me along the stone path leading to the porch. Beautiful annuals bloomed, their color lit by small garden lights. The wind was blowing just enough for me to feel the spray of the ocean's breakers, a gentle mist that would coat the many windows of my cottage—a former artist's retreat—with salt.

The air was rich with the heady scent of lilacs. There were several varieties planted alongside my cottage to ensure blooms well into June. I treasured those shrubs, which had come from cuttings from my mother's garden.

I loved this cottage. It was home.

Especially now that Sean would be living here, too.

I managed the few porch stairs, paused at the front door, then looked back at him.

"Are you okay?" he asked.

"I don't have a key."

His dark eyebrows drew downward. "Where is it? In the car?"

I shook my head. "No, not in the car. I have no idea where they are. Well, other than maybe in a kitchen somewhere."

Confusion slashed across his face.

"Long story," I said.

"You have a lot of those today."

"Tell me about it."

He pulled his keychain out of his pocket. "Well, I have mine."

"It's not going to work," I said. "Raphael changed the locks earlier. I forgot to ask him what he did with the new set of keys, though."

A voice rang out. "Yoo-hoo! LucyD!"

Dovie.

Sean's lip quirked. "I think I have a good idea what he did with them."

We turned and saw Dovie bustling down the hill, along the worn path that led from my house to hers.

It was a well-traveled path.

But Dovie's intrusion into my everyday life was a small price to pay for living here. Besides, I happened to adore her—even when she was pestering me about having babies.

She jangled a set of keys as she came up the steps. "LucyD, my God, girl. What did you do to yourself? Em said something about your foot?"

"I broke it."

Dovie smiled and waggled her eyebrows. "Bed rest?" She elbowed Sean in the ribs.

I rolled my eyes. "No, no bed rest. I can get around on the crutches just fine."

"More's the pity." She *tsk*ed. "Well, come on then, let's get you inside and get that foot propped up. I'm no stranger to broken feet, broken ankles, broken toes and what's best is time, plain and simple. Time in bed is even better."

Dovie had once been a burlesque dancer and then became a choreographer. She still worked at the local community theater and had the best moves in her Zumba class. Tall, lean, and lithe, she kept up her looks by eating right, staying active, and visiting her plastic surgeon regularly. "Let it go, Dovie."

Above her head, Sean gave me a smile. He used to find Dovie's attempts to get us to have a baby horrifying, but now he was amused by it.

I was still horrified.

"Party pooper. How long are you in that dreadful boot? Six weeks? Eight?" she asked.

"Six," I said as Sean took the key from her and slid it into the lock.

The alarm system beeped until Sean punched in the code. Grendel let out a huge meow and sprinted over to me, only to start hissing at the boot.

He looked at me like I had betrayed him.

Just wait till he met Ebbie.

Speaking of... I glanced at Sean. "You should probably go up and get Thoreau and Ebbie."

Dovie said, "No, no. I'll get them. You stay right here with Lucy, Sean. I've made some chili, too. I'll bring it down."

"Chili?" I said. "On the hottest day of the year?"

"Fight fire with fire, LucyD." She hurried out the door and scurried up the path.

I plopped onto the couch and Grendel immediately hopped up on me. I guess he'd forgiven me for bringing the boot in the house.

He was a creamy orange and white colored Maine Coon with expressive golden eyes and a weight problem. Maine Coons were normally extremely large, but Grendel tipped the scale. Marisol had put him on a diet, for which he'd yet to forgive her.

Bumping his head under my chin, he purred as I stroked his fur. Sean walked over to the mantel. Raphael had unpacked Sean's things and had mixed Sean's pictures in with mine. He stood there staring at the assortment of photos.

Finally, he turned around. Solemnly, he said. "They look good there."

I nodded. "You look good here."

He gave me a saucy smile. "Are you flirting with me?"

I lifted my foot and placed it on my coffee table. "I'm under the influence of Dovie."

Laughing, he kissed the top of my head as he passed by on his way into the kitchen. My small cottage had an open layout. The living and dining room blended into the kitchen. The one and only bedroom was at the back of the cottage. I could hear my hamster, Odysseus, whose cage sat on my dresser, running on his wheel. He was up early tonight—it was only a little past nine.

Sean brought me a glass of ice water. I stared at it. "What? No wine?"

"Wine doesn't mix with your painkillers. Doctor's orders." He took my tote bag and started emptying its contents. Discharge papers; my phone; the pink bear. He carefully set that in the bassinet that Dovie had gifted. I still hadn't figured out what to do with it.

I'd told Sean all about my experience in the radiology room—except for the part where Dr. Paul mentioned that Sean had strong spirit vibes around him.

He normally took all my psychic baggage in stride, but he'd already had a tough day and knowing that he had spirits around him might send him over the edge.

"To think I'd actually started liking Dr. Paul." I leaned over Grendel and picked up the pile of mail on the coffee table that Raphael must have brought in.

"He seems nice enough. A little strange, but nice."

"A lot strange, but nice." I pulled a magazine from the bottom of the pile and groaned.

"What is it?"

I held it up as he plugged my phone into the wall to charge. "*Parents* magazine. Apparently Sean and Lucy Donahue are new subscribers."

This magazine subscription was probably what my mother had warned me about. Or, at least I hoped so.

He laughed. I loved the way it sounded, deep and raspy. For now, he was content. Knowing him, it wouldn't last long. The arsonist was still at large. Sam was still in danger. And I hadn't yet told him about Graham's vision. It was bound to be a long night—Sean never slept well when he had a lot on his mind.

"She's tenacious," he said.

"Delusional is more like it. I don't know how to get her to stop."

He rummaged around in the kitchen. "The only way

might be to have a baby."

I whipped around so fast, I nearly knocked Grendel off my lap. Which was saying something.

Sean blinked at me innocently as he pulled a beer from the fridge. He twisted off its top and took a huge swallow. "It's true."

We'd never talked seriously about kids. Hell, we hadn't even been able to make a decision about moving in together until an arsonist forced us.

I swiveled in my seat so I wasn't craning my neck. "Do you want kids?"

He filled Thoreau's dish with dog kibble. "I'm not sure. You?"

"I never thought I did, until..."

As Sean popped the top off Grendel's cat food, he leapt off me, incredibly agile for only having three legs and being overweight. He darted into the kitchen and meowed pitifully until Sean put his plate on the floor.

I knew where Grendel's loyalties laid. In his food dish.

Sean washed his hands and glanced at me. "Until?" he prompted.

My throat was oddly clogged, and there was a sting in my nose. I bit my lip to keep my emotions in check. "Until I met you."

In my mind's eye, I could see a little girl with my blond hair, his gray eyes. And a little boy with Sean's dark hair and my brown eyes. I often had these thoughts, though sometimes the features were swapped. I wasn't sure whether these children were the product of a psychic vision of my future...or wishful thinking.

Sean came and sat next to me, his leg pressed against mine. "Even with all my baggage?"

"That baggage has helped shaped who you are today. You'd be a wonderful dad."

His jaw slid side-to-side, and I reached my hand out to hold it still. Sean captured my palm and placed a kiss on it.

Heat sizzled up my arm.

He pulled me to him, bringing his mouth hard against mine, crushing me with his intensity.

With his love.

Passion flared as we kissed, making me forget everything about this horrible day and giving thoughts only of the future.

A future filled with possibilities.

Of marriage.

Of babies.

Of happiness.

The anticipation was almost too much to bear.

His arms anchored me against his chest, and I'd never felt safer than at that moment.

Never felt happier.

"Well now, that's what I like to see," Dovie's voice rang out, along with a yip from Thoreau. "I'll be quick. Don't mind me none. Continue on. I need to work on my timing..."

I opened my eyes and found Sean still gazing at me. And in his pearly gray depths I saw his happiness, too.

My heart raced so fast, I was sure he could feel it against

his chest.

Thoreau leapt up on us, and we finally pulled apart, the spell broken.

Ebbie's carrier sat on my coffee table. Her green eyes peered out from behind the mesh. The poor thing had quite the day.

Thoreau dove off the couch and went looking for his favorite playmate—Grendel. The two rolled on the floor together.

Dovie was scraping a Tupperware bowl of chili into a pot. "I'm hurrying," she said.

"Take your time," I said, reaching for Ebbie's carrier. I set it on the floor.

"Are you sure?" Her eyes darted between Sean and me.

I sighed. "Yes." Though, honestly, I couldn't wait for her to go so Sean and I could pick up where we'd left off.

He slid to the floor and held his hand out for Ebbie to sniff. Grendel strode over and stared at the newcomer.

Thoreau didn't seem the least bit bothered by another cat in the house. He gobbled up his kibble and then plunked himself down in his doggy bed next to the fireplace.

Dovie pulled a couple of bowls from a cabinet. "Em said she'd check on you tomorrow morning, and your mother wants me to hire you a nurse."

My pulse was returning to a normal rhythm. "I don't need a nurse."

"That's what I told Judie," Dovie said, stirring the chili with a wooden spoon. "I'm perfectly capable of taking care of you."

Maybe a nurse wasn't a bad idea.

"I'm fine," I said. "It's not a bad break. It's just going to slow me down for a while. And really, since the office is closed for the rest of the week, the timing isn't all that horrible."

"The whole office is closed? I thought only your father was going on vacation."

I explained about the arsonist and elicited a promise that she wouldn't tell my mother.

Dovie abandoned the chili and sat on the edge of the coffee table. "And that's why you moved in here?" she asked Sean.

He unzipped the carrier and backed off a bit so Ebbie could venture out on her own. "Oscar evicted me."

Rubbing her temples, she said, "But you're staying, right? Even when this arsonist business is done with?"

Sean glanced at me. "Yes."

She smiled. "Good. This is where you belong. What's happening with the arson investigation?"

I looked to Sean for an update. We'd been avoiding the topic all evening. He said, "I spoke with a friend at the department today, and there isn't much to report. The fires were all started with a simple gasoline cocktail and lit with a match. No witnesses. The police are still investigating how Sam plays a role in it."

His jaw started sliding side to side again.

"Any useable evidence?" Dovie asked.

Sean nodded. He reached into his pocket and pulled out

a small evidence bag. "There are others identical to this one."

Inside the small plastic bag was a single unlit wooden matchstick.

"They let you have that?" Dovie asked.

"As a favor," Sean said. "This stick has already been processed, so it's safe to handle, but I have to return it tomorrow. I know Lucy's been working on reading objects... The hope is that she can see who owned the matchstick."

They both stared at me.

I held up my hands. "Whoa! I don't know how the whole object thing works. I can't control it."

"Well, LucyD, you can *try*," Dovie said.

I thought about Sam and his little girls. Of course I had to try. "Hand it over."

Sean shook the stick into my palm. I clamped it between both hands and thought about Sam, about the fires, about anything I could relate to the arsonist.

Nothing. Not so much as a flicker.

I shook my head and opened my eyes. "I'll keep trying."

"This is all so disturbing," Dovie said. "But Sam will be safe with Raphael, and let's hope that the arsonist keeps away from the office." She patted my knee. "And don't you worry none about the employees. I'll make sure they receive paychecks."

Sometimes I loved my grandmother more than I could say.

Ebbie stuck her nose out of the bag. Her whiskers

twitched.

Grendel looked curious.

"What's with the cat?" Dovie asked. "Raphael would only laugh when I asked him."

I told Dovie about Jeremy Cross. She laughed, too.

Standing, she said, "I should get back to the house and check on Preston. Chili is ready—it's just simmering. It's spicy, but not as spicy as you two." She wagged a finger at us.

I ignored the spicy comment. "How's Preston doing?"

Ebbie took a tentative step out of her carrier, her green eyes wide with wonder. Grendel wiggled his butt and pounced, diving on top of her.

I let out a cry, but before Sean could separate them, Grendel had rolled Ebbie over and was licking her face.

I stared. Sean stared. Dovie stared.

Well. That hadn't been the reaction I predicted.

"He likes her," Dovie said.

"A lot," Sean added with a laugh.

I watched as Ebbie playfully tapped Grendel's head with her paw. She was tolerating the attention well. "That's a good thing, I suppose."

"Maybe now," Dovie said, "Grendel will stop molesting Thoreau."

"Maybe." Though I doubted it. Grendel adored Thoreau. I glanced at Dovie. "Preston?" I reminded.

"Tuckered," she said. "Barely ate anything and went straight to bed. Is everything okay with her and Cutter? Because she has all the markings of a broken heart."

"I'm not sure." Was Dovie right? Preston had seemed perfectly fine this morning...

"Well, maybe Em can give her a checkup tomorrow and just make sure everything's hunky dory."

I smiled at the old-fashioned term. It sounded like something Preston would say. "Where is Em?"

"Dinner with Aiden." Dovie winked. "I'm not sure she'll be back tonight."

I was glad Em had finally gotten hold of him. It was strange that he hadn't called me back.

"And you?" I asked. "Where's Mac?"

She beamed. She'd been dating Mac Gladstone for a couple of months now. He and his dog Rufus spent many nights at my grandmother's place. Recently, they'd been talking about moving in together.

"Waiting for me at the house." Dovie gave me a loud kiss and rubbed the top of Sean's head. "Ta-ta! Don't do anything I wouldn't do," she called as she walked out the door, laughing the whole time.

"Your family is crazy," Sean said with a wide smile. "Lovable, but crazy."

"I know." I glanced up at the mantel, at the pictures gathered up there, old and new. My gaze lingered on one of Sean and me.

He was going to fit right in.

Chapter Sixteen

I woke with a start, pain throbbing in my foot, disturbing images of pink bears, dark trucks, and fires in my head.

Glancing around, I realized I'd fallen asleep on the couch. At some point, Sean had tucked a blanket in around me. Ebbie had curled up at my side. She slept peacefully.

Sean sat in my favorite chair—a club that rocked and swiveled. He had a notebook in one hand, a pen in the other. "You okay?" he asked.

I struggled to sit up and he came over and helped me. I noticed Grendel and Thoreau snuggled in the dog bed. Grendel hogged most of the space.

"Need some medicine?" Sean asked, tucking a piece of my hair behind my ear.

I nodded, wondering when I'd dozed off. Glancing at the clock, I saw it was close to eleven. After Dovie had left, we'd eaten, and I told Sean all about the purse snatcher and Graham's vision of my driver's license.

The happiness I'd seen earlier in his eye vanished in a

blink.

There was nothing like a potential stalker to kill a mood, and I'd apparently fallen asleep on the couch not long after.

Bending down, I picked up my crutches and slowly stood up. I wobbled a bit on my way into the kitchen.

"I would have brought it to you," Sean said, handing me a painkiller and a cup of water.

I swallowed the medicine. "I want to get my jammies on and brush my teeth."

"Need help?"

"I can do it."

He narrowed his eyes on me, clearly assessing whether I actually could. "Okay. Holler if you need me."

I crutched my way into the bedroom and peered in at Odysseus. He stopped running on his wheel long enough to evaluate if I came bearing a treat. He must have decided I hadn't, because he went back to running.

Odysseus, a one-eyed hamster, had been a gift from Marisol, as had Grendel. They'd been classified as misfits by potential adopters at the vet clinic where she volunteered. Unadoptable; so Marisol had brought them to me.

And maybe because I was a misfit myself, we'd bonded right away.

I pulled a tank top and pair of tiny drawstring shorts from my bureau drawer and slipped into them. It took longer navigating the bathroom than I thought possible and I finally emerged to find Ebbie sitting atop my dresser, staring at Odysseus.

"No," I said to her. "He's family, not a snack."

She blinked at me.

I wondered how much she understood and wished Jeremy Cross had filled me in.

"Come on," I said, scooping her off the dresser and setting her on the floor. She dutifully followed me out of the room.

On my way past the dining room table, a fabulous table that Sean had gotten me for Christmas, I picked up my laptop and tucked it under my arm.

Sean lifted an eyebrow. "It's okay to ask for help."

"I know," I said.

He smiled and went back to staring at his notebook. I fired up my laptop and said, "What are you working on?"

"A suspect list."

"Oh? Can I see?"

Sean turned the notepad around, revealing only doodles drawn on the page. "If it's true that the arsonist is from Sam's childhood, I can't come up with a single suspect." He dropped the pad of paper on the coffee table and his head into his hands. "It's so frustrating."

I could feel his tension. "Do you know Sam's history? What was his childhood like?"

"He doesn't talk much about it."

I was seeing a trend with that.

"All I know is that it was abusive and the state removed him from his home when he was little; around four or five."

"Do you know if he has biological siblings?" Could

these acts of arson be the ultimate in sibling rivalry?

"If he does, he never said."

Sean dragged a hand over his face. Ebbie tiptoed over to him and gracefully jumped in his lap. He picked her up and held her against his chest while scratching her ears.

My heart melted just a little bit more.

"Can you remember him having any enemies? How long were you two on the streets together?"

"Six months. And there's only one kid I can recall. His street name was Johnny Largo." He shot me a wry look. "He was a big boy. But Sam always managed to outsmart him, and it pissed Johnny off to no end."

"Do you know his real name?"

Sean shook his head.

"Do you think anyone in that neighborhood would know it? Or maybe his old school?"

"He didn't go to school, Lucy."

It was a whole unfamiliar world. My computer whirred quietly, warming up. "Maybe DCF?" The Department of Children and Families. I was grasping at straws, but this was Sam. *Sam.*

"Those records are sealed to the public. Not that it would matter if they weren't. All the foster and adoption records made during the eighties went up in smoke in that warehouse fire last month, remember?"

Goose bumps popped up on my arms. "A fire?"

Sean's eyes darkened. "Jesus," he whispered. "What are we dealing with?"

Sean continued staring at his notepad as if an epiphany would emerge from the college-ruled lines. We both agreed that this case was over our heads, but we were still ready to dive in to the deep end.

The problem was that we were looking for ghosts. The ghosts of Sam's past.

It was an impossible task.

But we were going to try.

Tomorrow morning we would get together with Sam and try to uncover more information. For now he was safe with Raphael.

We also planned to take a trip back to the neighborhood where Sean first met Sam on the streets. Maybe there were some old-timers there who would know Johnny Largo's true identity. Even if all the DCF records were gone, Johnny might still be able to be tracked down.

For kicks, I typed "Johnny Largo" into my web browser. Apparently there was a singer with the same name but wasn't the right age. Very little else.

I abandoned that search and typed in another name. I had my own ghost to search for.

Jeremy Cross.

There were too many hits to sort through. I narrowed it down to Jeremy Cross + psychic. Unfortunately, there were no relevant hits. I added "Massachusetts" into the search and the browser informed me that it had no matches at all.

I did another search, this one with Jeremy's name and "farm." Still nothing.

I stared at my blinking cursor. *Who are you, Jeremy?*

Glancing over at Ebbie, I frowned. For all intents and purposes, Jeremy Cross did not exist.

"What's wrong?" Sean asked. "Your foot?"

"No. It's Jeremy." I explained what I'd found. Or the *lack of* what I'd found.

Sean looked ready for a diversion. He turned on his laptop, too, and searched his P.I. databases. "There's nothing here that would match."

"So, 'Jeremy' is an alias?" I said.

"It's my guess," Sean said. "But why?"

I told Sean about the scar on Jeremy's face and what he'd said about my leg, and how I'd made the leap that he'd had a run-in with a psychopath, too.

He said, "You have the most interesting friends."

Ebbie was tucked next to him in the tiny space between his leg and the side of the chair. She slept peacefully. I smiled. "I wouldn't call him a friend."

"How are you going to find his match?"

"According to Jeremy, Ebbie's in charge. But I'm getting Cutter involved, too. However, I have to find Jeremy first."

Sean glanced down at the cat. "Do *you* believe she's in charge? That she's going to lead you to his soul mate?"

There was no mocking in his voice, just curiosity.

Inwardly, I searched for an answer. "Honestly? I don't know."

"But?"

"I'm willing to believe it."

"The Love Conquers All syndrome," he said with a drawn-out sigh.

Now he was mocking.

I tossed a throw pillow at his head. He often teased me about my belief that love could conquer all. I'd yet to convert him, but I was working on it.

Thoreau snuffled and rolled onto his back. Grendel lifted a sleepy eyelid and nuzzled deeper into the dog's side. The two adored each other.

Hopefully all three of the pets would continue to get along until I could figure out this Jeremy Cross situation. Why hadn't Orlinda called me back? Was she trying to teach me something? Was Jeremy part of another psychic lesson plan?

I glanced over at the bassinet by the front door. In it rested Bethany's pink bear. I thought about what I'd seen in that radiology room. The man. The license plate.

I knew well enough that the plate could have been misleading. Stolen. Bethany might not have even been kidnapped from Maine. I wanted more information.

Frowning at my blinking cursor, I deleted Jeremy's name from the search box and typed in Bethany + missing + Maine. My finger hovered over the enter button.

I wanted to find out as much as I could about Bethany's case. Her birth date. Her parents. Did she have siblings? Did anyone witness the abduction? Was the truck ever found? Was there a ransom note? Or any contact from the kidnapper afterward?

But I'd made a promise to Orlinda. To use only my psychic abilities to try and locate Bethany.

And really, the Internet couldn't answer my biggest question.

Was Bethany alive?

I pushed the delete button and closed my laptop.

Across from me, Sean was still staring with fierce concentration at the pad of paper. I was almost grateful for the arsonist's distraction. Otherwise, Sean would be worrying about the purse snatcher and Graham's vision.

I tried to push the thoughts out of my head. I had enough anxiety without dwelling on what may or may not be true. I needed a distraction.

I looked at Sean.

He sensed me staring and met my gaze. Slowly, he set his notepad on the table and dropped his pen. "What's that look in your eyes, Ms. Valentine?"

"My eyes?" I blinked dramatically. "Dust, maybe."

One of his dimples popped.

"You know, I was thinking about what you said earlier," I said.

"What's that?"

"About how it's okay for me to ask for help."

His other dimple popped. "And is there something with which you need help?"

I smiled at his very proper grammar. He had an English minor and sometimes it reared its head. "I believe so."

He eased out of his chair. "Do you want a drink?"

I shook my head.

"More medicine?" He knelt down on the floor next to the couch.

"No."

His hand slid up my thigh. "A book?"

I shook my head again, afraid my voice would crack. Just one look, just one touch, and he could make me melt.

"Well, what is it you want?"

"You."

"Well," he said, carefully setting my crutches aside and pulling me onto the floor with him, "I do think I promised to take good care of you."

The thick area rug was soft under my back as he tucked me beneath him. "Yes, yes you did."

His hand skimmed over my hip and dipped under the edge of my tank top. "How's your foot doing?" he asked.

"What foot?"

His fingers splayed across my ribcage, the tips barely touching the undersides of my breasts. "Let me help you with your shirt." In a flash, my shirt was off.

"Let me help with yours," I said, tugging his over his head.

I barely noticed the scar near his collarbone as my hands roamed over his chest.

This was the best distraction ever.

"And your shorts," he said, carefully sliding them down my legs and maneuvering them over my boot. He took his sweet time in kissing his way back up my legs, my stomach, my breasts. Finally, he reached my face and the desire in his eyes almost did me in.

"You're the best helper ever," I said.

He smiled, flashing his dimples. "You haven't seen anything yet, Ms. Valentine."

Chapter Seventeen

Enraptured, I watched the hand covered in a blue latex glove twist the cap off a generic water bottle and toss its contents in random arcs over the walls, across the counters, cabinets. He splashed the dining room cushions, the curtains.

Except it wasn't water. The sharp sting of gasoline filled my nostrils.

My heart thrummed as I watched the scene unfold. The hand set the bottle on the kitchen counter and pulled a wallet to him. He was precise with his movement, going straight for a driver's license.

With a red Sharpie, he drew concentric circles over a face.

My face.

Adrenaline coursed through my veins as the man turned the license over. On the back of it, he wrote five words.

CATCH ME IF YOU CAN

As he slid the license into a crack in the raised panel of a cabinet, I realized I was watching it all through his eyes.

A shudder rippled through me.

After picking up the water bottle, he turned and looked

downward, and I started when I spotted the body of a man on the floor. Face down. Unmoving.

The man stepped over him and turned back one more time.

Next thing I knew, he pulled out a matchbox. His hand didn't shake as he carefully removed a match, turned the box on its side, and placed the red match head against the strike strip.

With a quick swipe, a flame erupted. The man held it in front of his eyes for a moment, then he flicked it into the kitchen.

Flames burst from the floor. Licked across the floorboards and headed straight for the man on the ground.

My eyes flew open, and I bolted upright in bed, gasping for air. I clung to the sheets on the bed, trying to work through what I'd just seen.

It hadn't felt like a nightmare.

It had felt real. Very real.

Especially since I recognized the kitchen.

Sean sat up and placed his warm hand on my back. "Lucy?"

I tossed off the covers. "We have to go."

"Where?"

As soon as I put my feet on the floor, I crumpled in pain. I'd forgotten about my foot. Reaching down, I pulled my boot toward me.

The phone started ringing.

Sean rose out of bed, moonlight spilling across his naked body. He took a second to slip on a pair of pajama bottoms and ran for the phone in the kitchen.

I glanced at the clock. Two thirty-three.

My heart raced, and as I finished fussing with the Velcro

straps of the boot, I noticed Ebbie watching me carefully. She sat on the bed, next to my pillow.

I squinted in the darkness—there was something on my pillow. Sean's voice floated in, loud and clear in the silence of the night. "Who's calling?" he asked. "Hold on."

Turning on the bedside lamp, I groaned when I saw what Ebbie had done. The remnants of a chewed-up matchstick were spread like shrapnel across my pillowcase. It was the matchstick Sean had brought home.

Looking at Ebbie, I said, "You didn't."

She blinked innocently at me.

Suddenly, all I could think about were shards of wood in her digestive tract. I bent over her and opened her mouth. I couldn't see any sores, but I knew I'd have to have her looked at. The sooner the better. If a splinter pierced her stomach or esophagus or intestines... It would be bad.

But first...the dream.

The nightmare.

"Lucy," Sean said from the doorway, his hand covering the mouth of the portable phone. "It's Jeremy Cross."

I didn't have time for Jeremy right now. Had he somehow received a psychic message that Ebbie had eaten three-quarters of a matchstick?

I held my hand out for the phone, but kept the mouthpiece covered. To Sean, I said, "Use your cell and call 911, okay? Tell them there's a fire at Sam's house. And to hurry."

Sean blanched. "How do you know?"

Tears filled my eyes. "I don't know for sure. But I had

this dream...and it didn't feel like a dream."

"Lucy, I can't call with a hunch. A false report can get you arrested."

I stood up. "Call. Do it now. Please. There's a man in house. I think...he's dead. Do it. Please. Trust me."

He gave one quick nod and went to search for his phone. I took a deep breath and took my hand off the receiver. "Jeremy? I don't have t—"

"Damn it, Lucy Valentine, curse you and the day Orlinda brought me into your life. I should have known better. Now I'm dragged into this mess you're involved in..."

I reeled from the acid in his voice. "What mess?"

"The fires. The murder. Take your damn pick. I've called the fire department already with the address. I don't know whose house it is, but I know you're involved. I saw your driver's license."

I sat back down on the bed. Ebbie nudged my elbow with her nose. "You saw? The water bottle? The drapes? My wallet? The man on the floor? I was hoping it was a dream."

There was silence on the line for a moment. "It wasn't."

And he hung up on me.

Sean came back into the room, his face pale. With a cracking voice, he said, "The fire's already been reported. Trucks are at the scene."

I grabbed my crutches and a sweatshirt. "Let's go."

Sean reached for my arm and stopped me. "Who was the man, Lucy? The dead man?"

His pulse throbbed in his neck.

I shook my head. "I don't know."

Quietly, as if he'd used every last bit of strength in his body, he whispered, "Sam?"

I closed my eyes, and concentrated on the vision. I forced myself to recall the image of the man on the floor. I cupped Sean's jaw. "No, not Sam," I whispered.

The man I'd seen had been too short, his hair too dark and too long to have been Sam.

Lowering his head, Sean let out a breath. He released my arm and finally looked up. "Let me grab a shirt and we'll go. We can stop by Raphael's on the way."

"Grab Ebbie, too. I'll have Marisol meet us at Sam's."

"Ebbie? Why?"

"She ate your evidence."

"At least you provided eye candy," Marisol Valerius said, fanning her face.

Marisol and I sat on a curb across the street from Sam's house. Firefighters crisscrossed in front of us as they went back and forth from their trucks to the scene.

She checked out every male firefighter that passed by. "It almost makes it worth being called out of bed in the middle of the night."

"Thanks for coming over," I said, watching as crews continued to spray the house. Sean and Sam were together somewhere, talking to the police.

There was quite a bit of damage to the house, but it could have been worse. So much worse. Jeremy's call might have saved a man's life. The man I'd seen on the floor. He was severely burned, but he was alive. Barely, though. The EMTs didn't think he'd make it through the morning.

No one knew who he was, but the EMTs said the hospital might be able to get some fingerprints.

Might. The burns had been so bad...

"Of course," she said, peering into Ebbie's carrier. "She's a sweet girl, aren't you?"

Ebbie blinked.

Marisol stood and smoothed her hand down her shorts, brushing off pebbles and grass. "I should go. I'll take her to the clinic and run some tests. Wood doesn't show up on x-rays, though, so we might have to keep her for observation for a little bit. Most likely, she'll be fine."

"I know she's in good hands with you."

"You'll call her owner?" Marisol asked. Her shoulder-length black hair was pulled back in a tiny ponytail, and even though I'd dragged her out of bed at three in the morning, she still looked stunning.

I'd given her the Cliffs Notes version of how I'd come to care for Ebbie. "I'll try, but he's kind of off the grid, and kind of a jackass who doesn't deserve her."

But...he had saved a man's life. He didn't have to get involved when he had that vision. Yet he did...

"I hear a story there."

"A long one."

"Dinner this week?" she asked. "Maybe a girl's night in?"

"Sounds good." With the way my week was going, I'd

need a night of pure silliness.

"I'll call you with what I find out about this little one."

"Thank you." I gave her a kiss on the cheek. "And I'll take care of all her bills."

Marisol smiled. "I have your credit card on file."

"Not that it's going to do you any good. I had to cancel it today after my wallet was stolen."

An ache in my stomach worsened. How had my wallet ended up here? What did the purse-snatcher have to do with the arsonist?

What did *I* have to do with the arsonist?

Why had he drawn a bullseye on my face?

Concern filled her dark eyes. "As much as I love a firefighter—and I do, almost as much as Matt Damon, and you know that's saying something—what's going on here, Lucy?"

I balanced on my crutches.

"I don't know, Marisol. That's the terrifying part."

She glanced at the house, then back at me, a million questions in her eyes. But she only said, "Call me if you need me. And please be careful."

"I will," I said.

A moment later, she and Ebbie were gone, threading through the crowd of onlookers.

I sat back down on the curb and watched as small groups of firefighters went in and out of the house. Even though it was still hot and humid, I felt a chill. I zipped my sweatshirt up to my neck and wished I had put on a pair of yoga pants before I left the house.

Over the next hour, the crowd dispersed and Sean finally came back to me. Reeking of acrid smoke, he sat down. "Is Ebbie going to be okay?"

"Marisol thinks so."

"Good," he said, distracted.

His gaze followed the movement of the firefighters, and I knew he missed being one of them.

"How's Sam?" I asked.

"About as good as can be expected."

I imagined his family inside the house when the arsonist broke in, and it made me shiver. Thank God they hadn't been home.

"Where is he?" I looked around but didn't see him.

"Cutting through the neighbor's yard. Raphael's picking him up two blocks down."

I had thought we would bring him home, but realized how foolish that might be. Whoever lit this fire might have done so to flush Sam out of hiding. And even if we'd been careful driving him home, it was a chance we shouldn't take. As it was, Sean and Sam were using disposable phones to call each other.

Paranoia was now the name of our game.

"Was there an unlit matchstick found?" I asked.

He nodded. "Inside the mailbox."

I plucked a blade of grass from beside me. "And my license?"

"Right where you said it would be," he answered with an edge to his voice.

His jaw was working overtime, but I didn't reach out to

try and calm him.

We were beyond that point now.

Softly, I said, "I don't know what I have to do with this."

Sean put his arm around me. "Probably nothing. Whoever this is wants Sam to see that he knows all aspects of Sam's life. The guy is a stalker."

Probably.

I wanted desperately to believe him.

But I didn't.

Chapter Eighteen

By ten that morning, Sean and I were in his car, driving the streets of a quiet Boston neighborhood. He pulled up in front of a small two story house. A big oak tree shaded the front door, and the vinyl siding looked in need of a good power-washing.

"This is where the Donahues lived."

"Where *you* lived, you mean?"

He gave me a gentle nudge at the correction. "Yes, where I lived. From age fourteen until I graduated from college."

"Which room was yours?"

"Top left."

I studied the window, imagining Sean's face behind the glass. The branches of the oak brushed against the siding. "Did you ever use the tree to sneak out?"

"Not once."

I glanced at him.

Softly, he said, "I'd spent years wanting a room of my

own with a family who loved me. I wasn't about to sneak away from that. It was bad enough going to school every day, but I couldn't talk my mom into homeschooling."

His mom.

My heart swelled with love for the Donahues, and I wished I knew them.

"She didn't want you two under foot all day?" I asked.

He smiled. "She didn't want to admit she couldn't understand a bit of geometry."

Laughing, I said, "We have a lot in common."

There was a reason the math problems I did in my head were so simple. It was all I could manage without giving myself a migraine.

I adjusted the air conditioning vent so it wasn't blowing directly into my face, and said, "What did Sam say about his biological family?"

He put the car in drive and pulled away from the curb. "He was so young when he was removed from his home that he can't remember whether he had siblings."

"And were his records in that big DCF fire, too?"

Sean nodded. "I had to break that news to him this morning. He hadn't known about that fire."

"Did you call and ask Curt if a matchstick was found at that scene, too?"

"He says he'll look into it." He drummed his fingers on the wheel. "Sam doesn't even know his real name. At least I was old enough to remember mine."

I swallowed hard. There had to be a way to find out. This case was so frustrating.

Chasing ghosts.

Slowing, Sean turned right at the next corner and executed a series of turns that made me feel like I was lost in a maze.

We pulled up in front of a duplex in a working class neighborhood I didn't recognize. I had no idea where I was, other than the street name. Maple Drive.

With weathered gray shingles and old single-paned windows, the house looked like it could use some TLC.

"What's here?" I asked.

"That was one of the houses where I was placed after my mom died."

I tried to imagine a young Sean going in and out of the duplex, and the thought of it alone broke my heart.

"It's also the first house I ever broke into."

"What?"

"This was the foster family who threw away my things."

Realization hit me. "You broke in to see if they'd kept any of it."

He nodded. "Then I took things of theirs to show them how it felt."

"You didn't."

"I did," he said somberly. Then he smiled. "They moved not long after. Out of state."

I didn't know whether to laugh or cry. "You've got quite the colorful background. Were you ever arrested?"

"A few times. Nothing stuck. I was lucky, because I was able to have my record expunged. A lot of other kids in my situation weren't so fortunate."

I wondered what would have happened to him if Daniel Donahue hadn't taken him in and decided I probably didn't want to know. Fate had stepped in, and for that I was grateful.

Sean drove another few blocks and parked in the driveway of a fast food restaurant. He pointed across the street, to the site of a strip mall. "That's where the vacant building was that Sam and I accidentally burned down."

The scent of French fries wafted into the car, making me hungry. "Where did you meet Sam?" I asked.

"On these streets." He motioned all around us. "He took me under his wing, protected me from the bigger, badder kids."

"Like Johnny Largo?"

He nodded. "I've been thinking about him, and there's one person who might know what happened to him. If she's still alive."

Sean drove around the corner to a library that sat catty-corner on a tree-filled lot. It was picture perfect, even in this rough and tumble neighborhood.

"Mrs. Atterly never minded when I spent hours in here, reading everything I could get my hands on." He helped me out of the car and handed me my crutches. "She always encouraged me, brought me snacks, and slipped me money from time to time. I don't know how much she'd figured out about my life, but she had a giving nature and was a benefactor for a lot of the street kids. Giving what she could."

Street kids.

Sometimes my mind just couldn't wrap itself around what Sean must have gone through as a kid. A little boy. When I was taking piano lessons and going to the movies with Em and Marisol, Sean was foraging through Dumpsters for food and lighting fires in vacant buildings to keep warm.

I physically ached for that boy, but I was beyond grateful for the man he'd become.

I followed him into the building, breathing deeply of the cool library air. It was a special scent, musty and full of possibilities. I glanced around, noted the small nooks where a child could curl up and escape in the pages of a good book.

What a haven this must have been for Sean.

I blinked away sappy tears and watched him approach the information desk. He chatted with the librarian for a few moments, popping his dimples left and right, and finally turned back to me.

"Mrs. Atterly retired ten years ago, and now lives in an assisted living home down the street. Are you up for another stop?"

Catch me if you can.

"Lead the way."

Ten minutes later, we were standing in the lobby of Stonelick Retirement Village, waiting for Mrs. Atterly. The doorman had called her for us, and she'd said she would be right down.

Sean was unusually nervous, fidgeting and working his jaw side to side. I put my hand on his forearm and let my fingers slide down to his wrist. My whole hand tingled with electricity as I drew closer to his palm. I lingered near the base of his hand, teasing him by pulsating my fingers against his skin.

He snapped his head to look at me.

I smiled and said, "Just reminding you that you're not alone."

His jaw stilled. He calmed. His eyes brightened. "It worked."

Elevator doors opened and a tiny older woman stepped out, using a cane as she came toward us. Her back was stooped, but her eyes were alight with curiosity. Dressed in a trendy cream pantsuit and black pumps with thick heels, she didn't hesitate to come up to us.

Thrusting her hand out at me, she said, "Elizabeth Atterly." She tipped her head. "Do I know you?"

I shook her hand and was grateful she wasn't thinking of something she'd lost, and said, "I'm Lucy Valentine."

Sean held out his hand, and she took hold of it. "I'm Sean Donahue. I knew you a long time ago."

She squinted at him. "You came into the library when you were younger." In an aside to me, she said, "Those eyes are unforgettable."

I agreed.

"I called you 'Dimples.'"

Sean smiled.

"Ah, there they are. Come, sit down." She bustled toward a small lounge area with several couch groupings.

Sean helped me settle in and put my crutches on the

floor.

Mrs. Atterly gazed at him. "I've often wondered what became of you." To me, she said, "He'd spend hours reading. Anything he could get his hands on."

"He still does that," I said.

She smiled. "I'm happy to hear that."

Sean looked gobsmacked, as if the ghost of Christmas past had just plopped down in front of him. My guess was that he had good reason for not going to see Mrs. Atterly during all these years. After all, he knew where to find her.

But locating her meant dealing with a past he'd rather forget.

I said, "Sean and I are private investigators looking into a case, and a lead happens to intersect with Sean's past."

She *ooh*ed. "A *P.I.* He always did like the old Hardy Boys books. Did you?"

I found it odd that she kept addressing me, rather than him, but then I realized she was trying to make him comfortable. She sensed his unease.

"I did, though I much preferred books like *Watership Down.*"

Her hand fluttered over her heart. "Pipkin."

I nodded. "It doesn't get much better."

"Now what's this about a case?" she asked, finally looking at Sean.

He took a deep breath. "Do you remember a boy called Johnny Largo? Big kid, really rough around the edges?"

"Hard to forget, that one." She shook her head and said to me, "You simply know some children aren't destined to make it, no matter how hard you try."

Next to me, Sean stiffened. "Did something happen to him?"

Thin blue veins crisscrossed the top of her hand as she squeezed the handle of her cane. "He died in a street fight, probably fifteen years ago now."

Well, there went that lead.

"I see," Sean mumbled.

Softly, she said, "You were a lucky one, Dimples."

He met her gaze straight on. "I know."

We chatted with her for a few more minutes, catching her up on Sean's story before standing to leave.

I said, "Thank you so much. You've been a big help."

Sean's hand rested on the small of my back. "Yes, thank you."

"Take care," she said. "And come back to visit any time."

We'd taken a couple of steps toward the door when Sean suddenly turned around. "Mrs. Atterly?"

She hadn't budged from her spot—she'd been watching us go.

"Yes?"

"Do you mind if I give you a hug?"

A smiled bloomed across her face, and she opened her arms wide. "I've been waiting sixteen years."

Chapter Nineteen

Even though the lead to Johnny Largo didn't pan out, Sean had a calm demeanor about him. I think seeing Mrs. Atterly finally laid a few of his ghosts to rest. He'd promised to come back and visit with her again soon.

We were on our way to meet with Curt Meister, Sean's fire buddy. He'd called, wanting to talk to us.

My cell phone rang, and I fished in my handbag for it. The purse was practically empty since I hadn't yet replaced my wallet—or anything that had been in it.

A zing of anxiety swept through me as I imagined the flames melting my credit cards, my photos, and my driver's license.

The call was from Preston. "He asked me out," she said.

"Who?" I asked.

"Graham Hartman. Well, first he *accidentally* tried to cop a feel, then he asked me out."

"Accidentally?"

"He claims he tripped and reached out to grab on to me

to keep from falling. Thankfully, I was on to him, and sidestepped."

I smiled. "You let him fall?"

"Hell, yes."

I laughed. She sounded like her old self. Maybe her passing out yesterday had been a fluke, and Dovie had been wrong about a broken heart. "Serves him right."

"Anyway, I couldn't take it another minute. While we were in Starbucks, I excused myself to go to the ladies room and booked it out of there. I can't take a full day with him. In fact, I'm done with all of them. I cancelled on Annie for tomorrow. I'm going to have to use information I've already gathered for the article. My editor is just going to have to understand."

"Did you at least get some good tidbits before you bolted?"

"Definitely. The man enjoys talking about himself."

I knew that firsthand.

"I have lots to follow up on. Casework he's done with the police, clients who've agreed to talk with me for the article..."

"Did he mention anything about the missing little girl specifically?"

I suddenly realized that Preston didn't know I'd seen the little girl's name—or about her abductor and his car. We had a lot to catch up on.

"Actually, yes. It might be a big breakthrough," she said somberly. "He's called Orlinda, but she hasn't returned his call yet."

There was a lot of that going around. I'd tried several more times this morning to reach her. I had a million questions about the vision I had in my sleep.

"What did he see?" My pulse kicked up a notch. There was sadness in Preston's voice that warned me I wasn't going to like the answer.

Softly, she said, "He saw a shallow grave in the woods. He's pretty sure he can pinpoint the location."

My breath caught in my throat. "Did he say where?"

"Maine."

I bit my lip as tears sprung to my eyes. Sean kept casting looks at me, but if I turned to him now, I was going to lose it. "Is he sure the vision is related to the little girl?"

"He's positive."

My heart broke. Right then and there, it split in half and cracked open. All my hopes and dreams that Bethany was alive spilled out and evaporated.

"Lucy?" Preston said, gently probing.

"I'll be okay. I just need some time to digest the information."

"I wanted to tell you in person," she said, "but when I went to the office, the building was locked up tight and my key didn't work. What's going on?"

I swallowed over the enormous lump in my throat. "Dovie didn't tell you?"

"Tell me what? She was already at her Zumba class this morning when I woke up. What's wrong?"

"It's a long story." I glanced at the dashboard clock. "Can you meet me at my cottage in a couple of hours? I'll tell you all about it."

We set a time, and I hung up. Dropping my phone into my bag, I sighed.

"Bethany?" Sean said.

"Graham saw a vision of a shallow grave in Maine."

"Could he be wrong?"

"Maybe," I said. "But he was right about my wallet."

"I'm sorry."

"Me, too." Rain fell gently against the windshield, mimicking tears as the droplets slid down the glass. "I keep waiting for these cases, the ones without happy endings, to get easier to deal with. To be able to process the information and move on. But it just doesn't happen. Every time a person, especially a child, turns up dead, a bit of my heart dies, too."

I'd consulted on dozens of missing persons cases with the police, and most did not have happy endings. They were getting harder and harder to deal with. I'd spoken to Orlinda, who was a psychologist by trade, about it and the advice she had given me was to allow myself to grieve. And then move on to the next case.

Because the families needed me.

The missing needed to be found.

And I was one of the very few who could get the job done.

I had to suck it up and deal with reality.

Even if reality sucked. Big time.

I swiped a tear from my eye and took a deep breath. "Sometimes life is so unfair."

"I know."

Wipers rhythmically slashed at the window. Of course Sean knew how unfair life was. He, better than most, probably knew exactly how frustrated I was.

My phone rang again, and I pulled it out of my bag. It was Suz.

"Lucy Valentine, that Annie girl is one cuckoo kook. She crashed the voicemail system last night."

"I thought I told you to turn it off."

"I never do what I'm told."

I swiped another tear and smiled.

"Anyway, she left over a hundred messages. All begging for you to get in touch with her. I'm not sure whether you should call her back or get the police involved."

I supposed I'd let Annie suffer enough. "I'll take care of Annie."

"Thank goodness. But you'd think if she was a real psychic, she'd know how to reach you. I'm leaving the voicemail off for the rest of the weekend."

"Gee, what a good idea. Wish I'd thought of that."

"Smart ass. Any news on the arsonist? I saw there was another fire last night."

I filled her in about Sam's house, but left out the part about my driver's license. No need to freak her out.

She said, "This is scarier than I thought."

Much, much scarier.

"I'll let you know about any new developments," I said.

"Okay, then I'll see you on Monday, unless you decide to keep the office closed next week, too."

"My father would have a stroke."

"It's better than being burned to a crisp."

She had a point.

"Be careful, Lucy," she said as she hung up.

Sean said, "You mentioned Annie. From your group?"

"She called yesterday." I told him about her writings and how she'd called me a witch. "Honestly, I don't really want to talk to her ever again, but if she's so desperate to get in touch it makes me wonder why. It has to be important, right?"

"Maybe so, but the witch thing..."

"Yeah."

"Maybe make her suffer a little longer."

I smiled at him. "When did you get so vindictive?"

"Don't mess with the people I love."

The phrase reminded me of yesterday morning, when he realized Sam was in danger. Whoever it was lighting these fires didn't know how far Sean would go to track him down. Even if the leads were pitiful, Sean would never give up.

Traffic on the highway had slowed to a crawl. I saw flashing lights ahead that hinted there'd been an accident. Sean's fingers drummed on the steering wheel, and the calm that had washed over him after meeting with Mrs. Atterly was long gone.

Sean explained that we were meeting Curt Meister at a small coffee shop south of the city—and not at the firehouse—because Curt was taking a risk in talking to us.

It felt a little hinky to me, but it made me wonder what

he wanted to say.

As we slowed to a stop, Sean looked over at me.

"What?" I asked at the question in his eyes.

His fingers stilled on the steering wheel. "How did you see that fire last night? You don't have those kinds of dreams."

By just thinking about it, the scent of gasoline filled my nostrils. "I can't explain it. Maybe Orlinda's teachings are finally breaking through. Maybe this work on Bethany's case has opened up my *psychic channels*." I said that last part using finger quotes. Orlinda was always harping on about psychic channels, and I'd never paid much mind. It sounded so...*phony*.

Yet, clearly, it wasn't.

"The dream was so real. It was as if I was there, that I was the one dousing the place in gasoline. The one who lit the match. I saw everything through the arsonist's eyes."

"Did you feel what he was feeling, too?"

"No." Thank God. "My emotions were still in place. The horror at what I was seeing, the panic..."

"The readings you had on Bethany, were they the same? Seeing things through her eyes?"

"I was definitely seeing things through her point of view."

"Yet, with Bethany, you saw the past. And with the arsonist you saw the present."

Would I eventually be able to see the future? "I don't know how it works. It just happens, and I can't seem to control when it does."

Traffic inched along. "You'll figure it out, Lucy. Patience."

I playfully punched his arm. "When have you ever known me to be patient?"

His dimples popped. "You were really patient last night on the living room floor."

Heat climbed my neck. "That wasn't patience. It was savoring. There's a difference."

"We'll have to put that to the test."

Whoa! It was getting hot in here. I needed to put this subject back on track. "It'll be nice when Orlinda finally calls me back. I have so many questions..."

And not nearly enough answers.

Chapter Twenty

Curt Meister looked nervous.

Fidgeting. Looking over his shoulder. Tapping his fingers on the tabletop.

His anxiety was contagious, as I was starting to feel extremely agitated.

Curt's blue eyes darted between us. "All hell's about to break loose in the department over that missing matchstick," he said.

Sean said, "I can't tell you how sorry I am. I never thought in a million years the cat would eat it." He pushed his coffee mug between his hands. "I can take the blame. Say I stole it when I was at the station yesterday."

"I appreciate that," Curt said, "but I'd rather not visit you in prison. Listen, evidence is lost all the time."

That statement didn't exactly reassure me.

"Things are misplaced. Items are not labeled correctly. It happens. Unfortunate, but true. There are plenty of other matchsticks to build a solid case."

"But?" Sean said.

"There are whispers," Curt said, glancing over his shoulder. He looked back at us and ran a hand over his thick dark hair.

Sean stiffened next to me.

"What kind of whispers?" I asked. Condensation slid down the sides of my plastic cup. The mocha-colored iced coffee inside no longer held any appeal.

"I don't know how to say this," he said.

Sean gripped his mug. "Just spit it out."

Curt said, "You're under suspicion, Sean."

"What?" I cried. "That's crazy."

"It's not," Sean said.

I glanced at him. "Did you forget that I was lying in bed next to you last night when Sam's house went up in flames?"

Sean gave me a half-hearted smile. "There's no forgetting that. But that's not what I meant. It makes sense that I'm under suspicion. It's not unheard of for firefighters to turn into firebugs."

"Especially," Curt said, "when it's a firefighter who didn't willingly leave his job. One who has a girlfriend who mysteriously predicts when the fires are going to be set. I don't suppose you saw a face in your vision, Lucy? A reflection from a mirror or a window? Some sort of description to give the investigators."

I thought back to the vision, really concentrated on looking for anything that would reveal the arsonist's identity. "No."

"You said you saw his hands? Were his nails clean cut? Jagged? Did he wear a wedding band?"

"He wore blue latex gloves." Disappointment washed over me. "I can't even say for sure if he's black or white."

Curt stared at his own hands, twisted his wedding band back and forth. "That's too bad."

Anger bubbled up in me. This was ridiculous. "And what would Sean's motive be to target his own brother?"

"It might not even be about Sam per se." Curt glanced toward the front door, then at me. "Motive for fires is usually either revenge, or about being a hero."

"A hero?" I said. "How?"

"By solving the crimes," he said. "Or by putting out the fires himself. Saving the day."

My head started to hurt. "How would he solve the crime if he's the one doing it?"

"By having a fall guy," Sean said, his voice flat.

"Like the victim in the hospital," Curt added. "The one who wasn't supposed to live."

I let the information sink in. "So is someone framing Sean?"

"Maybe," Curt said. "Or maybe not."

That was clear.

"But now the investigation is going to focus on Sean, right?"

"Looks that way," Curt said.

"So whoever is setting these fires is going to get away scot-free."

"Not if I can help it," Sean said.

Curt leaned in. "That's why I came today. To advise you to lay low. If your search for the arsonist and the arsonist's path overlap, the investigators are still going to have you on their radar. Stay out of this, Sean. I'm asking you as a friend."

Staring into his mug, Sean said, "I'll think about it."

He was lying. I could tell by the tone of his voice. He was simply placating instead of arguing.

I suspected Curt knew so, too.

He threw another look over his shoulder. "I should go. It wouldn't be good for us to be seen together."

"Wait," I said. "Did you get an ID on the victim of last night's fire?"

"Yeah. Just a kid, only twenty-two. Petty crimes. Purse-snatchings, shoplifting, that kind of thing. The investigators think he was hired to steal your purse, and the arsonist was going to use him to take the blame for the fires."

I couldn't even fathom that the investigators believed that person was Sean.

"He's going to live?" Sean asked.

"Fifty-fifty. Right now he's in a medically induced coma. Hopefully, when he wakes up he'll be able to ID the person who hired him."

Curt's eyes lasered in on Sean, and for a split second I had the feeling that Curt didn't believe in Sean's innocence.

"Did you find out if there was a matchstick at the DCF fire?" I asked.

"There wasn't one that was found," he said, "but that doesn't mean there wasn't one there."

Big help that was.

Standing, Curt said, "Think about what I said about lying low."

Sean nodded, and Curt turned and walked out the door.

We sat side by side for a few silent minutes. Anger pulsed through me.

"What's going through your pretty little head, Ms. Valentine?" Sean finally asked.

"Screw Curt's advice. We have to find this guy."

Sean's lip twitched before he broke into a wide smile. "That's my girl."

"And then we're going to make him pay."

"Now who's the vindictive one?" he asked.

I grinned. "You've taught me well."

"Drink this," I said, shoving a bottle of water into Preston's hand. "You look like you're going to pass out again."

She leaned back on my couch and twisted the cap off the water. I leaned my crutches against the hearth and dropped into my favorite chair. Grendel immediately hopped into my lap and meowed until I rubbed his ears and scratched his back.

"The arsonist is after Sam?" Preston said, her face still pale. "I mean, I've been reading about the Beantown Burner, but I had no idea how close to home the story hit. Where is Sam now?"

"He's been hiding with Raphael." Sun peeked out from behind fluffy clouds and sent sunbeams streaming in the large windows of my living room. "But right now he and Sean are together, trying to come up with a bigger list of suspects."

Thoreau looked up from his spot on the floor, where he was basking in the sunshine. He yawned and put his head back onto his paws and closed his eyes. He looked as peaceful as could be, and I suddenly envied him for that.

I couldn't recall the last time I'd been truly stress-free.

I propped my booted foot up on the coffee table and reached down for Grendel's comb in the basket of his toys next to the chair.

"You should have told me," Preston said. A pout pulled the corners of her kewpie lips downward.

"If you hadn't snuck out of the hospital last night, you would have already known."

Her nose wrinkled. "But Lucy... Dr. Death. I had to get out of there."

I noticed her face still didn't hold any color. "Did you make a follow-up appointment with your family doctor? Because you don't look too well."

"I love you, too," she said sarcastically.

"You know what I mean." I rocked in my chair as I combed Grendel's fur. His purrs vibrated against my stomach. "I'm starting to worry."

She set the water bottle on the table. "Well, don't. I'm fine. It was just all that death. It got to me after a while."

I could understand that.

"Dr. Paul got to me," she added. "I can't believe you don't think he's creepy."

I wasn't about to admit I kind of liked him. "Is this about the skull collection?" I explained what he had said. And how yes, technically, he lived with his mother, but it was in a duplex. Each owned a side.

"Well, he's lying to you, Lucy."

I stopped rocking. "About what?"

"Those skulls." A guilty flush climbed her neck. It was nice to see some color brighten her up a bit. "I have a friend of a friend of a friend and he did me a favor."

Oh no. "What did you do?" Because I could tell it was something big.

She examined a fingernail. "He hacked into the hospital's system and counted all the death certificates Dr. Paul has signed off on. It's the exact number of skulls he's collected. How do you explain that? The exact number?"

"You counted the skulls?"

Another guilty flush. She was starting to look downright rosy. "Yes! I snuck back in there this afternoon, before I came here. I had to be sure."

I focused on Grendel's tail, gently tugging out the knots with the comb. His tail fluffed out, looking a lot like an orange feather duster. "Be sure of what?"

"Hello," she said. "That he's a serial killer?"

"Maybe it's a coincidence," I said, not believing it even as the words came out of my mouth.

"Right."

"Okay," I admitted. "That's creepy. But it doesn't make him a serial killer." I hoped. I would hate to think my instincts about him could be so wrong.

"You need to get out of that Diviner Whiner group. Whack jobs, every last one of them, including your crazy leader." She blinked at me. "Well, except for you."

I thought about Annie. When I went to call her back, I realized that I'd left her number at my father's penthouse. I tried calling her store, but no one answered. I also tried Suz, who told me that she deleted all Annie's calls, and defended the fact that even though she had listened to a bazillion messages, she hadn't memorized the phone number.

Annie was just going to have to wait. "You're still mad at Orlinda, I see."

Her lip jutted. "Why can't she just tell me what the big upheaval is? It's ridiculous to make me wait and see."

I dropped the comb back into the basket and told Grendel how handsome he was. He purred happily. Studying Preston, I dove head first into some tricky water. "Do you think the big upheaval has to do with Cutter?"

"What makes you say that?" she snapped.

Repressing a smile, I shrugged. "I don't know. You two are getting pretty serious."

"Are not."

Maybe Cutter was right about Preston's disposition lately. She had engagement anxiety. I thought about his silence when I asked him if he'd considered proposing and had the feeling Preston had no need to worry.

She stood up, and I noticed she was a bit wobbly. She tried to cover it with a stretch, but when she did that, I noticed how thin she was. "Have you been eating okay?"

"Like a horse," she said, walking to the fridge as if to prove a point. She opened the door and scanned the shelves.

I knew that wasn't true. She admitted yesterday at the hospital that she hadn't eaten all day. What was going on with her?

"I can make you some eggs," I said, hearing a bit of Dovie in my voice. She was a caretaker, a nurturer, and apparently she'd passed that trait along to me.

"That's okay. I'm not really hungry. I had a bagel on the way over here."

"Mmm-hmm."

She came back into the living room and said, "Don't you mmm-hmm me, Lucy Valentine."

"Mmm-hmm."

"You're impossible." She went to sit down, but something caught her eye.

Crossing the room, she took the pink bear out of the bassinet. Before I'd told her about the arsonist, I filled her in about the visions I had with the bear.

"Have you heard from Orlinda?" she asked.

"Nothing. I've called many times, and I know Graham and Dr. Paul have tried to reach her, too. She's not getting back to us."

Preston frowned. "Isn't that unusual?"

I opened my mouth then snapped it closed again. It *was* strange, as she had always been prompt in getting back to us. "I figured it was because she was at a convention, but now I'm a bit worried."

Gently, she placed the bear back into the bassinet. "Let me work on it. I'll track her down. I have some questions I want to run by her for the article, too. The sooner I get that thing done, the better."

She suddenly leaned forward, peering out the window behind me. "Em and Marisol are on their way down." She squinted. "It looks like Marisol is holding a cat."

Marisol had called an hour ago and told me that Ebbie was just fine and that she'd bring her home.

Home meaning here.

And I'd realized I missed the little fur ball. "Is it black? About this big?" I said, holding my hands apart a foot.

"Yes."

"That's Ebbie."

"Who's Ebbie?" Preston asked.

"My new cat."

"A new cat?" She threw her hands into the air. "What else, Lucy Valentine? What else are you keeping from me?"

Chapter Twenty-One

"Stop, stop, stop," Preston said, swatting at Em's hands as she tried to feel Preston's forehead. "I don't have a fever."

"You were asleep when I got home last night, and were gone this morning before I could look you over."

"I know," Preston said. "I didn't want to be looked over."

Ebbie hopped up in the chair alongside Grendel and me. She licked his face. He let her.

"A perfect match," Marisol said, sitting in the chair next to mine. Thoreau had awakened from his nap with all the commotion and was now sniffing everyone's feet. "Do you think her owner will let you keep her?"

"I thought you said she was your new cat?" Preston asked, still shooing Em away.

"Technically, she's Jeremy Cross's cat. I'm just caretaking at this point."

"Who's Jeremy Cross?" Preston asked on a long drawn-out woe-is-me sigh. "And why are you caretaking."

I told them all about Jeremy and his animal communication skills. And how Ebbie said that I was the one who'd find him his true love.

"Not another psychic." Preston stood up. "I can't take anymore of you. I'm going. I'll let you know about Orlinda."

"Oh, before you go," Em said. "Girls' night tomorrow at Dovie's. You in?"

"Are you bringing your stethoscope?" Preston asked oh-so-sweetly.

"No," Em said.

"Then I'm in." With a wave, she sailed out the door.

Em looked at me. "She's lost a lot of weight and her color is off."

"I know, but I can't seem to get her to agree to see a doctor."

Marisol said, "Get Cutter involved. She'll listen to him."

Ebbie pressed herself against me, plastered to my ribs. With all the body heat, I was going to have to turn the air conditioning down a few more degrees. "I'll call him. He's supposed to be back on Saturday, but maybe he can cut his trip short."

I glanced at Marisol. "Ebbie's tests were good?"

"Perfect. I don't think she actually ate much of the matchstick, if any. She probably just chewed on it. Keep an eye on her, though. Hopefully, she won't eat anything else that's not good for her."

Em said, "Can cats have pica?"

"Pica?" I asked. "What's that?"

"It's a disorder that usually affects women and small kids. They eat non-nutritious items like chalk, clay, paper, that kind of thing."

I frowned. I couldn't even imagine.

"And yes," Marisol went on, "cats can have it too. It usually means a nutrient is missing from their diet, but I tested her vitamin levels and all seem to be okay."

I nodded, taking in all the information.

"And there is one more thing," Marisol said.

"What's that?"

"I may be able to find her rightful owner. You said she was a stray, remember? When Orlinda found her?"

"Right, but how..."

"When I brought her to the office this morning, I scanned her for a microchip. The information popped up that she'd been chipped at a clinic I volunteered at, but didn't have any other info than the clinic's address and phone number. I'm going to stop by there on my way home today and see if I can find her file. It probably has her adopter's information in it."

I wasn't sure how I felt about Ebbie leaving. I'd grown attached to her. I also didn't know how Jeremy would feel about it.

Em tucked bare feet beneath her on the couch and yawned loudly. "This heat...," she said, lifting her hair off the back of her neck. "Makes me sleepy."

"Or was it your late night with Aiden?" I asked, trying to keep my mind off Sean and Sam. Had they come up with any more plausible suspects?

"What late night?" Em said. "I was home by nine, which is why I was surprised Preston was already asleep."

Marisol and I glanced at each other. There was a note of disenchantment in Em's voice. Marisol picked a piece of lint off her shorts. "Everything okay with you and Aiden?"

"No, everything is not okay." Em's cheeks flamed the same color as her hair. Brighter, even. Folding her arms across her chest, she said, "He's distracted, quiet, flustered. He must have spilled his drink three times at dinner last night, and I don't think he heard a word I said. He asked for the check before I could order dessert and practically raced me back to Dovie's. I don't know what's going on, but something is. I think it's time for a recon mission. What do you say?"

Marisol glowed. "You know I love a little recon. I'm game."

The last time there was a recon mission, Marisol and I had broken into Em's apartment. I had enough worries on my plate right now to add to them. "You two can tell me about it."

Em frowned at my foot. "It *would* be a little hard for you to get around."

"And blend in," Marisol added.

"And I don't think the kitties would let you go," Em said, eyeing the pile o' cat on my lap.

She might be right about that.

I couldn't imagine what was going on with Aiden. He was about as straight-laced as men came, and he absolutely adored Em. His behavior was out of the ordinary, and I was curious to see what the recon mission would uncover.

And if it would also explain why he'd yet to call me back.

Later that night, I stood in the doorway of my bedroom and watched Sean sleep. Ebbie and Thoreau were cuddled next to him, while Grendel sat in front of his food bowl with a hopeful expression.

It wasn't very late, only a bit before ten, but Sean had barely been able to keep his eyes open. It had been an exhausting day for him, more mentally than physically.

He slept peacefully now, and I hoped he'd stay that way. Most nights he tossed and turned.

Even Odysseus seemed to take notice and worked furiously at burrowing instead of running his usual late night marathon on his wheel.

I drew the door closed and crutched my way to the couch. My mind was spinning—too much to fall asleep.

Sean and Sam had little luck with their brainstorming session. The ghosts they chased refused to be identified.

Sam was back in hiding, working on trying to find out if he had siblings. So far, he'd had no luck whatsoever.

Sean had been quiet when he returned home and stayed that way until he went to sleep.

I sank onto the couch, and Grendel soon abandoned his food bowl and joined me. How do you solve a case with no leads? No suspects. Not knowing when the arsonist was going to strike next...

I glanced up as a flash of light streaked across my windows. The sound of tires on crushed shells came next.

Someone was here.

Carefully, I hopped over to the window and slid the drapes to the side a bit so I could peek out. The front of my cottage was well-lit, and it was easy to see who emerged from a small red hatchback.

Annie Hendrix.

I looked back at the bedroom, at the door slightly ajar. I didn't want to wake Sean. Especially not with a visit from Annie, who wasn't one of his favorite people.

Hopping back to the couch, I bent down and picked up my crutches. I hurried back to the front door and pulled it open before she could knock.

For a second, she simply stared at me. Her hair was frizzy and unkempt and rings of dark smudged makeup made the skin beneath her bloodshot eyes look bruised and wild.

"You have to help me," she cried.

I nodded for her to back up a step, and I slipped out the door. Her tiny tank top barely held her breasts in check, and she wore a skirt so short I could practically see her uterus.

It was quite the impression she gave.

"Come on," I said.

She followed me around the wraparound porch to two cushioned chairs that overlooked the ocean. The water was calm tonight, slapping quietly against the rocks at the bottom of the bluff. Moonlight spilled across the water like milk across black granite.

I motioned for her to sit. "I tried calling you today, but

you didn't answer."

"My cell?" She pulled out a phone that had been tucked into her ample cleavage.

Ew. "Your work. I don't have your cell number."

"But—"

I cut her off. "Long story, Annie. What do you want from me?"

The night was peaceful with barely any wind, and it reminded me of the calm before the storm. I shuddered and focused on the sound of the crickets chirping, the waves lapping.

Annie opened her purse and pulled out wads and wads of paper. All of them said "Lucy Valentine."

Tears shone in Annie's eyes. "The energy will not leave me alone. I was up all night, obsessed with writing your name over and over. I didn't sleep. I haven't eaten. I have to do a reading on you."

I noticed the lights on in one of Dovie's guest rooms and hoped that meant she'd badgered Preston into staying another night with her. Em's room was dark, and I wondered if she and Marisol were off doing their reconnaissance mission.

"Go ahead," I said. "Do you need more paper?"

She shook her head and pulled out a fresh pad from her purse. Taking a few deep breaths, she murmured something under her breath I couldn't understand. I took it to mean that she was opening her channels.

After a second, her pen, firmly in hand, began to move across the paper. Even though I'd seen her work before, it always fascinated me. She wrote three words, then the pen fell from her fingers.

She stared at the notepad, then said loudly, "That's it? Three words? You're freaking kidding me!"

It took me a second to realize that she was talking to the energy.

Annie shoved the wads of paper bearing my name back into her purse, cursing the whole time.

"What's it say?" I asked, nodding to her pad. I was fairly good at reading upside down, but the writing was terrible and I couldn't decipher it.

Annie slid it over. "Makes no sense to me."

I glanced at the words.

NOT SAM BLACKIE

"Does it make sense to you?" she asked.

"Not really." Of course I understood the Sam part, but what was blackie? And what did the phrase mean as a whole?

"Well, it's yours. I cannot even freakin' believe the hell I've been going through over three words. That's some energy looking out for you." She stood up.

I tucked the paper into my pocket and followed her across the porch, my crutches *thunking* along.

At the steps, she said, "I guess I'll see you Sunday. Unless the meeting's canceled now that we know what happened to Bethany."

Leaning against a column, I studied her carefully. "How did you know the little girl's name?"

She lifted a shoulder in a half shrug. "Google."

I must have looked shocked, because she said, "It really doesn't matter now that we know she's passed on, does it?"

"How'd you know what to look for?"

"Well, when Dr. Paul mentioned that he saw a Maine license plate, Graham suddenly got this vision about a shallow grave... I typed in Maine, missing girl, and kindergarten into the search box, and up popped Bethany Hill, age five, missing for two years."

"When was this?" I asked, my mind spinning with the details she spewed.

"Last night."

"You were with Dr. Paul and Graham last night?"

She pursed her lips. "Yeah."

Without me. Apparently, they'd met to talk about Bethany's case and decided not to include me. There shouldn't have been a stab of hurt, knowing how they felt about me, but there was. It was like a knife in the back. "I see."

"Nothing personal," Annie said.

"Of course not." She would have to be deaf not to pick up my sarcasm. "What else did you learn? About the case?"

I knew *I* wasn't going to break my word and Google the case, but Orlinda had wanted us to learn from each other so I saw no harm in asking Annie.

"Not much," she said, dismissing me with a wave. "There were never any suspects. The truck was never found. Her parents split up not long after the abduction. The case is still open."

And it would remain open even after Graham led the

police to Bethany's body.

Because there was still a killer on the loose.

She frowned and looked around. "Do you hear that?"

I glanced left and right. "Hear what?"

"I keep hearing someone say 'Hidden hollow.'"

I scrunched my nose. "A spirit?"

"They don't talk to me. There it is again. Do you have your TV on?"

"No." I glanced behind me at my screen door. There was a small shadow sitting in the doorway.

Ebbie's tail swished side to side and there was a knowing look in her eye.

Could it possibly been Ebbie's voice that Annie had heard?

Annie shook her head. "Weird. Anyway, maybe I'll see you Sunday."

"Maybe."

As I watched her drive off, my emotions warred. Hurt, angry, frustrated, sad.

I thought about Bethany. About how I'd been unable to find her.

And about how I was now determined to bring her killer to justice. I would never give up.

The taillights disappeared as Annie turned toward the main road. I probably should have told her about Ebbie.

But then again, she probably should have told me about the meeting last night.

Turning to go back into the house, the piece of paper Annie had given me fluttered out of my pocket. I bent down and picked it up, once again staring at the words.

NOT SAM BLACKIE

What in the world did it mean?

Chapter Twenty-Two

Early the next morning, I was once again watching Sean sleep. This time I was lying in bed next to him. He'd been tossing and turning for at least an hour, so I knew he was almost ready to wake up.

The automatic coffee maker had already made its first pot, and the scent was slowly luring me out of bed.

Thoreau nudged my hand as I sat up, and I patted his head. Ebbie glanced at me from atop my pillow (where she'd spent the night), and there was no sign of Grendel. Odysseus had long since gone to sleep, happily hidden inside his plastic igloo.

The first rays of morning light had slipped underneath the drawn shade, and the forecasters had predicted another scorching hot day. There was talk of probable brownouts across the city, and officials urged everyone to conserve as much energy as possible.

Which was kind of hard to do when it was going to be over one hundred degrees outside.

For the sixth day in a row.

I glanced at Sean's hand by his side. I bit my lip. I probably shouldn't do what I was thinking about doing... But I wanted to know.

I wanted to see.

Slowly, I leaned over and poised my hand atop his. Already I could feel the sparks. Taking a deep breath, I closed my eyes and pressed my palm against his.

Sean's hand jerked under mine. My eyes flew open, and I found him watching me.

My heart raced, and I was dizzy as I tried to figure out what I'd just seen.

"If you're going to have your way with me while I'm sleeping, might I suggest other body parts other than my hand?"

"Sorry. I couldn't help myself. I wanted to see..."

The sheet fell from his chest as he sat up. My gaze skimmed right over his scar and focused on the taut muscles, the tanned skin.

"See what?" he asked.

"What was in store for us."

"And?" he asked.

I shook my head. "I don't know what it is I saw. It's too cloudy."

Cupping my chin, he said, "Everything is going to be okay."

"Promise?"

"Cross my malfunctioning heart."

I smiled. "I'm going to hold you to that."

"I expect you to."

I batted my eyelashes. "And speaking of holding... What are those other body parts you would suggest to me? You know, for future reference."

He laughed. "I could show you. You know, for future reference."

The pets scattered as he pulled me into his arms.

An hour later, I was still cuddled next to his side when my eyes flew open.

"What is it?" he murmured.

My heart pounded. "I just realized what I saw when I touched your hand."

"The clouds?"

I rolled onto my side and looked him in the eyes. "It wasn't clouds."

"What then?"

"It was smoke. Lots and lots of smoke."

Sean was in the shower when Dovie blew through my front door an hour and a half later, carrying a basket in one hand and a gift box in the other.

Preston scuffled along behind her, looking like she needed an IV drip of caffeine.

I knew the feeling. I'd barely slept last night.

"Well," Dovie said after giving me a tight hug and a peck on the cheek, "aren't you the perfect picture of death warmed over?"

"Oh, the flattery," I teased as I poured a generous amount of coffee into a mug. I held the carafe up to

Preston, but if possible, she lost even more color to her already ashen skin tone.

"No thanks."

Talk about death warmed over.

Dovie rubbed Preston's back. "Preston's going to make an appointment with her doctor today. Aren't you, dear?"

Preston pressed her cheek against the cool countertop. "Yes," she droned.

I knew Dovie would wear her down. I'd called Cutter yesterday afternoon, but the airport had been fogged in, and he hadn't been able to get a flight out last night. He vowed to rent a car and drive down the coast to another airport if he had to. He was bound and determined to get back here as soon as possible. Preston had no idea he was on his way, and I warned him not to tell her that I let on she was sick.

Dovie held up the basket. "I brought fresh waffles, but first..." She slid the box across the counter to me.

The pipes in the walls quieted as Sean turned off the shower. I wasn't worried about him being caught *au naturel.* He'd learned the lesson to always wear clothes when there was a chance Dovie might pop in.

"What's this?" I asked, shaking the package.

Ebbie hopped up on the counter and sat next to Preston's head. "Pretty kitty," she murmured.

"A surprise!" Dovie said, her eyes aglow.

Preston dragged herself upright and scratched Ebbie's ears. "Brace yourself," she said to me.

"Oh you." Dovie gave her a little shove.

I balanced my weight against the counter and used both hands to reluctantly pull the top off the box. A beautiful sea foam green crocheted blanket was nestled in tissue paper. I lifted it out and held it up.

"Isn't it gorgeous?" Dovie cooed. "A friend of mine made it."

"A baby blanket?" I asked. "Isn't this taking things too far?"

Dovie dismissed me with a wave of her hand. "Phooey. It's not a baby blanket. It's a kitty blanket. For your new addition." She patted Ebbie's head.

Preston mouthed, "It's a baby blanket" behind Dovie's back.

"Well, thank you," I said, smiling. "I'm sure Ebbie will love it." I folded the blanket in half, set it on the counter, then picked up Ebbie and put her on top of it. "Perfect."

A little of the light dimmed in Dovie's eyes.

Preston, however, managed a smile. She slid off her stool and walked over to the couch and proceeded to lie down.

Dovie threw me a worried glance.

I shared her concern.

"And I have this," Dovie said, pulling an envelope out of the basket. She slid it over to me.

"What's this?"

"A little advancement from the Lucy Valentine rental fund."

I groaned. That's what she called the rent money I gave her every month—the money she socked away.

I opened the envelope. There were ten crisp one hundred dollar bills.

"You'll need some cash until you can get a new ID and your credit cards replaced. Just let me know if you need more."

I hopped around the counter and gave her a kiss. I slid the envelope into my purse and went for the basket of waffles. I was starving.

As I pulled a plate out of the cabinet, a shrill ring came from the counter near the fridge. I turned and hopped over to the cell phone charging there. It was the throwaway phone Sean used to contact Sam. I picked it up and answered before it could switch to voicemail.

"Lucy," Sam said, his voice high, "is Sean around?"

"Just getting out of the shower."

"I need to talk to him."

Sean appeared in the bedroom doorway, wrapped in a towel.

Dovie fanned her face, and I rolled my eyes at her.

Though, really, Sean was face-fan worthy.

"It's Sam," I said, holding out the phone.

I saw the worry in his eyes as he took the cell from my hand.

Preston popped her head up from the other side of the couch. She, Dovie, and I eavesdropped shamelessly on Sean's side of the conversation.

"What? When?" His eyebrows drew downward, and his lips set into a thin line. "Where?" Shooting a glance at me, he said, "That doesn't make sense."

"What doesn't?" I whispered.

Sean said, "There was a fire last night at 869 Maple."

Why did that address sound so familiar? Then it hit me like a sucker punch to the stomach. "One of your foster homes?"

He gave a sharp nod.

"Did Sam live there, too?" I asked.

"No." Then into the phone, he said, "Sam, I'll meet you there in forty-five minutes."

Drawing in a deep breath, he disconnected the call, and said, "It doesn't make sense. Sam never lived there."

"But you did," Preston said from the couch.

I gasped, my eyes growing wide. My pulse hammered in my ears.

NOT SAM BLACKIE.

"What?" Sean reached out for me.

I held up a hand and hopped one-footed to the mantel where I'd put Annie's note under a picture frame.

Tears flooded my eyes. "Not Sam," I whispered.

"LucyD," Dovie said, "what's going on?"

I hopped back into the kitchen and met Sean's gaze. "Who's Blackie?"

His eyes flew open wide, and he took a step backward as if I'd just shoved him. "What did you say?"

"Who's Blackie?" I pushed the note toward him.

"What is this?"

I quickly explained Annie's visit the night before.

Sean's jaw worked side to side, and the sheen of moisture in his eyes was unmistakable.

"Who's Blackie?" I whispered.

His Adam's apple bobbed. "I am. It's the nickname my mother used to call me."

Chapter Twenty-Three

It was bedlam at the scene of the fire on Maple Street. The media was out in full force, and dozens of firefighters and police milled about. Onlookers crowded sidewalks and front porches.

Sean, Sam, and I stood at the street corner, looking on in silence.

Thankfully no one had been hurt in the blaze, but there was barely anything left to the house. It lay in blackened ruins.

Sean's jaw was locked in a clench, while Sam looked ravaged.

I was still reeling from the revelation that Sean's mother had been the energy bothering Annie, and I also took some satisfaction in that.

Annie deserved to be bothered.

A lot.

I was grateful to Sean's mom.

On the way here, I shared with Sean what Dr. Paul had

said about the spirit surrounding Sean. He hadn't said anything in reply, and we spent the rest of the drive over in silence.

When he fell in love with me, he probably hadn't counted on all the psychic baggage that came along. Even more of it now that I had psychic sidekicks and more and more abilities.

I was starting to wonder if it would be too much for him to handle.

Maybe not right now... But someday.

Was Cupid's Curse at work?

Sam shifted his feet and said, "We couldn't have known."

It was a sentiment that had been voiced several times over the past hour.

We couldn't have known it was Sean the arsonist had been after all along.

That the fires hadn't been targeting places that related to Sam but to *Sean*.

Everything from the DCF fire to Sam's house—where Sean had temporarily lived for a few months. Someone had researched Sean's life. Knew it inside out.

Eating at me was the fact that it should have been Sean in hiding not Sam. Yet, we'd been oblivious to the danger.

Why hadn't the arsonist simply burned down my cottage?

Why was he toying with us?

Despite the heat, I shivered. I couldn't help but feel that we were pawns in some evil game.

One of the firefighters on the scene broke away and walked over to us. As he neared, I could see it was Curt Meister. And he didn't look happy to see us.

Dark ash dusted his coat, his helmet. His face shield was pushed up atop his helmet and his scowl would have made me shudder if I didn't already have the chills.

"Damn it, Sean," he said tightly. "You shouldn't be here."

Angrily, Sam said, "Wait a second, Curt. You don't understand. The arsonist is after Sean." Sam explained about the relevance of the house that had burned down, and how Sean was tied to the other places on the list.

Curt swore under his breath. "Go home, Sean. I'll try to steer the investigation in another direction, but your name keeps coming up. You're making things worse for yourself being here."

I nudged Sean with my elbow. "We should go."

Sean looked at me, long and hard. Finally, he nodded. He turned on his heel and walked away.

Sam followed, jogging to catch up to him.

I said to Curt, "You've got to catch this guy."

His eyes narrowed at me. Sweat and grime covered his face. "Just keep Sean away, okay?" Pivoting, he stomped away, the acrid smell of extinguished fire trailing after him.

I watched him go until he was undistinguishable from the other firefighters; all dressed alike in their heavy coats.

Finally, I turned and started making my way back to the car. My crutches were rubbing raw the skin under my arms, and my hands were slick with sweat.

The forecasters hadn't been exaggerating the heat.

Ahead, Sean and Sam waited for me at the corner. I could tell by the set of Sean's shoulders that he was absolutely beside himself. With anger. With sadness. With helplessness.

In turn, I felt those things, too.

And as I neared them, I couldn't help the kernel of suspicion growing in my head. About firefighters who liked to be heroes.

About how desperately Curt wanted to keep Sean away from the scenes of these fires.

"I found her!" Preston threw open my door, startling Ebbie, who bolted for the bedroom.

Grendel paid Preston no mind. He had a new favorite spot in the house—inside the bassinet. He was beside himself with happiness. Sean and Sam were outside, walking Thoreau. All the way home, we'd bandied ideas on who could be the arsonist. Who would frame Sean. Who were his enemies.

They both dismissed my suggestion of Curt Meister.

I, however, hadn't crossed him off my list.

"Who?" I asked, setting aside my laptop. I'd been searching Sean's P.I. databases for Curt's name to see if anything suspicious popped up. No red flags yet. Good credit, money in the bank, responsible homeowner. No arrest record.

Damn him.

"Orlinda! It took forever to track down the hotel the

convention is using. I left her a message to call you as soon as she could, that it was an emergency, life or death, blah, blah, blah."

She sat across from me, and despite the enthusiasm in her voice, she looked even worse than she had this morning. Pale, drawn. Not healthy at all.

"If that doesn't make her call you back within the next couple of hours, then we start worrying about her."

"You're amazing," I said. "I didn't even think to contact the hotel."

"I know. I'm a genius."

"Modest, too."

"Don't forget cute as a button."

I smiled. "Cuter than a button."

"Don't make me blush."

I wish I could—it would add color to her cheeks. As nonchalantly as I could, I said, "What time is your doctor's appointment today? I can go with you. Nothing is going on here except waiting for someone to come burn down the house."

"You have a sick sense of humor, Lucy Valentine." She shook her head. "Waiting for someone to burn down the house. Sheesh."

I sat up straight. "Say that again."

"Sheesh?"

"No, the part before that!"

"Waiting for someone to burn down the house?"

I snapped my fingers. "That's it!"

She grinned. "Glad I could help. Now, what's '*it*?'"

"We've been going about finding this arsonist the wrong way, trying to figure out who it could be, who would have motive, that sort of thing."

"Isn't that the way investigations are usually done?"

I peered out the window, wondering where Sean was. I couldn't wait to share my plan with him. "Sometimes you have to think outside the box."

"I hate that saying. Think outside the box. What does that even mean?"

I said, "It means that we need to set a trap."

"That doesn't answer my question."

"Your question has no answer."

"I'm confused," she said, holding her head.

"What time is your appointment?" I asked, smiling.

She peeked out at me through one eye. "I hate you."

"You love me."

"You think you know me so well."

"The appointment?"

"At three, and I don't need a chaperone. I'm a big girl."

I gave her the hairy eyeball, not sure I believed her. She stared back, unblinking.

"I'm coming with you," I said.

"We'll see about that."

We continued to have a stare-down before she finally said, "Have you talked to Em today?"

I wasn't fooled by the change of subject, but I let it go for now because my eyes were getting gritty from not blinking. "Not yet. Have you heard how the recon went?"

"Complete dud. Aiden didn't leave his house all night.

No one went in or out, either. They tried to sneak a peek inside the house, but Aiden had all the blinds closed. He went to bed at eleven, and they went home."

"How high was their disappointment level?"

"Marisol's was off-the-charts. You know how she likes catching people in the act. But Em? I think she was plain-old relieved. What do you think is going on with Aiden?"

"I'm not sure." If I had time this afternoon, I'd try to track him down. I'd be able to get a much better feel for what was going on if I saw him face to face.

Preston said, "My article about the Diviner Whiners is almost done. My editor wants me to hold off on finishing it until Graham...you know."

I glanced at the pink bear, which shared the bassinet with Grendel, and felt the ache in my heart. The editor would want the conclusion to the story. "That makes sense, I suppose."

The phone rang, and thankfully I had the portable sitting on the coffee table. I didn't recognize the number and almost let it go through to voicemail until I remembered that Orlinda was supposed to call.

I cautiously answered, ready to do battle with a telemarketer if need be.

Orlinda's voice came across the line loud and clear. "What in the hell is going on up there, Lucy Valentine?"

Chapter Twenty-Four

"I leave for a couple of days and all hell breaks loose?" Orlinda said. "Start at the beginning and tell me everything. And don't you dare leave out one single detail."

I spent the next ten minutes filling her in and wondering where Sean and Sam had gone. Thoreau's walk should have been long over with.

Preston had fallen asleep on the couch.

Orlinda explained that she hadn't called me back because she never received the messages. She'd lost her phone between leaving my office and flying out to Chicago.

"You have to find a safe house," Orlinda said.

I'd been thinking about that. Staying here wasn't the wisest idea. Dovie would have to move out, too. And Em.

I was suddenly mad at this arsonist for disrupting our lives.

I watched the rhythmic rise and fall of Preston's chest. I could feel in my bones that there was something seriously wrong with her. "A hotel, I guess. But I have to find somewhere that takes a dog, two cats, and a hamster."

"I'd let you stay at my place, except I'm allergic to cats."

That's right. It was why she had dropped Ebbie off at Jeremy's.

Or so she claimed. I still wasn't convinced about her motives.

Now wasn't the time to get into that, though. There were many more important things to think about.

Sean and I and our menagerie couldn't stay at my mother's house like the last time a psycho had forced us from our home. The arsonist undoubtedly knew to look for us there. Same with Raphael's. I couldn't put him and Maggie in danger.

"Let me think, let me think..." Orlinda said, and I could easily picture her tapping her chin.

"While you're thinking, I should tell you that you missed several other calls as well." I told her about Dr. Paul's and my visions. And about Graham's.

Silence stretched along the line. "I'll call and speak to them," she said softly.

Preston shifted, letting out a sigh.

"Orlinda, do you remember when you healed my stomach?"

It was at our first meeting, and I'd been utterly perplexed by what happened.

"Of course."

"Can you heal over the phone?"

I heard the smile in her voice. "I cannot heal broken bones, Lucy Valentine."

"It's not for me," I said. "It's Preston."

"What's wrong with her?"

"I don't know. Do you think you can help?"

"Not until I return. My energy to heal comes through palms. I will try to get on an earlier flight. I feel my presence is needed more with you than with the psychologists' association."

Selfishly, I wanted her here. She was a safe harbor in what was turning out to be quite the storm.

I heard her inhale sharply. "I have an idea about where you can stay."

"Where?"

"With Jeremy Cross. I'm sure he'll agree."

"No."

"Why not?"

"I don't like him."

She laughed. "You don't know him. Give him a chance. You can trust him. I promise."

I frowned.

"I can sense your frown, Lucy Valentine. You must remember that some scars run deeper than what's on the surface. Wounds run deep."

What was she trying to say? I pictured Jeremy's scar, the one that ran along his jaw, and wondered how he got it. "Who is he?"

"A friend," she said. "I'll have him call you. Stay strong, Lucy. Your inner strength is your greatest strength, but your impulsiveness is your biggest weakness. Look before you leap."

"'Leap and the net will appear?'" I quoted a famous saying.

"Not always," she said darkly.

I hung up with her feeling as though I'd just been warned.

About what, I wasn't sure I wanted to know.

Five minutes later, the phone rang. The Caller ID was blocked. I had a good idea who it was.

"You cannot stay here," Jeremy Cross said after I answered.

"It wasn't my idea," I countered, watching Preston nap. She looked out for the count.

"Be that as it may, it's a horrible idea."

"It's been good talking to you," I said, ready to hang up.

"Wait."

"What?"

"You can't stay here, but I can help."

"How?"

"I know people."

I laughed. It sounded so gangster. "People who own hotels? Because I need a place to sleep tonight."

"You can stay where you are."

"Didn't Orlinda give you the memo about the arsonist?"

"I didn't need any memo."

Right. I'd almost forgotten how he'd seen the vision of Sam's house going up in flames.

"A security force is already on the way to your house. They'll remain hidden unless there's a disturbance. You have my word that the arsonist will not get within one hundred feet of your or your grandmother's houses."

A shiver ran through me. Not only because he knew where I lived and who lived next door, but because of the hard tone of his voice. It brooked no argument. He meant business.

I didn't quite trust his word, but I did trust Orlinda. If she said he was a friend, then I'd believe her.

"Give me a safe word," he said.

"A what?"

"If you happen across someone on the property, you'll know who's who. Pick a word, a phrase. The security officer will know it. A prowler will not."

"Fuzzy navel."

"Fuzzy navel?"

"That's right." I could practically see him rolling his eyes.

"Fine."

"Good."

"How's Ebbie?"

I glanced over my shoulder. She was asleep on my pillow. "Good. I'm thinking about keeping her."

He laughed, but there was no humor in the sound.

"I'm not joking."

"We'll discuss this tomorrow. I'll stop by and see what Ebbie has to say."

"Who are you?" I said. "Really? Because I know your name isn't really Jeremy Cross."

There was a long silence before he said, "I'm a ghost of

a man" and hung up.

Preston stirred and sat up. "Who was that?"

"A ghost of a man."

She blinked at me, then said, "I'm going back to sleep." Closing her eyes, she tipped her head back.

I set the portable phone on the table, stood up, and hopped over to the window. Sean and Sam sat in a pair of Adirondack chairs perched at the edge of the bluff. Not talking, just sitting.

Both, I was sure, were formulating plans.

But as soon as they came in, I'd run my idea past them. Sean had lived in limited places. If each of those homes were staked out overnight, the chances of catching the arsonist in the act were much greater. We would need more manpower, but with Sam's connections, I wasn't worried about that.

Jeremy's security force had Dovie's and my house covered. We would need someone at my father's penthouse. At Valentine, Inc. At all of the homes Sean could remember living.

We would catch the arsonist. I was sure of it.

I felt something brush against my leg and looked down to find Ebbie sitting next to me. I scooped her up, amazed at how light she was compared to Grendel.

Her purrs vibrated my hand as I held her against my chest. I thought about what Jeremy had said about asking her opinion on whether she wanted to say.

I rested my chin on top of her head and hoped her answer would be yes.

Chapter Twenty-Five

Hours later, Dovie handed me a glass of wine. "Drink."

Flames from tiki torches flickered around us on her deck. The ocean looked peaceful in the moonlight. It was the only peaceful thing in my world right now.

Well, the ocean and Thoreau, who slept at the top of the deck stairs.

Dovie settled next to me on a wicker loveseat and put her arm around my shoulders. "Telling you not to worry probably wouldn't help."

I shook my head and sipped the wine. My foot was aching a bit—I'd cut back on the painkillers, switching to ibuprofen, but the pain was tolerable.

The ache in my chest was much, much worse.

The arsonist stake-out had begun. Without me.

Sean and Sam had insisted I stay home.

I hadn't been happy about it, even though I understood their reasoning.

With my foot, I couldn't give chase, and if I tagged

along with Sean, he would be more worried about me than catching the arsonist.

So here I was, at girls' night in at Dovie's.

Worried sick.

Sean was watching the Donahue house; Sam was watching Valentine, Inc.; and they'd enlisted various others to help with different locations.

Aiden had regretfully sent his apologies that he couldn't help out tonight.

I was worried about him, too.

"I spotted one of the guys in the woods," Dovie said. "Ha cha cha. Dressed all in black, muscles galore. Drop dead sexy."

I hadn't seen anyone, and it was rather creepy knowing they were there.

Creepy yet reassuring.

"Should Mac be worried?" I asked.

She smiled. "Always."

She wasn't fooling me. She adored Mac Gladstone. Unfortunately, how long their relationship would last was in the hands of fate.

Mac had cancer. Originally the doctors had predicted a fairly quick death, but he was beating the odds.

But for how long?

I breathed in the salty night air. The temperature had dropped into the high eighties, but it was still oppressive. Half the city had lost power, and I felt bad for those who didn't have a cool ocean breeze to take the edge off the heat.

Dovie pressed a kiss to my temple. "Have you heard from Sean?"

"A couple of text messages." He promised to keep me informed throughout the night. "So far he's bored, sweating to death, and wishing he'd brought more snacks."

"No sign of the arsonist."

"Not yet."

The French doors behind us opened, and Marisol came out carrying a tray of tapas. Em followed with a full bottle of wine, and Preston brought up the rear, looking like she was about to fall over.

And she hadn't even been drinking.

The sneak had lied to me about her doctor's appointment. It had been at two, not three, so by the time I made it up to the house to demand she take me with her—she had already returned.

The doctor had taken blood for testing and sent Preston home to rest.

She still wore the Band-Aid that the nurse at the doctor's office had put over the puncture site. The wound was being stubborn about clotting.

"You two didn't tell us we moved the party outside," Marisol said.

It didn't feel much like a party.

I was a nervous wreck. Preston looked like death. Em refilled her wine glass and stared at it morosely.

"What a lively group," Dovie said as if reading my thoughts.

I smiled. Leave it to Dovie to point out the obvious.

"Do you think he's having an affair?" Em asked.

"No," we all answered at the same time.

She frowned. "Then what's going on?"

"Give him time, Emerson," Dovie said. "He's obviously working through something."

"Then why doesn't he tell me about it?"

"Maybe *you're* what he's working through," Preston said, demonstrating yet again her lack of tact.

Em stuck her tongue out at her, downed her wine, and refilled her glass.

"Well," Marisol said, "things are great with me. Business is wonderful, and I have a date this weekend." Beaming, she glanced around.

We all stuck out our tongues at her.

"Well, fine. Be that way."

Dovie smiled. "Who's the man?"

"Tall, blond, gorgeous. He's a pastry chef." She rubbed her hands together. "And he's delectable."

"Ew," Preston said.

I grinned.

"We can't all be so lucky to have a Cutter McCutchan in our lives," Marisol said, poking her.

"I know," Preston said softly.

Dovie leaned forward. "Wine, Preston?"

She shook her head.

"Tapas?"

"No thanks."

Dovie threw me a worried glance. I wondered how long the blood work would take to return.

Thoreau stirred from his sleep and came over to sniff the goodies on the table. Marisol lifted him up onto the chair next to her. "By the way, Lucy, you're not going to believe what I found out about your little cat."

"What?" I asked.

"Remember how I told you her microchip came from a clinic where I volunteered?"

"You told me that this morning. I'm not senile. Of course I remember."

"Cranky," Marisol said.

Dovie nodded.

I was cranky. It had been a bad idea to come up here tonight. I wasn't fit for company.

"Go on," Em said to Marisol. "Lucy's just worried about Sean."

"Sorry," I mumbled.

"You're forgiven." Marisol's hair gleamed in the moonlight. "Anyway, I went to the clinic this afternoon, and they let me peek at her paperwork. You're never going to believe who placed that microchip in Ebbie."

The hairs raised on the back of my neck. "You?"

She nodded. "Isn't that crazy? And as soon as I saw that file, I remembered her. Such a sweet cat. She'd been a stray when she came in nearly starved. I even took her home with me and fostered her until she put on some weight. I can't believe I didn't recognize her today."

I bit my lip, recalling a recent conversation I'd had with Jeremy.

"And Ebbie told you she wanted to see me?"

"Yes."

"Why?"

"Apparently," he said, "only you can find my soul mate."

Ebbie had once known Marisol... "When did you microchip her?"

"Late November. Why?"

"Just trying to piece a timeline together. It's not long after that she was placed with Jeremy Cross." He'd said just before Christmas.

"That makes sense. It was right around the time she ran away from the clinic."

I set my wine on the table. My stomach was too topsy-turvy to finish it. "She ran away?"

"Apparently. I didn't know about it, because by then my stint volunteering there was over. One of the techs told me today that Ebbie was their one and only escapee."

"That's really strange," Em said. "That she'd somehow find her way back to you."

"Not strange," I said. "Fate."

"Does she have any thoughts about who your soul mate might be?"

"She says that you can find her."

"What do you mean?" Marisol asked.

I smiled. "It means you might have to cancel your date with Mr. Delectable. You're already spoken for by Dr. Doolittle."

A couple of hours later, Thoreau and I made our way back down to my cottage. I had fully intended to spend the night at Dovie's, but I hadn't been able to sleep, and decided I'd rather be at home.

Ebbie and Grendel met me at the door as if I'd been gone for weeks not hours. I showered them with love and affection and crutched my way into the kitchen for some more ibuprofen.

While there, I pulled out a piece of processed cheese and removed the cellophane. I broke the cheese into quarters and tossed three to Grendel (who liked to chase his treats), and one to Ebbie, who sat daintily on the counter.

I leaned down and said, "It's Marisol, isn't it?"

She blinked at me.

I rubbed her ears. "Okay. We'll figure this out."

Because as much as Ebbie wanted the match between Marisol and Jeremy, I wasn't so sure about it.

A ghost of a man.

What kind of best friend would I be to set Marisol up with someone who claimed he was a ghost of a man?

Ebbie nibbled at her food while I made my way to the couch. As my laptop warmed up, I checked my cell phone. Sean hadn't answered my last text, and it had been more than fifteen minutes.

I texted again: **sleepy?**

He wasn't one to fall asleep on the job, but it was hot, he was bored, and he was exhausted. I couldn't rule it out.

While I waited for him to write back, I typed "Jeremy Cross" into a search engine again, and came up with the same results as last time.

Grendel hopped up beside me, looking for attention. After I gave him lots of scratching and rubbing, he hopped down again and sniffed Thoreau, who was curled up in the dog bed next to the hearth. Ordinarily, he would join him there, but tonight, he crossed the room and leapt into the bassinet.

Ebbie ran in from the kitchen and joined him.

He flicked an ear in her direction, and she nudged him with the top of her head.

I thought for sure Grendel was going to pitch a fit, but he sank down, curling up to go to sleep. Ebbie did the same.

I thought again about opposites attracting. Which led my attention back to the computer screen. As far as I could tell, Jeremy and Marisol were about as opposite as they could be.

I typed in everything I could think of having to do with psychics and animal communicators. Marshfield farms. Orlinda. Anything.

Needing a break, I texted Sean: **Anything new?**

When he still didn't text back, I called him. It rang and rang, and finally his voicemail picked up. I left a message asking him to call me back. That I was getting worried.

Which I was. But I tried not to let it overwhelm me.

Biting my lip, I stared at my cursor, and pondered what I knew about Jeremy. Which led me to thinking about the men in the woods.

I typed in "FBI Psychic Jeremy."

The very first hit was an article about FBI profiler, psychic Jeremiah Norcross.

Bingo.

For the next hour, I skimmed articles and pieced together Jeremy's life.

Gifted psychic, recruited by the FBI while in college. He worked the toughest cases, tapping into the criminal minds of some of the most depraved people in the world.

Until one of those people killed his wife and his daughter.

And almost killed him.

Jeremiah Norcross then fell off the map.

I guessed that's when he'd changed his name and became a farmer.

He'd gone into hiding.

You must remember that some scars run deeper than what's on the surface. Wounds run deep.

Orlinda was a wise, wise woman.

On a hunch, I typed the words Annie Hendrix had heard on my front porch last night. The words I suspected came from Ebbie—and also added the town Jeremy had given me as well.

"Hidden Hollow + Marshfield."

Up popped a yellow page listing for Hidden Hollow Wildlife Sanctuary in Marshfield, Massachusetts.

I leaned back, feeling a sense of relief.

I'd found this ghost.

But what did I do with this information?

Chapter Twenty-Six

I looked down at my hands, shocked that they were so small. And dirty. Until I realized I was finger painting, making big smiling suns and colorful rainbows on a large piece of construction paper.

Until I realized they weren't my hands at all—I was once again in someone's head, watching the world through another set of eyes.

Paint splashed, and looking down, I saw it had splattered onto a pink skirt.

A woman came into the room and said, "Almost done?"

The woman looked familiar to me, and I tried to place her. Streaky blond hair, big blue eyes.

"Almost."

"Five minutes, okay?"

"Okay."

The small hands took a moment to paint a large flower onto the paper, and I noticed the stack of mail on the table. I didn't recognize the man's name on the bill, James Rockwell, *but took note of the address—it was in Phoenix.*

Then we were moving, keeping arms straight out in front so as not to get paint on the walls.

Down a hallway, past a pink bedroom filled with toys. To a small washroom.

"Annabeth!" a male voice called.

Turning, I saw a man in the doorway.

He smiled. "Hurry, hurry!"

My heart nearly stopped. I definitely recognized the man. He had been the one who took Bethany, minus the beard.

Paint ran into the sink, the colors blurring together. More soap. More scrubbing.

And finally—finally!—a glance into the mirror.

I nearly cried as I looked into the almond-shaped brown eyes of Bethany Hill.

I bolted upright, my eyes flying open. Breathing hard, I looked around. I was on the couch in my cottage. All was quiet.

At some point Ebbie had moved from the bassinet to the couch alongside me and had brought a friend with her—the pink bear. It sat on the couch pillow, right next to where my head had just been resting.

I picked it up and stared at it, trying to make sense of what had just happened.

What I had just seen.

I glanced at the clock. It was just after three in the morning. I grabbed my phone. It had been hours since I heard from Sean.

My heart pounded. He should have called by now. He'd promised me no more disappearing acts...

I dialed Sam.

"Lucy?" he asked, sounding bored.

"Have you talked to Sean?"

"Not since earlier."

"He's not answering his phone."

"He's probably asleep," Sam said.

I wanted to believe him. Prayed he was right. But I knew it wasn't. *Felt* it. "Something's wrong."

There was a beat of silence before Sam said, "I'll drive over and check."

"Hurry. And call me when you get there."

I stood, picked up my crutches and the bear.

Was it possible Bethany was alive?

It was a ridiculous hour to call someone, but I picked up the phone to call Orlinda. Only to be told she'd already checked out of the hotel. Apparently, she'd gotten an early flight out, but that meant I didn't have any means of communicating with her—she had no cell phone.

I couldn't help but hope that Bethany was in fact alive. There was no reason to doubt it. The other visions I'd had like this one had proven true.

Then I thought about what Graham had said, about the shallow grave. It was entirely possible he'd been wrong. That his vision had misled him, as so many of mine (when I touched Sean's hands) had done to me. Psychics were not infallible.

I wanted to do a jig.

I was taking several deep breaths, trying to get my heart rate back to normal when a pair of headlights swept across the windows.

Sean? I hobbled quickly to the door to peek out. Hope bubbled, and then burst when I saw who was getting out of the car in the driveway.

Dr. Paul McDermott.

As soon as he took two steps toward my door, he was flanked by two intimidating men dressed all in black. He looked about to pee his pants, so I pulled open the front door. They helped Dr. Paul up the steps and said to me, "Do you know him?"

I gazed at them, at how intensely scary they were. "What's the safe word?"

I saw a flicker in the eyes of the man closest to me. He leaned in and whispered into my ear. "Fuzzy navel."

I tried not to smile—it wasn't really a humorous situation—but I couldn't help myself. This rock-solid, scary-as-hell man saying "fuzzy navel" was about the funniest thing I'd seen in days.

If Dr. Paul had come with nefarious intent, these men had undoubtedly changed his mind. "You can let him go," I said.

They nodded and dropped his arms. Spinning, they disappeared into the darkness.

Dr. Paul stumbled into the cottage. His face had gone pale. "Holy ninjas! Who the hell are they?"

"Protection."

"Effective."

I nodded and set the pink bear back into the bassinet. If Dr. Paul saw that I'd been holding it, he didn't say anything. "What are you doing here?" Suddenly, I noticed he wore a pair of sweat pants and a t-shirt along with a pair of flip-flops. There were still pillow markings on his face. He'd obviously just tumbled out of bed.

"I had a dream," he said, taking off his glasses and pulling a hand down his face.

"About Bethany?"

"Bethany?" He slid his glassed back onto the bridge of his nose. "No, it was—"

The sound of footsteps on the front porch interrupted him. The screen door pulled open and Preston stuck in her bedhead. "I saw the commotion," she was saying, "and came down to check it out." Her gaze zeroed in on Dr. Paul. "But I'll be going now."

"Get back in here," I said, "and sit down." By the looks of her, she wasn't going to make it back up the hill. "Dr. Paul was just going to tell me about a dream he had."

Preston sat. "What dream?"

He gazed at her with such intensity that it made me uncomfortable.

She looked at me. "Make him stop staring at me."

I nudged Dr. Paul. "The dream?"

"It's Sean."

"My Sean?" I asked. My pulse jumped and started racing again.

"I didn't know if it was real. I came here to find out. Is he here?"

I shook my head. "He's on a stakeout."

"Does he have a black car?"

I nodded.

"Do you know where he is? Exactly?"

"I could find it, yes."

"Then, we need to go. Grab some shoes. Well, *shoe*."

"Dr. Paul," I said, trying to fight back a wave of nausea, "what did you see?"

"Is Sean dead?" Preston blurted.

I sat on the arm of the couch. I'd been thinking the same thing. After all, Dr. Paul was Dr. Death.

"What? No! No! Not that I know of." His bald head glistened. "All I saw was a masked man sneak up behind Sean and hit him over the head. He put him over his shoulder and walked away."

"Over his shoulder?" I asked. "Like a fireman's carry?"

"Exactly like that."

My stomach started aching.

The phone rang. I snatched it up. It was Sam.

"His car is here, but he's not," Sam said, cursing a blue streak.

"Call the police. I'll be there as soon as I can."

I hung up and hopped over to the door and slipped on a flip flop.

Preston stood up, wobbled a bit, and said, "I'm coming, too."

Dr. Paul handed me my crutches. "Oh no you're not, Preston."

"Says who?" she demanded. A feeble demand, but still.

The air grew eerily still. Dr. Paul walked to over to the table, picked up the phone, and punched in a couple of numbers. Into the receiver, he said, "This is Dr. Paul

McDermott. I need an ambulance sent right away." He gave my address, and then hung up.

Preston's jaw dropped. "What? Tell me that ambulance is not for me. I'm coming with you two."

Dr. Paul took a step toward her, and she took a step back. Softly yet sternly, he said, "No, you're not. There's someone who needs you a lot more than Sean right now."

She crossed her arms over her chest. "Who's that?"

Yeah, who? I wondered. Because Sean being knocked out and carried away by a madman seemed pretty life or death to me.

Dr. Paul said, "The baby you're carrying is clinging to life right now. If you don't get to a hospital, he will die. No question. You have to go. Right now."

As if her legs had given out, Preston slowly sank into the chair behind her, her face filled with shock. "Baby?"

"Baby?" I echoed, glancing at her. She was rail thin, not even a trace of a baby bump.

"You didn't know?" he said to her.

She shook her head and tears sprang to her eyes. Her hands pressed against her stomach. "What's wrong with him?"

Orlinda hadn't been kidding when she predicted a huge upheaval in Preston's life. Upheavals didn't get much bigger than unexpected dangerous pregnancies.

"I'm not sure," Dr. Paul said.

Her tear-filled eyes were wide as she stared. "But if I go to the hospital right now, the baby will be okay?"

His silence was telling. "I'm not sure, Preston, but for

right now, he's alive."

Chapter Twenty-Seven

Dr. Paul drove.

I fidgeted in the passenger seat of his Mercedes, wishing I could be in two places at once. Preston needed me.

Yet Sean needed me more.

We'd driven Preston up to Dovie's house and filled her in before we headed out. Dovie woke Em, and both would stay by Preston's side. I called Cutter, but he hadn't answered. I left him a message to call Dovie immediately. I could only hope he didn't answer because he was on a plane on his way here.

We'd crossed paths with the ambulance on our way to the highway.

"Is it really a boy? The baby?" I clarified. "You kept saying 'him.'"

He nodded.

"Did you know she was pregnant the day she followed you around the hospital?"

"Yes, but I didn't realize how severe her condition was

until I saw her tonight. The baby's spirit was already starting to leave her body."

"Is he going to die?"

"I hope not, Lucy. Right now, it could go either way."

Tears stung my eyes as I thought about a little boy with Cutter's brown eyes and Preston's spiky blond hair. *Please let him pull through.*

Dr. Paul sped along the highway, pushing his car to eighty, ninety miles an hour. There was hardly any traffic, but the city looming ahead looked spooky, half of it in blackness.

The brownout.

Nausea rolled through my stomach, and I stared out the window, trying to keep the queasiness in check.

Dr. Paul said, "Can you connect to Sean psychically?"

"Only when I touch his hand."

It reminded me of the vision I'd had. The one where we were surrounded by smoke.

I would find him.

I just didn't know when. Or how.

Directing Dr. Paul to Sean's old neighborhood wasn't as easy as I remembered, but we eventually found the street. There was one lone police car at the scene, sitting behind Sean's Mustang. Sam stood off to the side, speaking to an officer. Several neighbors had emerged from their houses to try and see what was going on.

The neighborhood was in the dark. Not a single light shone from inside the houses.

Dr. Paul pulled up to the curb in front of Sean's car. I

pushed opened the door, took a deep breath to quell the queasiness and pulled my crutches out of the back seat. Sam was by my side in an instant. I made a quick introduction to Dr. Paul and explained about the vision he'd had.

"Why is there only one police car?" I asked.

"The department's spread thin with the brownout. There's looting going on downtown."

Who cared about a couple of stolen TVs when Sean was missing? "Are there any witnesses?"

"Not that we've found."

I glanced at him. "Do the police even believe that Sean's been kidnapped?"

His face paled. "The note helped convince them."

"Note?" I asked, swallowing hard.

He motioned with his head for us to follow. He walked along Sean's car toward the back window. He took out a pen flashlight and shone it onto a message written in red on the glass.

FIND ME IF YOU CAN

I sucked in a breath. "Is that written in blood?"

"Yes," Sam said.

My knees buckled and Sam and Dr. Paul each grabbed onto an arm. They helped me over to the sidewalk and sat me on the curb.

Tears filled my eyes and spilled over as they sat next to me, one on each side. I glanced at Sam, "Why is someone doing this to him? Why?"

Dr. Paul cleared his throat. "Lucy?"

Tears dripped off my cheeks as I looked at him.

"It's my feeling," he said, "that this might not be about Sean."

"Then who?" I asked.

His gaze bore into me. "It could be about you."

After spending hours at the police station, Sam drove me home while Dr. Paul went to the hospital to check on Preston. The morning sun was glowing brightly in a clear blue sky when I opened my front door. Thoreau came bounding out, and Sam said, "I'll take him for a quick walk."

I filled food bowls as Grendel and Ebbie circled my feet, washed out their water dish, and tried not to fall apart.

I would find him. I'd seen the smoke.

Sam came back inside, flanked by two men dressed all in black. "It's okay," I said to them, not even bothering to make them say "fuzzy navel." "He's with me."

They nodded and disappeared out the door.

"Who are the commandos, Lucy?" Sam asked.

"A gift from a friend. Remember? He was sending over security to watch the house?"

"Wasn't quite the rent-a-cops I was expecting, but it's assuring to know you're in good hands. I'm going to go now."

"Where?" I asked.

There was no place to go. Nowhere to look.

"Curt Meister and I are going to go back to the scene and scout for more clues, ask more questions."

Curt Meister. I hadn't wanted to rule him out as a suspect until Sam confirmed that Curt had been at the firehouse all night long, in the company of at least ten people who could vouch for him.

I'd finally accepted the fact that Dr. Paul might be right.

These fires were about me.

Hurting the people I loved.

Especially Sean.

"You'll call?" I asked.

He nodded and gave me a hug. "Try to get some rest."

He was kidding, right?

I watched him go. As soon as he was out of the driveway, I hopped around the house, gathering anything I could find of Sean's. By the time I was done, there was a mountain in the middle of the living room. Thoreau yapped and brought me a ball to throw as I sat down on the floor. I tossed it behind me and he took off.

Piece by piece, I picked up Sean's things and held the item between my hands and tried to get a reading.

One by one, my hopes were dashed.

"Come on!" I cried, picking up one of his books. I squeezed my eyes shut and focused on Sean. On everything I loved about him.

I saw nothing.

With a scream, I threw the book across the room.

Who was doing this to us?

To me?

Thoreau pushed his nose into my arm. I picked him up and cuddled him close. "I'm sorry if I scared you."

My cell phone rang, and I hurried to answer it. It was Dovie.

"Any news?" she asked.

"None," my voice cracked on the word.

"My love," Dovie said softly. "My heart is breaking for you. Where are you now?"

"At home. I don't know where to look for him. He could be anywhere."

"What do the police say?"

"They're patrolling, but they have nothing to go on. Plus, all these brownouts now. The looting..."

"And the fires."

"What fires?" I asked, shooing Ebbie out of the laundry area. I closed the bi-fold doors.

"It's all over the news. Dozens of fires have broken out across the city, set by the looters, they're saying."

Goose bumps rose on my arms. Set by the looters? Or an arsonist?

"Come to the hospital, LucyD. It's better than being home alone, waiting."

I swallowed hard. I'd never felt so helpless. I wasn't a wait-around kind of girl. "Okay," I said. "How's she doing?"

"It's worse than we thought, Lucy. It's all still very much touch and go. Right now, the baby's still alive. Preston was so severely anemic she had to get blood transfusions. Cutter is downstairs right now donating a pint."

My heart felt like it was breaking into pieces. "He made it, then."

"About an hour ago."

"How's he doing?"

She paused. "Not well. I think he really loves her."

I knew he did. "I'll be there soon."

I hung up and hopped back to my pile of Sean's things. I belly flopped on top of it, tears spilling from my eyes.

All my anger, frustration, helplessness and desperation seeped out. I bunched up one of his shirts and put it under my head.

Closing my eyes, I pictured his smile, his eyes when he laughed. The way he held me, touched me.

The way he made me believe in love. In happily-ever-afters.

I blinked and saw a baseboard running the length of a room. Wiggling, I rolled over, feeling the carpet beneath my arms, and realized I lying was on the floor.

I sat up and looked around.

What had just happened?

I'd been seeing a scene through someone else's eyes again. Sean's?

But how? I hadn't been holding anything of his.

I lay back down, closed my eyes and took a deep breath, trying to focus.

I struggled to sit up, rolling this way and that, and I realized my hands and feet were tied. I lay back down and looked up at the ceiling, at the swirls. Then I looked left and right, at the bare walls painted a soft tangerine color.

I sat up again, my heart pounding, and the vision was gone.

How the hell was this working?

I looked down at the pile I'd been laying on and picked up Sean's shirt, which had been tucked under my head. I held it in my hands and concentrated as hard as I could.

Nothing.

Then I thought about the other visions I'd had... How there had been a matchstick on my pillow, and the bear next to my head.

Slowly, I lifted Sean's shirt to my face and breathed in the trace of his scent on the fabric.

I rolled again, back and forth trying to get momentum. Finally, I was able to sit up. I looked around. At the walls, the desk, the chairs, the lamp.

I drew the shirt away from my face. "Holy shit," I cried. "He's at the office!"

I jumped up and held the shirt to my face again, breathing in, focusing.

From the sitting position, I was able to stand up. I hopped over to the door, turned so that my hands tied behind my back could grab the handle. It was locked. Using my shoulder, I rammed the door, but nothing happened.

Throwing Sean's shirt over my shoulder, I hopped over to the bassinet and picked up the pink bear. I held it to my face and breathed in, thinking about Bethany.

I was on a swing, my feet kicked out in front of me as I glided through the air. "Higher!"

Ohmygod, ohmygod.

The visions were related to *scents.*

I hopped back through the living room and into the

kitchen for my cell phone.

My heart sank at the scene before me. Ebbie had gotten back into the laundry area and dragged out several plastic grocery bags.

They were shredded on the floor, and a piece hung out of her mouth.

I dropped down next to her. "Tell me you didn't eat the bags."

I quickly tried to put the bags back together, jigsaw-style, and it became obvious several chunks were missing.

"Oh no. Oh no!"

I tried to think fast. I had to get to Sean. But Ebbie... I dialed Marisol. She answered on the first ring. "Are you still at Dovie's?"

"Just getting ready to leave."

"Ebbie ate a plastic bag, can you come and get her? I have to go."

"No problem. I'll be right there."

I hung up and looked at Ebbie. "Marisol will be right here. Don't eat anything else." I picked her up and placed her in the bassinet.

I had to think quickly. What did I need to bring? In the vision, Sean's feet had been bound with duct tape. I hobbled into the kitchen and rooted around until I found a small Swiss Army knife. I stuck it in my pocket.

I wasn't exactly schooled on what to bring when facing off with a potential arsonist, so I tried to think like Sean. What would he do?

A gun.

I knew he'd taken his with him last night, but he had a spare in a box under the bed. In my room, I dropped to my knees. My hand shook as I worked the combination dial lock and lifted the lid.

I grabbed the small pistol, made sure it was loaded and stuck it in my purse.

It had been a few months since I'd been to a firing range, but I had no doubt that I could handle the weapon. Especially if my and Sean's lives were on the line.

In the kitchen, I gathered up the shredded bags and stuffed them in the trash. I grabbed my car keys, my phone, my crutches, and made sure I had Sean's shirt as I headed out the door.

I'd call the police while on the road. Until then, I mentally prepared myself for the fight of my life. Because I knew that soon Sean and I would be together, surrounded by thick smoke.

And where there was smoke, there was fire.

I was headed straight into it.

Chapter Twenty-Eight

Route 3 through the Weymouth and Braintree area wasn't bad, but at the 93 North merge, it became bumper to bumper traffic. I'd tried calling the police several times but either my phone would lose its coverage or the 911 number had a busy signal.

As soon as I saw the Boston skyline, it was apparent why.

Smoke plumed over the city, and it looked like something out of an end-of-the-world action movie. I half expected alien spacecrafts to swoop in and start firing.

Unfortunately, with this scene there would be no director yelling, "Cut!"

The scent of the smoke drifted into my car even with the windows rolled up. Cars around me honked, and panic was quickly setting in. I turned on the radio and listened as broadcasters announced that the governor had declared a state of emergency. Millions were without power all across the state, cell phone towers were down, landline phones weren't working, and looters had taken over many of the streets as dozens of fires burned out of control.

This heat wave hadn't only brought out the kooks, but every criminally-minded resident of the city.

Traffic inched forward. I tried to call Sam, but my cell phone showed no service. I tossed it on the passenger seat and beat my hand against the steering wheel. This couldn't be happening. Not now.

Several T subway trains had stalled on the track, and I felt bad for those trapped within the cars. They couldn't be let off—there wasn't a safe place for them to disembark, and it had to be boiling hot on the train with no air conditioning.

I glanced to my right and off in the distance, the ocean water glittered in the sunshine. With all my heart, I wished I had taken the ferry into the city. There would have been no traffic there at all.

Tears of frustration built in my eyes, and to keep myself sane, I pulled Sean's t-shirt from my bag and held it to my nose.

Through his eyes, I saw nothing at all.

I tried to think what that meant and reasoned he was either sleeping or out cold or...

No. I refused to go there. It was impossible, anyway. I'd seen us together in the smoke.

I tucked the shirt back into my bag and angrily zipped my car into the breakdown lane. I'd gone about twenty feet before I realized everyone else and their brother had the same thought. This lane was just as jammed.

Concentrating on taking deep breaths, I tried not to

have a full-blown panic attack. I couldn't very well walk into the city—not with my foot—but there had to be some way to get there.

There was a marina in Dorchester that wasn't too far away. I could probably limp my way there in an hour or so. Which was probably faster than I'd get there by car. Once there, I could offer to pay someone with a boat to take me to Rowe's Wharf. From there it was a long walk to the office, but it was better than sitting in my car growing more and more frustrated.

I gathered up my purse and pulled my car key off my keychain. I'd leave it in the ignition. If someone wanted to steal my car, they had my blessing.

I opened my door and was just about to get out when in the rearview mirror I caught sight of a motorcyclist weaving in and out of the breakdown lane.

A savior on a Harley.

I jumped out. I glanced at my crutches in the backseat. There was no way they'd fit on a motorcycle. I left them where they were and started waving my hands in the Harley's direction. When he didn't look like he was going to stop, I jumped in front of his bike. Tires squealed as he braked.

Lifting his visor, he scowled at me. "Jesus, lady! You have a death wish?"

"A thousand dollars if you can get me to the Public Garden in the next half hour."

He narrowed his eyes. "Show me the money."

I fished around in my bag for the envelope Dovie had given me. I flashed the cash.

"Hop on," he said.

I crisscrossed my bag over my body, and slung a leg over his seat. The man in the car behind me started yelling that I couldn't leave my car in the middle of the highway. I wanted to argue that the car was in the breakdown lane where it was perfectly reasonable for a car to sit unattended, but instead, I yelled, "The key is in the ignition!"

The man's wife, in the passenger seat, could take it. Keep it for all I cared.

"Hang on!" my knight on shining Harley said, revving the engine.

I latched on to his jacket and he zoomed off, toward the clouds of smoke hovering ominously above the city.

The man dropped me right in front of the Porcupine. There were cars tipped upside down in the middle of the street, and several fires burned nearby.

Miraculously, this neighborhood hadn't lost its power, for which I was extremely grateful since my keycard to get into the building wouldn't work without electricity.

I handed over the envelope containing the money. "Can you do me one more favor?" I asked.

Grizzled eyebrows slashed downward. "What's that?"

"Find the closest police department and report an abduction. Give them this address. Tell them the Beantown Burner is inside."

"Are you kidding?"

"Do I look like I'm kidding?"

He studied me.

I said, "There's another thousand dollars in it for you if you do. I don't have the cash on me now, but I'm good for it. I work here," I said, pointing to the building. "Second floor. My name is Lucy Valentine."

Recognition flashed across his eyes. "The psychic?"

I nodded.

"My wife loves those articles about you written by..." He snapped his fingers.

"Preston Bailey."

"Right. Can you do a reading on me? I lost my watch a while back..."

"If you go to the police, I'll find anything you lost. I promise. Just go. Please."

"I'll see what I can do." He took off.

Now that I was here, I didn't know how to approach the situation. What if the arsonist was inside, lying in wait for me?

I could wait for the police, but I didn't have the patience. Despite what Orlinda advised, I was going to have to leap before looking.

I slid my keycard through the reader and took a second to prop open the door. Everything inside looked the same as always. The cherry wood steps gleamed, and it was hotter than hell. I glanced up three flights of stairs. Nothing seemed amiss.

My foot ached as I took the first step. I debated about taking the elevator, but with the brownouts, I didn't want to risk getting caught inside. I'd deal with the pain.

Slowly, I climbed the steps, my pulse pounding in my throat.

I took one step at a time, trying to be as quiet as I could in case Sean and I weren't the only ones in the building.

When I finally reached the third floor landing, I nearly cried in relief. My foot throbbed and my nerves made me feel like I could jump right out of my skin.

I pushed open the door to SDI and scooted inside, keeping my back flat against the walls. The reception area was empty except for a filing cabinet, a sofa and some chairs.

In the hallway, I stopped to listen. I couldn't hear much other than the beating of my heart. I hoped and prayed that the police were on their way. That my Harley rider had convinced someone to at least check out the building.

Sam's office door was wide open, but Sean's was closed tight with a chair wedged under the door handle. I quickly removed it and turned the handle.

Inside was my worst nightmare.

Sean was lying face down on the floor, blood seeping from a head wound. Duct tape bound his hands and feet.

"Sean," I said, shaking him.

He groaned softly. I made quick work of the duct tape using the handy-dandy Swiss Army knife and rolled him over.

"Sean!" I slapped at his cheeks and tried not to look at the blood on the floor.

He winced and moaned but didn't open his eyes.

I crawled to the desk and grabbed the phone. I dialed

911 only to once again get a busy signal.

I tried again and again and finally gave up. As I went back to Sean, the lamp in the corner flickered but stayed on.

I wanted to cry, but instead took a deep breath and slipped my hands under his armpits. He was dead weight and it was slow-going to get him out of his office and down the hallway. I paused to take a breath in the reception area. Sweat glistened on my hands, my arms, my chest. My clothes were soaked through.

As I looked at the stairs, I tried again to revive him. There was no way I could make it down those steps with him on my own.

"Sean!" I whispered fiercely. "Mr. Donahue!"

He squeezed his eyes tight, then slowly opened them. He took a look at me, smiled, and passed out again.

I glanced at the stairs, then the elevator. I had no choice.

I pushed the call button, and the sound of the cables in the shaft echoed shrilly in the silent building.

A loud ding punctuated the elevator's arrival. I wrestled with the doors and dragged Sean inside. I managed to get the doors closed and as soon as I pushed the down button I let out a sigh of relief.

Bending down, I tried again to revive Sean. With no luck whatsoever.

The elevator lurched and the lights inside flashed. It was the longest elevator ride in history. Finally, we reached ground level. My hands shook as I reached for the doors to open them. The inside door opened easily, but the outer door wouldn't budge.

I tugged and tugged and finally started kicking at it. Sweat poured off me.

"Temper, temper," a voice said from the vestibule.

I jumped and let out a startled cry.

Graham sat on the bottom step watching me calmly as he poured gasoline from a plastic water bottle onto the stairs and splashed it onto the walls.

"Graham?" I said, unable to believe my eyes.

"You were expecting someone else?" he said. "Like the Beantown Burner? Ooh, so scary. The big bad Burner."

I thought about the visions I'd been having and how they'd all proven true. I'd seen Sam's house set on fire. I knew Sean was in his office. And I fully expected Bethany Hill to be alive.

There hadn't been a mistake, a misunderstanding of his shallow-grave vision, at all.

He'd out-and-out lied.

As my brain began to connect the pieces, I realized that when Graham had told me about my license, it had been the afternoon—hours before the arsonist drew a bullseye over my face and set Sam's house on fire. Yet, Graham could only have visions of past and present events. Not future.

There was only one explanation of how he knew what the arsonist was going to do to my license.

Graham was the arsonist. He hadn't been predicting anything that day in the Porcupine—he'd been telling me what he planned to do.

I'd fallen hook, line, and sinker for his lies.

Was he even psychic?

"The police will be here any second," I said, trying to sound as though I was full of confidence and not shaking in my orthopedic boot.

"Sure they will. Just as soon as they deal with the thousands of looters and all the fires."

"Did you set all those fires?"

"Some," he said. "The rest are copycats. Some people can be so jealous."

I recalled what Dr. Paul had said about Graham and Annie.

They're the jealous sort, and there's only room enough for one teacher's pet in our class, don't you think?

"Is that what this is all about? You're jealous of me?"

"Don't make me laugh. It's you who should be jealous of me. You and Paul and that slut Annie. Even Orlinda. I have more abilities than all of you put together."

"Yet I'm the one who knows Bethany is still alive and not you," I said.

His nostrils flared and he slowly, deliberately took out a box of matches.

"You're making that up," he said.

"Am I?"

"You're nothing but a fraud. A phony. You make me sick," he hissed.

"Then how did I know Sean was here?" I countered. I had the gun, but there was no way the muzzle would fit through the outer door's delicate brass pattern.

"Lucky guess. How did I know about all the places Sean

was connected to?"

"Because you broke into the DCF warehouse."

He smiled a sickly, twisted smile. "You have no proof of that."

"I don't need it. I'm psychic, remember?"

"You're a liar!" he shouted. "It took you weeks to even figure out that your beloved Sean was a target." He over exaggerated a frown. "Poor Sean. He's not so tough when a baseball bat hits his head, is he?. How come you didn't see that coming, Ms. Psychic Pants?"

Anger boiled in me, setting all my nerve endings on fire. I had to keep my calm. Not let him goad me. "I found your wallet, remember?"

He ignored me. "I even left you those matchsticks. But no, you couldn't even get a reading on those, even with your so-called new gift of psychometry. Admit it! You're a phony. A fake!"

"If I'm a fake, how did I see you in Sam's house? Dousing the walls? Drawing the bullseye on my license? Stepping over that body on the floor?"

Insanity filled his eyes. "It doesn't much matter. There's only room enough for one teacher's pet in Orlinda's group and that's going to be me."

He struck the match, held it up, and smiled as he flicked it toward me.

Flames leapt.

I slammed the inner door of the elevator and jabbed the button for the second floor, hoping that he would think I went to the third, to the roof. As the elevator climbed, my hands shook as I dug in my bag. I grabbed the gun and my keys.

There was a loud ding, and I lifted the door and managed to get the outer door open a few inches before Graham was there, leering at me from the landing.

Smoke was rising from the first floor, stinging my eyes.

My hand shook as I took aim at him. His eyes narrowed on the gun, then zipped back up to my face.

I fired.

The bullet went wide.

He dove for the stairwell closest to him, which was the one going upstairs. I summoned all the strength I had and pushed the outer door of the elevator open. I heard a footstep and turned and fired, hitting Graham in the arm. He let out a scream and dove back into hiding.

I dragged Sean out and over to the Valentine, Inc. door.

"You're not getting out of here alive," Graham taunted.

"Oh? Did you have a vision of that? Because I know your visions don't come true."

Unlike mine.

This was the image I'd seen when I'd touched Sean's hand.

Smoke completely surrounded us, and I had to feel with my fingertips to get the key into the lock.

I coughed, my lungs starting to burn. I couldn't tell where Graham was, but as I opened the door to the office, I fired another shot toward the stairwell, hoping he'd be scared off. I grunted and groaned as I dragged Sean into the office and closed and locked the door. I was halfway down the hallway when I heard a loud crash.

The glass door panel.

I doubled my pace, tugging and hobbling and nearly tripping in haste to get to my office. Graham appeared at the end of the hallway, looking like a ghost surrounded by all the smoke. In his hands he held a lit match in his hand. I raised the gun and fired again.

He dove for the floor. As he fell, the match extinguished.

I slammed my office door closed and barricaded it.

I sprinted to the window, twisted its lock and lifted it up. The fire escape was our only hope. I climbed out and tried my best to lower the ladder to the ground. It was stuck.

I cursed and climbed back in the window. I'd get Sean outside, then deal with that ladder.

My office door vibrated as Graham rammed something into it. As I dragged Sean closer to the window, I saw fingertips slide under the door and drop a lit match onto the carpet. I stomped out the flame.

When I turned back around, I let out an ear-splitting scream when I saw a man standing on the fire escape, peering in.

He said, "It's good to see you, too."

Jeremy Cross no longer looked like a bad boy but rather an angel. A dark angel, but still. I wasn't in any position to be picky. "How'd you get here?"

"The roof."

The door vibrated again. I could hear the frame splitting.

"I can't get the ladder down," I said.

Jeremy gave it a good push, and it creaked downward. He leaned in and grabbed hold of Sean's upper body. I took hold of his feet. Together, we maneuvered him through the window.

Jeremy hoisted Sean onto his shoulder and said, "I've got him. Stay close behind me."

But just as he headed down the ladder, the door to my office finally splintered. There was another crash and the door thrust open. Graham, with a crazed look in his eye came running toward me.

"Go! Go!" I shouted to Jeremy.

I raised the gun and fired off a shot, but it was as if the bullet that hit Graham in the upper chest had no effect. He dove headlong through the open window toward me. I sidestepped his body and went back in through the window before he could stand up.

I made a run for the hallway, my boot slowing me down quite a bit. Smoke filled the reception area, and I could barely see my hand in front of my face. I raced for the steps, but immediately realized that going down was out of the question. Intense heat emanated from the first floor. When I turned to go up the stairs, I felt a hand lock around my bare ankle.

I stomped on Graham's wrist with my boot. He yowled and I went for the stairs going up.

I'd taken one step when he once again latched on to me. This time my arm. I twisted out of his grip, thankful for the self-defense class I'd taken, spun and jabbed toward his face, aiming for an eye. I hit something, and he cried out. I then grabbed on to both railings and lifted my leg and kicked toward his abdomen with all my might. I heard him tumble backward. The sound of him falling down the stairs echoed along with crackling flames.

I could barely breathe as I dropped to my knees and crawled back through the Valentine, Inc. doorway, past Suz's desk and down the hall. I'd just reached the windowsill to my office when Jeremy reappeared, took my arm, and helped me out.

"Sean?" I asked.

"Is damn lucky you found him."

Not as lucky as I was. Because I didn't know what I would do without him.

"The guy?" Jeremy asked.

"Fell down the stairs to the first floor."

"A fire engine just showed up." His gaze locked on mine. "Should I run ahead and tell the firefighters there's a victim on the first floor?"

I knew what he was asking me. Graham's survival was up to me.

Finally, I nodded.

He gave a short nod and leapt off the ladder and sprinted around the corner.

I found Sean on a stretcher in the back of an ambulance. He'd finally opened his eyes. The EMTs had an IV in him and an oxygen mask over his face.

He tugged it down so he could say something to me.

"I apparently missed all the fireworks," he said.

I wanted to say something snappy and sassy in return, but as I looked into his eyes and knew he was going to be okay, I threw my arms around him and burst into tears.

Chapter Twenty-Nine

Dr. Paul pulled some strings and had Sean transferred to the same hospital as Preston so they could share a room.

"Come on," Preston said to Dr. Paul early the next morning. "Admit it about the skulls. They're souvenirs, keepsakes."

"I should have your head checked while you're here," he said, smiling.

There was something behind his smile, though, that had me believing that Preston was right. I wasn't sure why I wanted to know what was truly behind the skull collection. I'd had enough traumas for the week.

His head wrapped in gauze, Sean sipped from a cup of water and glanced at me. "Do I want to know?"

He'd needed thirty stitches and had a severe concussion, but nothing was permanently damaged and in a few weeks he'd be just fine. Except for the emotional scars.

"No," I answered.

Dr. Paul said, "I'll go sign the paperwork for your

discharges. You," he said to Preston, "need to stay on bed rest for at least a week. You," he said to Sean, "need to stay on bed rest for at least a week."

"What about me?" I said, hoping to stay in bed for a week, too. Especially if Sean was there.

"You," he said to me, "are out of luck."

He'd already expressed to me how lucky I was that my foot hadn't been injured worse by running around without my crutches.

I rolled my eyes.

He took something out of his pocket and tossed it up and down. "Guess I'll have to keep this for another person."

It was a small ceramic skull.

He winked at me and walked out.

Preston glared at me as I laughed. "He is not funny. He's sick! Twisted."

"He's kind of funny," I said. "And he did save little baby Valentine's life."

She lovingly placed her hands over her stomach. "I'm grateful, but I still think he's a serial killer."

Sean chuckled as Dovie came bustling into the room, carrying a box. She set it on Preston's lap. "A present for the baby."

The baby was hanging on. Preston's anemia would need to be closely monitored for the rest of her pregnancy, but the obstetricians on staff here were confident she and the baby were going to be just fine. She was almost three months along—there would be a new addition to our family around Christmastime.

"Where's Cutter?" Dovie asked.

"Getting breakfast. He'll be back soon."

I glanced at the engagement ring on Preston's finger. My brother had proposed to her last night.

Heaven help her.

Preston pulled open the box and her eyes grew wide as she pulled a sea foam green blanket out.

"Hey!" I said. "That's Ebbie's blanket."

"No," Dovie said. "It's for my great-grandchild. And I'll be taking back the bassinet, too."

"Over Grendel's dead body," I said.

"He'll deal," she said airily.

"Maybe Grendel can keep the bassinet," Preston said, trying to keep the peace.

"No," Dovie said, adjusting the blankets. "It's for the baby."

"But—"

Dovie cut her off. "No."

Suddenly, I couldn't help but laugh.

"What is so funny, LucyD?" Dovie asked.

"Yeah," Preston echoed.

I smiled at her. "Welcome to the family."

Later that afternoon, Orlinda, Marisol, and Jeremy sat in my living room. I tugged the bedroom door closed so Sean wouldn't wake up.

I crutched my way to my favorite chair and sat down. Grendel hopped into my lap and Ebbie sat in the middle of the coffee table. Thoreau was snuggled next to Sean in the other room.

Orlinda said, "The Phoenix police just confirmed that Bethany Hill has been found alive and well."

"Was her mother really behind her kidnapping?" I asked.

"It looks that way," she said. "Apparently the parents were on the verge of divorce and the mother didn't want to share custody with the father. She staged it so it looked like Bethany was gone forever and blamed their breakup on the abduction. Bethany lived with her mother's boyfriend until her mom joined them in Phoenix permanently."

"That's sick," Marisol said.

"There are many deranged people in this world," Orlinda said.

I glanced at Jeremy, but he didn't add to the conversation. While waiting with me at the hospital last night, he'd told me how he'd come to help at Valentine, Inc.

Of how when he came here to discuss Ebbie with me, he'd found her with Marisol.

Of how Ebbie told him where I was.

At first, I didn't remember saying anything aloud, but then I remember shouting that "he was at the office" when I had the vision of Sean.

Ebbie had probably saved our lives.

She swished her tail.

Jeremy had called in another favor, and an FBI helicopter had picked him up here and flown him into

Boston, dropping him onto the roof of Valentine, Inc.

And suddenly, I wondered how involved he still was with the Bureau. Even though he changed his name didn't necessarily mean he didn't work for them anymore...

I noticed how Marisol kept looking Jeremy's way and he at her, and I wondered if Ebbie had really known the two were meant to be together.

At this point I believed anything is possible.

Orlinda swirled the ice in her drink. "I'm still in shock over Graham."

We all were.

"I don't know how I misread him so badly," she added. "Lucy, I'm so very sorry I introduced him into your life."

She'd already apologized a dozen times. "You couldn't have known," I said. Just the other day, Sam had said something similar when we thought the arsonist was targeting Sean...and only Sean.

Graham had kept us all guessing.

"People like him wear good masks," Jeremy said softly.

Graham had been pulled out of the building alive, but he had died on the way to the hospital from severe burns. I wasn't the least bit sorry that he was dead. Only that Sean had been dragged into a vengeance plot against me.

I'd received word this morning, too, that the twenty-two year old skateboarder had died as well. The only comfort I found in the news was that Graham would no longer be able to hurt anyone else.

"What will happen with our group?" I asked. Grendel purred loudly in my lap.

"I'm not sure at this point. Let's wait and see for a while."

Jeremy said, "He wants you to stay home more." He motioned to Grendel.

"No kidding," I said. "He has separation anxiety."

"He claims he doesn't. Just that he misses you."

"He misses me giving him treats all day."

"That, too," Jeremy said with a smile.

"What about Ebbie?" I asked. "What does she have to say?"

Orlinda and Marisol watched on silently.

Jeremy's tone was serious as he said, "She says her job here is done."

I bit my lip.

Marisol said, "How did she know to go to you in the first place, Lucy?"

"I can answer that," Jeremy said. "Apparently while Ebbie was under your care at the vet clinic, you talked about Lucy a lot. It was right after her psychic abilities had been revealed and her name was in the paper. She heard you tell people that Lucy was your friend. She never knew your name, but she remembered Lucy's."

Ebbie's tail swished.

"Wow," Marisol said. "She's tenacious."

Jeremy tried to look nonchalant when he said, "You made a big impact on her."

I glanced at Orlinda and wiggled my eyebrows.

She smiled. She claimed she had nothing to do with any of the matchmaking, but I wasn't sure I believed her.

Trying not to sound too eager, I said, "Did you ask Ebbie where she wants to live?"

Jeremy clasped his hands together—but didn't clench his fists. "Like I mentioned, she said her job here is done."

"Oh," I murmured.

"But," he added, "she'd really like it if she could stay with you."

Joy bubbled in me. "Really?"

"Really."

I bent over and scooped her up, nestling her next to Grendel on my lap. He put a paw on her back and licked her face.

A perfect match, as Marisol had called them the other day.

I glanced between her and Jeremy.

Were they a perfect match, too?

I'd soon find out. Cutter was sitting on Dovie's deck with a pair of binoculars, waiting for Jeremy to leave.

Operation Jeremy's Aura was underway.

"Is she going to stop eating things that aren't good for her?" I asked.

He laughed. "She only did that so you'd call Marisol."

"Sneaky," I said to her.

She purred.

"Well," Orlinda placed her glass on the table. "I should go. I just wanted to stop by and give you an update on Bethany."

I hobbled over to the bassinet and picked up the pink bear. I handed it to her. "She might want this back."

Orlinda nodded and tucked it into the bag on the back of her wheelchair. I opened the door and she rolled out toward the ramp we used when she visited.

"I should go, too," Marisol said, standing. "I've got to grab a quick lunch before heading back to the clinic."

Jeremy rose. He walked over and patted Ebbie's head, then turned toward the door. "I was going to get some lunch, too... Maybe you'd care to join me?" he asked.

Marisol nodded shyly.

Shyly! Marisol! I never thought I'd see the day when a man made her shy.

As Jeremy helped Orlinda navigate to her car, Marisol turned back to me.

"He's really not my type," she whispered.

"I know."

"But...I'm curious."

"Curious is okay," I said.

"And I think he'd be good in bed—all that bad boy energy."

"Get out of here," I said, playfully shoving her through the door.

She turned and waved, and I walked to the edge of the front porch and glanced up at Cutter.

He was giving two big thumbs up.

A perfect match.

Chapter Thirty

Later that afternoon, Sean and I sat on the porch, looking out at the ocean.

"My parents are on their way back," I said. "My mother is beside herself worrying about Preston and you, and Dad's beside himself worrying about the Valentine, Inc. building."

Sean cracked a smile. "He'll be relieved that the upper floors are just smoke damaged."

I was relieved, too. It was going to take a while to set the building back to rights, but most of it was intact, thanks to the man on the Harley who'd driven me into the city. He hadn't just gone to the police, but he'd also gone to the nearest firehouse, where Curt Meister happened to have just returned after helping Sam look for Sean.

Fate? I wondered. Or something else? Like Sean's mom looking out for him?

I probably wouldn't ever know, but my motorcycle-riding friend was coming by tomorrow for a reading on his lost watch—and his thousand dollar bonus. I planned to double it. It was the least I could do.

Happily, the Porcupine hadn't been damaged at all. The fire separation wall that had been installed when Maggie renovated the place had withstood the worst test possible. She and Raphael were already back in business.

The water glittered like diamonds, and sailboats dotted the horizon. It was still hot as hell, but the breeze was cool and there was a cold front on the horizon.

The National Guard had regained control of the city overnight, and all of the fires were out. Now it was time to clean up and rebuild.

Sean said, "How do your parents feel about the engagement?"

"We didn't talk about it too much," I said.

"How do you feel about the engagement? The pregnancy?"

"I'm..." I searched for a name to my emotion. "I'm not sure."

He said, "Do you wish it was you?"

"Marrying and having a baby with Cutter? Ew, that's gross. He's my brother. There are laws against that."

He laughed. "You know what I meant."

I glanced at him and got lost for a second in his gray eyes. "I know."

"And?"

I shrugged. "A little. But, I have issues. My parents are crazy. My grandmother barges in at all hours, I have these visions, and oh, yeah, I deal with my fair share of psychopaths. That's a lot of baggage for someone else to help carry."

Biting my lip, I waited for him to say something. If he wanted out, now was the time to speak up.

He nudged my chin. "That baggage has helped shape you into who you are today. You're going to be a wonderful wife. And mother." Leaning over, he kissed me slowly. "I love you."

"I love you, too," I whispered.

He picked up his glass of lemonade and took a drink.

I waited and waited for him to continue the conversation, but when he put his head back against the cushion and closed his eyes I finally had to speak up.

"That's it?"

A dimple popped as he cracked open an eye. "What? You're expecting a proposal here and now?"

"Well, yeah, kind of. That was quite the build-up."

His other dimple popped. "Patience, Ms. Valentine. Patience."

I leaned back in my chair. "You know how I feel about patience."

"That's right," he said, his voice suddenly husky. "We still have to put the patience versus savoring issue to the test."

I smiled. "When you're feeling better, we'll put that to the test."

"I'm feeling much better."

I glanced at him out of the corner of my eye. "How much better?"

"I don't know about you, Ms. Valentine, but I'm ready to savor every minute."

His eyes told me that he meant so much more than what was on the surface. He was talking about our life together. The good, the bad, the ugly. He was talking about marriage and babies.

Love.

My heart soared.

"Me, too, Mr. Donahue. Me, too."

Early the next morning, I was pouring a cup of coffee when the doorbell rang.

Glancing at the clock, I frowned. It was a little past seven. I knew it couldn't be Dovie—she would have come right in.

I patted Ebbie's head on the way to the door and quieted a barking Thoreau. I peeked out the window and was shocked by who stood on my porch.

Pulling open the door, I said, "Well, Aiden Holliday, where have you been hiding yourself?" But as I teased, I noticed the wild look in his eye, the way his normally neat short hair stuck out all over his head. Stubble covered his cheeks. I immediately started to worry. "What's wrong?"

"I need your help, Lucy."

"Of course. With what?"

He held up a finger, spun around, and marched to his car. He pulled open the back door and reached inside. What he pulled out had my jaw on the ground.

A beautiful little girl, maybe eighteen months old, clung

to his neck.

Aiden carried her to the porch.

"Who's she?" I asked.

"My daughter."

I stared at him for a long, hard minute. Finally, I found my voice. "Where's her mother?"

"That's why I need your help," he said. "She's missing."

Did you know Heather Webber
also writes as Heather Blake?

Keep reading for a sneak peek at
Heather Blake's debut novel.

It Takes a Witch

January 2012
Obsidian

Chapter One

Usually I'm not in the habit of tiptoeing through strange houses under the cover of darkness.

It was unsettling to say the least, and I felt completely out of sorts. My outfit only added to my discomfort. The flouncy, frilly pink satin bodysuit, tulle tutu, and pink ballet slippers were a far cry from my usual jeans and tee.

It didn't help that my every move was being watched closely.

As I crept up aged wooden stairs of a large house along the coast of Salem, Massachusetts, Amanda Goodwin followed behind me with her mother-in-law, Cherise, bringing up the rear. They'd ushered me straight upstairs as soon as I'd arrived, their eyes lit like they were two little girls sneaking a peek at Santa.

At the top of the steps, a long hallway branched into four bedrooms, one of which had its door closed. Pink and black polka-dotted block letters attached to the wood paneling declared it as my destination: Laurel Grace Goodwin's bedroom.

"Have you done this before, Ms. Merriweather?" Amanda asked softly, tugging on my gossamer wings. "Played the tooth fairy?"

I sized up Amanda immediately as a hip suburban soccer mom, in her designer jeans, beaded tank top, and Grecian-inspired sandals. A natural blonde, she wore her hair long and straight, parted down the middle. Lots of lip gloss and mascara but not much else.

I smiled, trying to hide my nervousness. "Please call me Darcy, and this is my first time." I truly hoped it would be my last. Tulle and I didn't get along. My legs were itching something fierce, despite the thin protection of a pair of tights.

"Well"—Cherise had a strong Boston accent of someone who had been born and bred in this area—"your aunt Velma highly recommends you, and we trust her and As You Wish implicitly."

I had been working at my aunt Ve's business, As You Wish, for only two weeks. The company blended the tasks of a virtual personal assistant and a personal concierge service. Our clients' requests were diverse, often challenging, and sometimes just plain strange. They ranged from administrative tasks to running errands, to shopping for a gift, to providing an extra pair of hands to clean up a messy house, and much, much more. As You Wish's motto was that no request was too big or too small and no job impossible—as was proven by the fact I was standing before the Goodwins looking like a character from a fairy tale.

I transferred my velvet drawstring purse from one hand to the other and noticed I was leaving a trail of glitter behind me. It sparkled on the rich dark oak floors.

Short and pleasantly plump with chin-length snow-white hair, heavily layered and teased, Cherise wore a bit too much makeup, and overaccessorized with several ropes of beaded necklaces and heavy chandelier earrings. "I was glad to hear of you and your sister moving in with Velma. I imagine she's been glad to share the *family business* with you?"

Ve had told me that she and Cherise were old friends, though they hadn't spoken in a while. Even still, I wasn't the least bit surprised Cherise knew of my arrival to the Enchanted Village, the unique Salem neighborhood where my aunt lived.

A new witch in town doesn't go unnoticed in these parts.

And two new witches? Rumors were flying faster than some broomsticks.

Cherise either was fishing for a little gossip or was genuinely curious to know if my sister, Harper, and I were aware that the family business she referred to wasn't the brick-and-mortar As You Wish, but the fact that we could actually grant wishes through a wishing spell.

It was a reasonable inquiry. Until three weeks ago, Harper and I were living in Ohio and dealing with lives that weren't what we'd imagined. When we received a note from Aunt Ve asking if she could visit because she had something important to tell us, we had no idea how our lives would change. Within a week we had packed up what little we had and moved to the Enchanted Village.

"We're glad to be here." Well, I was. Harper was still adjusting.

Putting my (disastrous) divorce and my inability to find a decent job behind me and getting Harper out of Ohio before she caused any more trouble may have been the perfect incentive to move, but learning about our heritage of the Craft, or in my family's case *Wish*craft, was now a priority. I was still learning the Wishcraft Laws, and all the ins and outs that came along with the revelation that I was a witch.

Thankfully some of the laws were easy to remember. Like the fact that I can't wish death on anyone. Or prevent death. Or interfere with true love. Or that no Wishcrafter can grant her own wishes (or other Wishcrafters' wishes). I also can't solicit or refuse to grant a wish without severe consequences. However, the biggest rule of all was that I (or any Crafter for that matter) couldn't reveal to any mortal the truth about my powers or I risked losing my wish-granting abilities forever.

Unfortunately, some of the laws were a little fuzzy. Like the law about wishing for money—granting that wish meant the money would have to be *taken* from someone else. To follow the Crafters' basic principle of "Do no harm," the Wishcrafter Laws also required that only wishes made with motives pure of heart would be granted. How that was actually determined was still a mystery to me.

Cherise pressed. "How do you enjoy working for As You Wish?"

The Goodwins were Curecrafters, healing witches, and were apparently quite nosy to boot. "It's going well," I said. "So far this week I've tracked down sold-out tickets to tonight's Boston Pops performance, created a gift basket for a basset hound recovering from surgery, searched online for an out-of-print romance novel, and now this." I gestured to my costume. I didn't mention anything about the Wishcrafting, and how I'd been able to use a spell to help a client get last-minute tickets on a sold-out flight to Paris so he could surprise his girlfriend with a weekend getaway.

As You Wish was both popular and highly successful. Most of the requests received were accomplished through hard work and sheer determination. However, sometimes magic was needed to get the job done right. Often, because of the name of the shop, people simply made wishes—which made our job a whole lot easier. Other times, seeking the help of other Crafters and *their* unique abilities gave us an edge.

But mortals, who were the majority of our clients, didn't know about the magic. And though the average customer wouldn't be surprised about something mystical happening in a place called the Enchanted Village, disclosing our family powers wasn't a risk Aunt Ve was willing to take, especially after having an ancestor nearly burned at the stake.

"Well, you make a lovely tooth fairy," Amanda said as a grandfather clock *dong*ed at the far end of the hallway.

It was nine. I had to hurry this along—or I'd be late for the emergency village meeting that was due to start at nine thirty. Ve had insisted Harper and I attend. Our aunt was still introducing us around the village and was eager for us to get acclimated. She wanted nothing more than for us to put down solid roots among the other Crafters. Well, that and take over As You Wish when she retired.

"Do you mind if I tape this?" Cherise asked, holding up a small video camera. "For my son? He couldn't be here tonight."

"I'm sorry," I said. "We don't allow videotaping of our services." For good reason. Wishcrafters emitted a blinding glow, a white aura, on camera. Which explained, after all these years, why there weren't any baby pictures of Harper and me, and why every picture we were in was always "overexposed."

I was surprised Cherise had asked. Didn't she know about the auras? I made a mental note to ask Ve how much Crafters knew about one another and their limitations. How secretive were Crafters with one another?

Cameras were definitely out. Not that I would even recognize myself right now, with all the costume makeup and glitter I was wearing. It took a lot of effort, and some amazing false eyelashes, to look fairylike.

"Dennis was welcome to be here tonight, Cherise." Amanda's cheeks flushed. "He declined. It's his loss."

"He's stubborn," Cherise said. "You know this."

I tried to blend into the woodwork—rather hard to do when one looked a lot like a giant glittery stick of pink cotton candy. The last thing I wanted was to get involved in the middle of a family dispute. Been there, done that.

Amanda must have sensed my unease. She said, "I'm sorry. My husband and I recently separated. I'm sure you don't need all the gory details. Suffice it to say that *he's* the one who moved out."

My heart ached for her. I was much better off without my ex, but it had taken me two years to realize that.

Cherise's eyebrow rose. "He's *very* stubborn."

Amanda flashed her an irritated look. "Besides, if you recall, it's his fault we had to contact As You Wish in the first place."

As You Wish had received a frantic call from Cherise this morning, needing to hire someone to play the tooth fairy. Amanda's daughter, five-year-old Laurel Grace, had lost her first tooth, and had been excited for the tooth fairy to come—until her father told her there was no such thing.

Aunt Ve, who had taken the call, had somehow deemed that this was the perfect job for me to take on. I had my doubts. Especially when I saw the gossamer wings and the pink tights. Not to mention the dreadful tulle.

Cherise looked pained. She explained, "He wasn't thinking. Once he realized what he'd said, he tried to convince Laurel Grace he'd been kidding, but the damage had been done."

"Not the first time," Amanda murmured.

"I just wish . . . ," Cherise began.

I sucked in a breath, waiting. My every nerve was on alert, standing on end, prickling, getting ready to react. Adrenaline surged, flowed.

"I just wish . . ." She shook her head. "Never mind."

I let out the breath I'd been holding.

Wringing her hands, Amanda said, "Five-year-olds shouldn't have to grow up so soon. Darcy, we need you to convince her that sometimes grown-ups can be wrong. The last thing we want her thinking is that magic doesn't exist, especially when she doesn't know about her Craft yet."

"I'll certainly do my best," I said. "Shall we give it a try?"

Aunt Ve had gone over exactly what I should do. I ran over the instructions in my head as I slowly turned the doorknob to Laurel Grace's bedroom. I held my breath and entered.

Moonbeams slipped through striped curtains, spreading muted light across the room. The walls were painted pastel pink and trimmed in creamy white. Touches of pale green were everywhere from curtains to the overstuffed chair in the corner, to the duvet on the bed. Stuffed animals overflowed a toy chest, books were piled high on a corner bookshelf, and a dollhouse sat on a tiny table in the middle of the room, filled with delicate-looking miniatures.

I turned my attention to the four-poster bed. Tucked under a lightweight comforter, Laurel Grace slept on her side. I crept closer. Blond ringlets fell across a lace-trimmed pillowcase. Her little face, slack with sleep, was angelic and peaceful.

I was aware of Amanda and Cherise lurking in the doorway as I carefully slid my hand under Laurel Grace's pillow. I pulled out the little ribbon-edged, tooth-shaped pillow that had been delivered by courier earlier in the day for Laurel Grace to tuck her tooth into. I felt the lump of the tiny tooth under the fabric as I brought the keepsake over to Amanda and handed it to her.

I then walked back over to the bed, opened my purse, and pulled out a small satin pouch trimmed in white ostrich feathers. Laurel Grace's name had been embroidered in pink on the bag. Inside, two one-dollar gold pieces clinked together. I gently slid the pouch under the pillow.

I smiled in the twilight, thinking about how expensive that little tooth had been. Two dollars from the tooth fairy, fifty dollars for accessories, and one hundred dollars for half an hour of my time.

I bent my head close to Laurel Grace's and whispered the words Aunt Ve had me memorize.

"Hello, hello, little one,
A tooth you have lost,
More you will lose,
Put them under your pillow,
And take a sweet snooze.
For upon that eve,
You will receive
A visit from me,
If you just believe."

Laurel Grace's eyelids squeezed into a wince—I couldn't blame her—it was a horrible, horrible rhyme—then popped open.

Filled with a warmth that came from being part of such a special moment, I suddenly had visions of being the area's go-to tooth fairy, spreading love and happiness and gold coins across the state, heck, all of New England. Even the tulle didn't seem so uncomfortable anymore.

Laurel Grace stared at me for a second, probably taking in the tiara, the eyelashes, the wings, the makeup and glitter. I kept quiet, giving her a moment for it all to sink in.

Abruptly, she sat upright, looked me straight in the eyes, and started screaming at the top of her lungs. Long, shrieking cries that hurt my ears. "Stranger danger! Stranger dan-ger!"

Startled, I screamed back.

Amanda rushed into the room, saying, "Shhh, shhh."

I wasn't sure if she was talking to me or her daughter.

Clamping my lips closed, I backed away as Amanda sat on the bed and gathered Laurel Grace close. "Shhh."

"Stranger danger! Stran-ger dan-ger!" Laurel Grace continued to howl.

"No, no," I said, gathering my wits. "I'm not a stranger! I'm the tooth fairy." Heaven help me, I even twirled.

My skirt billowed out, raining sparkles on the carpet.

"No, you're not." Tears flowed from Laurel Grace's eyes.

Ve had not prepared me for *this* scenario.

"Yes, I am," I reassured, fluffing layers of tulle as though that would help my cause.

"She really is." Cherise sat on the other side of the bed, rubbing Laurel Grace's back.

"No, she's not," Laurel Grace insisted.

"Why isn't she?" Amanda asked her daughter.

"She's—she's . . ." I was waiting for the words "a fraud" to fall from her lips, and was shocked when she said, "She's not blond!"

I held back a smile as I fingered my long dark hair, trying to think of what to do, what to say. I knelt by Laurel Grace's bed and improvised as best I could. "Fairies are just like people." *And Crafters*, I added silently. "We come in all different shapes, sizes, and colors."

She gazed at me with big blue eyes as though I wasn't even close to measuring up to her idea of a fairy. It was true I more resembled Esméralda from Disney's *Hunchback of Notre Dame*, which might be a tad bit confusing to a five-year-old looking for the Tinkerbell sort, so I tried really hard not to be offended when she started wailing again.

I saw Cherise's lips moving but couldn't hear what she was saying, and then her left eye blinked twice. Laurel Grace immediately quieted but still wore a tremulous pout.

Cherise had used a curing spell to calm the little girl.

Amanda quickly said, "Why don't you look under your pillow, honey?"

I recognized a chance to escape when I saw one. "I should be going. Lots of stops to make tonight. Lots of teeth lost!" I backed out of the room as Laurel Grace pulled the satin pouch from beneath the pillow.

"How did she know my name, Mommy?" I heard from the safety of the hallway.

"Because she's magical," Amanda answered. "Do you believe now?"

"Maybe," Laurel Grace whispered.

I had to smile at her noncommitment.

Cherise had followed me out. "Thank you, Darcy," she said as we walked down the stairs. In the kitchen, she pressed a check into my hand. "I'll let Velma know what a great job you did."

I was ready to put this whole night behind me—and hang up my wings for good. I tucked the check into my purse. "You're welcome."

Cherise rubbed her ears as if they were still ringing. "She's tiny, but she has a pair of lungs that can rival an opera singer. Sometimes spells come in handy, don't you think?"

I fidgeted, not sure what to say.

Before I could come up with a response, she added, "I just wish Dennis could be here right now. He's really missing out on an important event in his daughter's life."

She stared expectantly at me.

She had me. As a Wishcrafter, I was obligated to grant the wish. However, if Cherise wasn't pure of heart in her motives for making the wish, my spell wouldn't work no matter how hard I tried to grant it. *Do no harm.*

My nerves tingled as I said softly, "Wish I might, wish I may, grant this wish without delay." I winked my left eye twice, which would look merely like a twitch to a mortal, but other Crafters would know my spell had been cast. "You're sneaky."

"I know. Sorry about that." She gave me a mischievous smile. "You just can't trust anyone these days."

It Takes a Witch

is available at bookstores everywhere.

Coming Soon:

A Witch Before Dying – August 2012

The Good, the Bad, and the Witchy – Spring 2013

www.heatherwebber.com

www.heatherblakebooks.com

Printed in Great Britain
by Amazon